BEFORE WHITE NIGHT

BEFORE WHITE NIGHT

Rescue from Jonestown

Joseph Hartmann

BELLE ISLE BOOKS
www.belleislebooks.com

Printed in the United States

ISBN: 978-1-9399300-8-8

Library of Congress Control Number: 2013949949

BELLE ISLE BOOKS
www.belleislebooks.com

Some events do not occur at the right time, and others do not occur at all. It is the proper function of the historian to correct these faults.

—Herodotus

To my loving and lovely wife, Roxana,
who has unfailingly provided encouragement,
and for my children,
Laura Alexandra and Mark Andrew

Preface

Two very different worlds come together in this story. The first is the world of an affluent businessman who has it all, but is besieged by a wife who cannot find inner satisfaction except through the promises of a religious leader—Jim Jones. Her fascination with Jones directly affects their daughter, Katrina. The second is the world of a Vietnam-era college graduate who served his country as a special forces officer and subsequently pursues his goal to be an American diplomat. Grounded in the truth of historical events and told with insights that can come only from firsthand knowledge, *Before White Night* centers on the efforts of several strong-willed individuals to rescue a thirteen-year-old girl from a cult stronghold in the middle of Guyana's jungle, known as Jonestown.

The majority of the characters depicted in the book are real people. Their names have been changed to give me a free hand in developing character scope and personality. Fact and fiction are woven together to highlight the importance of the events that occurred and to reflect the unadulterated truth about Jim Jones and his Peoples Temple as seen through the eyes of an American diplomat in Guyana.

The epilogue and afterword chronicle the actual events surrounding the horrendous assassination of Congressman Leo Joseph Ryan and four members of his party in Guyana on November 18, 1978, as well as the mass murder of 913 men, women, and children at Jonestown.

Prologue

Summer 1978

It was a hot, humid night like any other when the alert sounded, rousing the people of Jonestown from their beds. Thirteen-year-old Katrina Olsen awoke sluggishly, her mind and body too exhausted to be yanked from sleep even by the shrill wail of the alarm. Her face tickled, just as it always did now when she woke. Her right hand reflexively brushed her lips to fend off beads of sweat. Around her, other small bodies were moving, groaning, rising from their dorm bunk beds.

These midnight alarms were becoming more frequent in recent months. As Katrina stood in her dormitory, her friend Judi voiced a tired complaint, saying that she only wanted to go back to bed. The other ten girls in their group of nine- to thirteen-year-olds were already walking out through the screened door like zombies in their sleeping shirts. Katrina and Judi caught up with them, and they settled into their usual place at the pavilion.

Once everyone was assembled, Father Jones began his lecture, broadcast over the loudspeakers. Katrina craned her neck, not really listening, trying to locate her mother among the women in attendance.

Failing in finding her mother's face in the throng, Katrina turned her eyes to the reverend. He was talking somberly into the microphone, telling them all that the time had come for courage and heroism. Katrina and Judi both knew what was eventually coming. The only question was how long it would take Father Jones to get there. To entertain each other, the girls whispered among themselves, picking out odd words from his sermon to roll around on their tongues. It was all they could do to stay awake.

Finally, nearly two hours after the alarm drew his followers from their bunks, the reverend reached his conclusion: "We are all in imminent danger!

But there is no need to fear being captured and tortured by Satan's minions. I will not allow that to happen! To defend ourselves in the name of all that is holy and from within the union that we have made with one another, we are called upon now to ultimately sacrifice ourselves in protest against the injustices of Satan's world." The word "sacrifice" sent a ripple of murmurs around the pavilion and caused Katrina and Judi to rally to attention.

As the Reverend Jones spoke, his assistants had been opening packages of powdered drink mix, preparing vats of flavored water for the thousand people present in the pavilion. And so the ritual began again. One by one, Jones' followers stepped in line to take their "poison" in a communion of revolutionary suicide with their fellow Temple members. As they did so, Father Jones assured them that the end would come peacefully after forty minutes or so.

Katrina lined up behind Judi and the other girls in her dormitory and eventually moved to the front, where the purple water gleamed black in the moonlight. As she got close to the vat half-full of liquid, she saw a strange grey foam floating on its surface, and a tremor of alarm ran through her. Katrina racked her brain, trying to remember if the concoction had looked like that before, during other rehearsals. Or was this different? Was this finally the real thing?

As Judi stepped forward and took a cup, Katrina scanned the assembly one more time, seeking out her mother's face for reassurance. Then a woman pressed a paper cup into her trembling hands and coaxed her, ever so calmly, to drink.

This was life in Jonestown.

CHAPTER 1

August 1973

In the dining room, on top of the long mahogany table, right next to the freshly cut flower arrangement, something was out of place. After studying the object in dim light, John finally recognized it as the Waterford Crystal paperweight—a golf ball—that should have been on his desk in the study upstairs.

That's odd, he thought as he moved closer, turning on the overhead chandelier. Pinned beneath the golf ball was a cream-colored envelope, his name written in ink across the front. *Now what?* he thought. Notes from his wife were usually left on the corkboard in the kitchen designed specifically for that purpose. Instinctively, he scanned the rest of the dining room, then the sunken living room, to see if anything else was awry.

His eyes moved across the red Karastan rug that started under the dinner table and ran down the steps into the soft Florentine atmosphere and pale oranges of the living room. From there his gaze swept out to the patio and pool, where the colors got lighter still, finally fading into the sage-green grasses and tawny mesquite of the Santa Monica foothills. The house looked just as it always did: clean, well ordered, everything where it should be . . . everything except that paperweight. So why were John's nerves suddenly on razor's edge? As much as he wanted to believe otherwise, he knew the note must be important to have his senses twitching like this.

He picked up the paperweight in one hand and the envelope in the other. He had just opened the flap when the Hamilton Grandfather Clock in the hall rang out.

"Judas Priest!" he exclaimed, jerking his head to the side. His blood pressure was swelling to a new high for the day. Agitated now, he tore the letter from the envelope and unfolded it.

Now John. The handwritten note surged beneath his grasp, and immediately he knew it concerned their eight-year-old daughter.

> *I know you will take this the wrong way, because of all the arguments we've been having lately. But I've thought it through and had several sessions with the Temple's counselors.*
>
> *I've taken Katrina to the Temple. I should be back by the time you get home. Tonight she goes by bus to Ukiah to attend girls' camp. I thought over what you said. This is what's best for Katrina.*
>
> *Priscilla*

"God damn you!" John roared. His arms flew up and the right fist, the one still holding the paperweight, crashed into the chandelier above him. "Shit," he mouthed involuntarily. Falling crystals left gouge marks on the table; several shattered upon impact. The mishap and the pain in his knuckles sent John's anger surging. He started to heave the paperweight but caught himself at the last second.

Wait a minute, John, he said to himself. *What are you doing? Are you going to throw this lousy golf ball at the brass trophies on the mantle . . . at the sliding glass patio doors?*

"Damn you, Priscilla," he swore at his wife again and kicked one of the dining room chairs in frustration. After replacing the crystal paperweight safely on the table, he read the note a second time. Then he shredded it and the envelope, dropping the pieces among the broken crystals on the table.

Trying for composure, he went down to the stereo and began rifling through his classical music collection. John always retreated to his music to regain control. He wasn't sure what he wanted, but he wanted something quick. Bach! Bach would help. Bach, with his measured, rational tones, was perfect for the moment. He put on Glenn Gould playing the Goldberg Variations and turned up the volume. It helped a little. He wasn't a drinking man, actually felt guilty ordering more than one drink, but he headed to the liquor cabinet anyway and poured a two-finger glass goblet of Chives Regal Scotch and then added some ice cubes for good measure.

As the soothing progression of piano tones filled the room, his breathing slowed. The sounds rose around him, the bass went through him, and he began to think clearly again. He got up and decided that he would barbecue anyway, just like he had done every Friday night for more than a decade. He went outside, consciously breathing deeply, sipping at the scotch, and making a little face at each sip. In no time he had the charcoal going. As he poked the coals, he began to feel the comfort of the routine work its way through him.

John popped a meloril for his blood pressure and chased it with an aspirin. Then he settled back into one of the lounge chairs by the pool, gazing out at the clear blue water, the Mediterranean tiles, the manicured lawn. Aside from the music, the house was still, but he could feel the electricity in the air like a summer night's lightning storm. He took another deep breath, followed by a bigger dose of the scotch, finishing it off.

After a long moment of reflection, John got up and went into the house to get the meat out of the fridge. He opened the patio door and headed into the almost-liquid music, turning it up even higher, so it filled the whole house. John splashed another drink, and it occurred to him that at thirty-two, he was the same age Gould had been when he recorded the album. On the refrigerator door, Yellowstone National Park magnets held in place several small watercolors that Katrina had brought home from school. He opened the door and pulled out the pan full of marinating steaks. As he did so, he noticed a strange object protruding from the saran wrap.

A purple plastic barrette pierced one of the T-bone steaks. He set the metal tray on the kitchen counter. There was a little note in the clip.

> *Daddy, I don't want to go to camp. Mommy made me. Some church people skare me. Last time, they made Paula stand nayked in front of us to ponish her for telling a lie. I don't like it! Don't tell Mommy, please.*
>
> > *Love,*
> > *Katrina*

He began shaking in rage. In a flash, he heaved the tray of steaks against the tiled kitchen wall. Pots and pans clattered down; juice and blood splashed onto the wall, then onto the floor. He picked up one of the high-back kitchen chairs and struck it against the hardwood floor until it cracked and broke, and he went down with it, landing heavily on his elbows. He rolled onto his back and lay there amid the smells of the peppercorn, meat, and Worcestershire sauce.

He remained still—vividly aware of his banging heart, his ragged breathing, and the rise and fall of his stomach where it protruded above him.

It was not just the act itself of Priscilla openly defying him. He was used to that. At some point during their ten years of marriage, he had grown accustomed to being overruled and having his opinions discounted as only so much noise. Assertiveness was an effort for him, one he labored at out of necessity at his job. It came naturally to Priscilla, though, and so at home he had slipped comfortably into letting her have her way. Even when he didn't understand or agree with her decisions, he found it easier to appease her than to fight.

When she'd begun attending services at the Peoples Temple, a Pentecostal church with a reverend who apparently talked about socialism as much as he did about God, John had been uncomfortable with it, but he hadn't fought it. He'd even gone with her to a service, though the experience had only confirmed his suspicion that the atmosphere was just too bizarre for his liking. This time though, he had put his foot down. He'd told Priscilla in no uncertain terms that she was not to involve their daughter in her religion. They'd fought about it last night, and in an almost unprecedented moment of victory, John had won. Or so he'd thought. Priscilla had conceded that she wouldn't make Katrina go to camp if she didn't want to. But now Katrina was gone, against her will and his.

He sat up. As he pulled himself heavily to his feet, he had the sinking feeling that he was losing control. He felt the kind of panic the Trojans must have felt when they realized their gift had turned on them. This Trojan horse of a religion had been brought inside the gates by the wife he loved, and now their only daughter was caught up in all the drama that accompanied it.

With heavy shoulders, he walked slowly through the shadowy living room, toward the patio again, deliberately not turning on the lights. The piano music was still loud, so he didn't hear Priscilla's car enter the garage. Outside, beyond the shimmering blue pool, beyond the darkening ridges, the tangerine California sunset began to gather. The sky took on the mystic aquamarine he loved so much. This had been his favorite part of the day for years, ever since he fell for this house with its red-tile roof and Spanish graces. Suddenly the music stopped mid-track.

"Why did you destroy my chandelier?" Priscilla cried out from behind him. "My chairs! You destroy my chandelier, my dining room—just because I disagreed with you? Is there anything else you destroyed? Well?"

John didn't answer. He didn't turn around. He tried to focus on the calm of the sunset. A coyote yipped in the distance. He felt emotionally shot—bone-tired from a day spent wrangling over lost shipping orders and bungled sales from his top men. He didn't feel up to arguing right now, especially over something this explosive. He just wanted to lie still with his drink by the pool and let the sunset wash over him. His veins felt watery, his jaw slack. He knew that his blood pressure had gone to the sky and back several times now. If he argued, he would have no control and it would be terrible—shattering, because he would burst.

"Well, I'm waiting," she said as she walked onto the patio with a chandelier crystal clenched in her hand. "Damn you, John! I deserve an answer."

Without looking, John could smell her freshness, her just-washed fragrance. He could tell she wanted nothing more than to pounce, just like the coyotes out there. Her voice was hard-edged, primed.

Wearily, he said, "I don't want to discuss it or anything else tonight, Priscilla. I'm just too beat and disgusted for—"

"You're disgusted? Ha! That's rich. Haven't you noticed what's going on around here? You're an absentee landlord, pal. Whenever there's something important to discuss, you cop out and won't focus. You aren't even taking responsibility for the family. I seem to be the only one who is interested in Katrina, her schoolwork, and the parent-teacher conferences. Now, whenever I want to discuss something, in this case a very important new decision in my life, you're a whimpering, lifeless pile of decadent shit!"

"Decadent shit," he repeated, almost smiling.

He gulped at his drink and half-turned toward her in his chair, making a sweeping motion with his arm, palm up, mutely gesturing to the house, the land, the fine furnishings and art collections he'd worked so hard for—his contributions to the wife and child she was accusing him of neglecting. His mouth moved but no words came out.

"You know," she continued, "I knew you would react like this. Fortunately, before I made this decision, I consulted with the Peoples Temple counselors, several of them. And finally, you're not going to believe this, I even had an audience, a private audience," here she clapped her hands, "with Dad himself, and he predicted this. He predicted you would react in a typical bourgeois, white male fashion—violence, destruction, insults. You know I spent months looking for that chandelier. How could you?"

John's brain recoiled from her scathing accusations as much as it did from hearing her reverend's politics roll off her tongue. She never used to talk like that. He almost pointed out that of the three offenses she'd listed, he was only guilty of destruction—that he hadn't insulted her or been violent. But he was too weary to form a rebuttal. He saw how fruitless it would be to bring up Katrina's note or his fears about his daughter and the Peoples Temple. She was primed for battle and he wasn't.

"Let's just discuss this in the morning when we're both rested and rational," he said. "I'm beat, and you're full to the brim with your Temple dogma crap."

"No!" she yelled. "Dad said you wouldn't back down. You're stalling for time, and you'll be the same in the morning. Things aren't going to change."

"Well . . . I thought we agreed, explicitly agreed, that you could explore this Peoples Temple thing to your little heart's content, but that we were going to *leave Katrina out of it!*" In spite of himself, his voice began to rise. He moved uneasily on the lounge chair.

"That's just it," Priscilla said. "I'm not exploring anymore. Don't you get it? I've decided to contribute to society for a change, instead of being tied to you and your petty little stationery business. What a laugh. And all the groveling, fanny-kissing dinner parties with boring business types. You know, when was the last time you helped somebody for God's sake?"

"Priscilla. We give to at least four or five charities."

"When did you ever help somebody of a different race, for instance? Huh? When have we ever had a black family over or had Katrina play with a black girl?"

John felt the hairs on the back of his neck prick up defensively. It was an old accusation—one she'd flung at him numerous times since getting involved with the Peoples Temple the year before. She'd noticed his discomfort when he'd accompanied her to the temple. Her shrewd eyes had detected the way he kept to himself after the service, but more so when surrounded by the black congregation members, of which there were many. Now she never missed an opportunity to drive that knife in when they fought. She never ceased to remind him that she had embraced de-segregation and developed friendships with black people, while he remained a product of his parents' generation of conservative attitudes and selective separation. He'd reminded her once that she hadn't always been so color-blind before she joined the Peoples Temple, but she had flown off the handle at that. So now he bit his tongue and let the attack continue.

"No. You give shit, and your life is worthless. All grabbing—me, me, me. And my life will be worthless if I stay tied down to you. Simple as that. Always working on Saturday—work, work, work. We haven't been out of town in a year. Like all those weekend trips we used to take. And you haven't taken me abroad or to the Caribbean in something like six years. You just don't give a damn." Here her voice wavered and broke and she began to cry. John could hear it, but he didn't turn around. He felt the usual conflicting feelings of guilt and anger battling inside of him. He'd grown to resent those tears, which always sprang up when she was insulting him, if only to complicate the rage her words incited in him. She warbled on, "You haven't really made love to me in a year. All you care about is grubbing for money!"

He rose out of the chair and turned toward her. "Priscilla . . . ," he began. But she shook her head and dug her knuckles into the corners of her eyes as though to stanch the leak.

"The film has been lifted off my eyes and I don't have to be tied to you anymore, Dad says."

"Oh Jesus! Don't refer to that megalomaniac bastard as Dad!"

"What Dad and the counselors suggest—half of them black, by the way— is that Katrina and I separate from you for several months. They have special living quarters for just these kinds of cases."

"Cases!" he yelled. "What cases? What the hell are you talking about?"

"I'm—No! Don't come toward me," she said, her arms outstretched defensively. "You're reacting with violence, just like they said. I said you would be rational. But no, I'm not waiting till morning, because it's all too late. I'm going now, right now." She turned and ran back through the house.

"Priscilla!" John called out. He took a few trembling steps, afraid to do anything more. "Jesus Christ," he was talking to himself now. "Don't overreact. Don't do anything rash. Just slow down a minute. Just—"

But she was gone. He heard her car start up and the garage door open, and just like that, she was gone.

Stunned for a long minute, he finally moved toward the bar, grabbed the bottle of scotch and some ice, and took it out by the pool, switching on the watery pool lights. Everything else he left dark. It was quiet now. He dangled a hand in the pool, watching the water ripple in the slight breeze. Beyond his brick wall, far up the foothills, coyotes began yipping again from their darkened arroyos. He listened to the water lapping as he leaned back in the lounge chair.

What a day. John could feel panic welling up in his chest, a panic that might turn into his own tears if he let it. But he wouldn't. *You're a businessman,* he reminded himself. *Be rational, don't break down. Cut your losses if need be, but keep on going no matter what.*

He was a businessman and he would rise above this just as he had climbed up and over everything else. You had to be hardhearted sometimes. Get cold with cold figures, unemotional bottom lines. He began to compute his losses.

First he started to figure how many three-finger glasses of scotch it would take an overweight, out-of-shape, two-hundred-and-ten-pound male to get drunk, because he'd been drinking but didn't feel anything yet. He really didn't like to drink, but tonight might be an exception. He didn't even smoke. No, all he did was work and grub for money and stay out of bars and *never*, in all his years of marriage, ever fool around. No, all he did was have white people over sometimes who furthered his business, put food on the table, and kept the mortgage spiraling downward.

Then he began to compute how much he was still in love with Priscilla, which was not as much as he wanted it to be, but maybe more than was good for him. Then he began to compute how much of this house was still his, based on California law. Half of the house—down the middle? The entire first level? Or the entire second level? He remembered the story of the guy with the bulldozer cutting his house in half during a messy divorce while the wife was out of town. He smiled. Maybe he should have been a little more attentive. Hell! How many women wouldn't love to be in Priscilla's position? Maybe he was being unfair with this Reverend Jim Jones. Then he began to compute the lawyer fees. He swore to himself. Then he began computing Katrina. And that was when the computations broke down. In the dark, next to the long, luminous blue pool, he fell asleep, quietly weeping.

CHAPTER 2

August 1973

It had taken John a night of tossing and turning and a morning taking in the ocean's breezes to recuperate and sort things out. He took a long walk on the Santa Monica beach with his shoes off, letting the waves wash over his feet as he strolled. Though they lived twenty minutes away, he hadn't been on the beach in three or four years. And he was too deep in thought to appreciate it now. He knew he loved Katrina, but it took some hard thinking to finally come to the conclusion that he still loved Priscilla as well.

By noon, he was packed and on California Interstate 5 North to Ukiah. He was only vaguely aware of where the town was, but he had a map. He had no idea where the Peoples Temple might be.

While driving, he went over in his mind the one and only visit he had paid to the L.A. Peoples Temple on Figueroa and Silverwood streets. He had relented after Priscilla's badgering. That would have been just two months ago, in mid-June. John remembered the experience as vividly as if it were yesterday.

The temple was located in a fairly seedy part of the Silverado area. The building had four heavy Corinthian columns out front. They certainly weren't marble, but some kind of sandstone, weathered and chipped in places. The interior was equally impressive, although the furnishings had a faintly used, secondhand-store quality. Where an altar would normally be, there was a sturdy stage about three feet high with another raised platform in the middle.

On either side of the stage, slanting away, purple-garbed choir members were singing, chins upraised. The singing, which reverberated through the stone and tile interior with its high ceilings, was unlike any church music he had ever heard.

As he made his way down one of the aisles, he saw why. Tucked almost out of sight behind the right choir platform was a rock band, blasting away, yet somehow melding with the singers. On the other side, there was a traditional organ, and this too somehow blended in. Huge speakers amplified an almost oceanic sound, filling the auditorium completely.

The congregation was large—maybe seven hundred people, more than half of them black. These members, though dressed up, wore the most outlandish color combinations John had ever seen, inside or outside a church. Men wore pink silk under dark suits. Women garbed in cadmium red, cobalt blue, and chartreuse were waving fans, their hair piled high. Everyone was smiling, swaying, humming along to the music.

John had instinctively headed for a pew where a well-dressed white family already stood, but Priscilla had grabbed his arm and steered him into a pew alongside a large black woman who was clapping with the beat. He thought he saw a hint of reproach in Priscilla's smile as she released his arm.

Then the music stopped and the crowd grew still and expectant. John felt his attention pulled to the center of the stage, where a white, square-faced man sat on an elaborate, high-backed chair that looked like some sort of a throne. Huge floral displays featuring lilies, begonias, zinnias, giant yellow sunflowers, and yellow and purple orchids reached almost up to the armrests on either side. On the wall behind him, an enormous diorama depicted the traditional Christ on the left and a Moorish Christ on the right.

The man stood and John belatedly realized that he must be the Reverend Jim Jones, though he didn't look like any preacher John had seen before. He was dressed in a black suit with a cream-colored shirt—not a business-type shirt, but rather one made of undulating, pleated silk, like John had seen men wear in the Caribbean. No tie. His straight black hair flopped casually across his tanned forehead, and his eyes were hidden behind dark glasses, completing the impression that he had strolled off a boardwalk and onto the pulpit.

Jones opened his mouth as if to start his sermon, but instead, he began to emit a deep-toned mantra that sounded like nonsense to John. Occasionally he would pause and one side of the choir would answer in a musical counterpoint.

Members of the audience began to chime in now with murmurs and cries of "Amen, brother," "Tell it like it is," and "Lord helps those!" Periodically, young girls in white would enter the room, one from each side, lay a long-stemmed rose at Jones' feet, kiss him on the cheek, and exit from center stage. John detected movement out of the corner of his eye and turned to see a small cluster of people approaching the stage with a woman in a wheelchair in their midst. They stopped just in front of Reverend Jones.

Then, as if on cue, the volume of every participant began to rise. The congregation got more animated. The black woman seated next to John was enthralled, not knowing whether to sit or stand, to clap her hands or sing out God's praises. She was captivated by the Reverend Jones' every word and gesture. Priscilla, too, was fixated on Jones with wide eyes and swayed in concert with the music.

"There is a Godliness coming through me now," Jones suddenly boomed in his deep, rich voice. "Can you feel it Sister Kalena?"

"Oh Lord," the woman in the chair moaned. "Oh come to me Lord."

Suddenly, one of those attending the woman dramatically pulled the wheelchair out from under her. The congregation gasped; some rose to their feet. The woman went down hard on the floor, her lap coverlet flying. She struggled like a dying bug for a moment.

"Lord says get to your feet, woman!" Jones intoned, the bass aspects of his voice reverberating around the ceiling. John watched the prone woman with a mixture of revulsion and anticipation. The air around him seemed to crackle with excitement.

Her legs were moving with more purpose now. Tentatively, she got to one knee, then, with a halting step, she stumbled toward the raised stage, her arms stretched out in supplication to the Reverend. The crowd started to cheer and whoop. "Hallelujah, hallelujah!"

The woman cried out, "Dad! Dad! You did it! You healed me. You done healed me!" The others rushed to her and she fell or fainted back into their arms.

Suddenly, the band and organ cranked up. Both halves of the choir joined in with a spirited anthem. The baritone voice of Jim Jones broke through again. Jones was standing on his throne, leaning forward.

"Did I do that? Did I do that healing just now?" he inquired with sweeping gestures. "My brethren. My flock. My brothers. My sisters. Or—" Here Jones stretched out his hands. "—did Sister Kalena heal herself?"

Jones paused and the crowd shifted uncomfortably as he waited for a response. "God is within," offered a woman's voice. "Be here now," said another. "God is in our midst," cried an old man.

Jones began again: "I will tell you. I healed her because I am God! Let no man here today doubt me. I am not the Sky God the honkies been pushin' for two thousand years of oppression. I am not the Sky God of myth, of myth derived from whitey to control you. Did the astronauts see Him on the way to the moon, if He lives in the sky? No! Didn't we have an astronaut here just last week? Didn't he tell us that in so many words? Astronaut Gordon Cooper, that's right, came and stood right where I'm standing. Help Sister Kalena back to the pew there. Well, maybe the Sky God has moved! Maybe he done moved a little further away from you-all. Maybe he moved on to another solar system. So-laar system. Or is that *sold-out* system in this here world? As in, white, organized religion has sold you out!"

The congregation sat motionless with rapt faces, black and white. Even the children in the audience were still. Jones continued in a choppy cadence.

"And what I have been preaching for—for I don't know how long—for some time, at any rate…"This was greeted, as if on cue, by a chorus around the auditorium of "alleluias" and "Keep it goin', brother."

Jones continued, dropping his inflections, modulating his perfectly controlled voice: " . . . is that We Will Heal Each Other. We *will* look *out* after each other. Oh, *I am* GOD. I think I have proven that often enough up here. Is that right, Sister Kalena?"

A huge cheer went up.

"Hand me one of them bi-*bulls*," Jones shouted toward the right wing. "And we will love one another, like the early Christians say, before the Word was polluted." He was handed a bible. "We don't need no Sky-false-whitey God here in this temple. Every man's temple!" Another great roar went up among the throng.

John glanced at Priscilla, eyebrows arched, as if to say, *You're not really buying this, are you?* But she wasn't looking at him. Her eyes were glued on Jim Jones, and her mouth was set in a grim line that was anything but skeptical. Jones was quoting:

"Vex not thy spirit at the course of things;

They heed not thy vexation,

How ludicrous and outlandish is astonishment

At anything that may happen in life."

Jones looked out at the congregation. "Who said that?" he asked quietly. A few tentative voices said: "Isaiah 2:4." Others said, "John" or "Luke."

"No!" Jones shouted. "Marcus Aurelius, and he hated Christians. He was an atheist. It's okay. Don't be misled by this book! It is inaccurate. Haven't I been telling you that for some time now?" His voice was pleading.

"The fact is that you must only believe in what you see. If you see me as your friend, I'll be your friend. If you see me as your father, I'll be your father. If you see me as your God, I'll be your God." The Reverend Jones then raised the bible high, paused, and flung it down on the stage and spit on it. Lurching forward, he stomped on the book and then kicked it, sending it skittering across the stage several feet until it came to rest, pages askew. A kind of rolling murmur went through the crowd; people watched him with puzzled, concerned faces. A few souls voiced, "Amen, brother."

Jones raised his eyes upward and said, "I just said 'God does not exist.' Sky God, whitey God. Would any of you dare to do that?" Another wave of murmurs. "Of course not. 'Cause you all are brainwashed. Why doesn't Sky God strike me dead then? Can't he hear me? Why doesn't he blind me for blasphemy? I'll tell you why. I am the living New Age Christ and I can heal, and you know I can 'cause you all have been witness. But it hasn't got done without you. You can heal *yourselves*. We can *all* heal each other. But the answer is . . . we got to stick together! Brothers and Sisters!"

At his closing words, a bevy of young women appeared on stage to escort him to the wings as a thunderous roar filled the huge auditorium.

When the service was over, Priscilla lingered outside the temple to exchange greetings with other members of the congregation. John hovered awkwardly at her side, nodding stiffly and shaking hands with people who seemed too nice and normal to agree with the speech he'd just heard. He wondered if all of them did. Nobody mentioned the fact that Jim Jones had claimed to be God, though one woman approached Priscilla with wide eyes and a whistle, whispering, "Whooeee, how 'bout that sermon?" Priscilla merely laughed softly before changing the subject to the woman's kids.

Once they were in the privacy of the car, John couldn't contain his incredulity: "What *was* that? I thought this was a Christian church, Priscilla. Please tell me you don't believe that load of crap."

He expected her to turn on him defensively, or else to share his reaction. But all she did was laugh apologetically and say, "That was a little more out there than most of his sermons, but you have to realize what a genius, what a prophet he is. He doesn't think like you or me. He says some shocking things just to get you to sit up and *listen*. Because we don't listen enough, John, we don't think enough. And did you see the way he healed that woman? Have you ever seen a miracle like that before?"

John wanted to tell her he didn't believe for an instant that the woman had been crippled to begin with. But he stopped himself, suddenly realizing that he was talking to a stranger. They drove the rest of the way home in silence.

———————

A road sign announcing twenty miles to Ukiah slipped by, but John Olsen remained lost in his thoughts. The memory of the Peoples Temple had left a foul taste in his mouth and a knot of dread in his gut. His mind lingered on the dark glasses Jim Jones had worn throughout his sermon. At the time, John had chalked them up to an attempt to look cool—a prop to go with his unconventional theatrics. But now John couldn't shake the notion that those glasses were intended to conceal something. He imagined Katrina mounting the altar steps in a white dress to lay a flower at Jim Jones' feet before disappearing out the door behind him, her little body swallowed up by the hole in the temple wall. John's foot pressed the gas pedal all the harder. He knew a confrontation with Priscilla was coming. He had to do everything he could to keep Katrina away from Jim Jones and the Peoples Temple.

CHAPTER 3

1956

James Warren Jones stared up at the white clapboard building he had just purchased for his own. It wasn't much to look at, but soon it would be brimming with believers, white and black alike.

Though located in the Old Northside area of Indianapolis, in the Kingspark section of the city, 1502 North New Jersey Street was not a particularly prestigious address. Nonetheless, Jim Jones had a vision. There'd be no other congregation like it, he thought. The sign reading "Restoration Baptist Church" would have to go. He planned to call his church "Wings of Deliverance," as he would deliver his flock from the chains of racism, and perhaps from capitalism, if they would follow him.

Even though his parents were not churchgoers, Jim had been fascinated by religion ever since he was a small boy. Born right after the Great Depression, on May 13th, 1931, in the rural village of Crete, Indiana, Jim knew poverty firsthand. Because his father, James, was a seriously disabled World War I veteran, Jim's mother, Lynetta, had to work to support the family. The elder James was soured by his personal lot in life and bitter that the government wasn't doing more to help him and others like him. Jim lived under this blanket of resentment throughout his time at home and found it difficult to experience the joys and happiness that other children relished.

Not having any siblings, and with his father immobile, Jim spent most of his free time alone, entertaining himself in his own, self-imagined world. Neighbors saw Jim and his family as odd and exhibited little sympathy for their plight. At the time, the majority of rural residents were just able to make ends meet, and everyone was struggling to try to get ahead. The neighborhood kids enjoyed coming to the Jones' house to play, because they knew that they would not be bothered by Jim's father and would be free to do what they wanted. At nine years old, already Jim was holding mock church services with his neighborhood playmates, with Jim playing the role of preacher. More often than not, these mock religious events were funeral services for some dead animal, which gave rise to suspicions among the neighbors that Jim had killed some of the animals himself.

The teenage years were harder on Jim. He didn't have any close friends, was withdrawn in social settings, and was considered a loser by most of his classmates. That all changed in 1948, when he met Marceline Baldwin.

Jim had already begun his college education at the young age of sixteen. To pay his way, he took a summer job as an aide at St. Vincent's Hospital in Winchester, Indiana. A petite girl in a candy-striper uniform caught his eye during his second week on the job. Seizing the moment, Jim used the ploy of needing some comfort to initiate contact. Marceline seemed amused at least, and responded kindly. They took their relationship seriously from the start and were married in June of 1949, both still in their teens.

Marceline shared Jim's fundamental belief that everyone should help those in need. It was one of the things that attracted her to him. Jim just wanted to make the world a better place. To accomplish that, he first tried to be the junior pastor at an already established church, but he quickly found that he didn't see eye-to-eye with the elder pastor. Jim was just too exuberant, too passionate, and with his strong pro-integrationist vision, wanted to create an interracial church. This wasn't a popular notion at that time, to say the least. And so, Jim found himself standing in front of 1502 North New Jersey Street, ready to go it on his own.

As he passed through the poorly maintained white picket fence that marked the front of the church and ascended the three concrete steps to enter, he paused for a long moment, laying a hand on the large front door. His thoughts were reflective—of thanks to God for His goodness in providing him this opportunity.

Thus began in earnest Jim Jones' career as a man of the cloth.

Over the next few weeks, as Jim settled into his role as church pastor, he reveled in the potential of the opportunity and the sweetness of this new beginning. It had taken him two full years of soliciting donations for his church and saving every penny. He'd even worked a side job selling exotic pets before he finally had enough for the down payment on "1502," as he called it. Now he had a building and enough followers to make his dream a reality.

Unlike most other churches of the time, Jim Jones' Wings of Deliverance Church was a racially integrated church that focused on helping people in need. During a time when segregation was rampant, Jim offered a different, utopian view of what society could become. From the start, he was a charismatic preacher who demanded commitment and loyalty from his followers. He preached a Pentecostal message of Christianity and social justice. He had an incredible ability to quote and cite scripture. Yet at the same time, he also chastised people who relied too heavily on the Bible as a guide.

A philosophy of socialism underpinned much of his vision, a vision that bled through everything that Jim did as a preacher. This was driven in part by his strong belief that American capitalism had caused an unhealthy balance in the world following World War II, where the rich had too much money and the poor worked hard to receive too little.

A year after founding Wings of Deliverance, Jim renamed it the Peoples Temple, a name that better honored his socialist vision. While still small in size, the Peoples Temple established soup kitchens in greater Indianapolis, and homes for the elderly and mentally ill. Jim also cultivated a network of businessmen who would help church members find good jobs. When someone was sick, a member from the temple visited. Jim thereby became part of every family in the church and, with the sincerity of his convictions, earned the trust of his followers.

CHAPTER 4

1972

B ill Hausman blinked, and in that instant, Phuoc's Claymore mine shook the earth and sent clouds of shrapnel, jungle debris, and smoke into the air to hit their intended targets like lethal hailstones.

Bill felt the explosion where he lay on his stomach, thirty meters or so from the enemy. It wasn't far enough. The onslaught of gunfire from the North Vietnamese continued unabated.

Knowing instinctively that they were outnumbered, Bill got on his PRC-77 radio and called the ops control center, requesting an air strike on his team's location and an evacuation helicopter to get them out of there. There were only six of them— himself, three South Vietnamese soldiers, their commander, Captain Phuoc, and Val. The command center responded that a chopper was en route and would be at the requested landing zone at 0650 hours. They had forty-five minutes to get there. Fortunately, the North Vietnamese fire, while intense, was not well coordinated. They hadn't yet pinpointed the exact location of the small recon team.

Crawling over the jungle floor to Special Forces Sergeant Eddy "Val" Valentine, Bill gave him his orders. Then he briefed Captain Phuoc. They would all blow their individual Claymores and use the pause in enemy fire to get out of the area.

After Phuoc passed the word to the other Vietnamese soldiers, Bill blew his Claymore—the signal for the others to do the same. Yelling for everyone to move, Bill set out in the direction of the landing zone, some 375 meters directly west of their position. He sensed the footsteps of his team behind him and, glancing back, saw Val hot on his heels . . . They were all running for their lives.

Bill awoke with a start, soaking wet. It took him a moment to realize that he was back home in Elmhurst, Illinois, at his girlfriend's apartment, safe in bed.

He glanced to his left where she lay, still snoring softly. Careful not to wake her, he slid out from beneath the damp sheet and made his way to the bathroom, where he washed his face and downed a glass of water.

He knew it would be some time before he could fall back asleep, so he went to the kitchen next and withdrew a bottle of Johnny Walker from the cupboard. The army medics had advised him to keep busy and keep his mind occupied in order to repress memories that were best forgotten, and this often worked during the daytime. But at night, he needed something stronger.

With a generous pour in hand, he settled into a chair in the dark living room and drank to forget.

As usual, this particular nightmare stayed with Bill well into the next morning. He was outside, waxing his prized '49 Ford two-door sedan, when his mind was again back in Vietnam. His arm stopped its buffing motion and he leaned heavily on it, feeling the warmth of the car hood work its way through the rag and into his palm.

"Bill? What's wrong, honey?"

Elaine's face hovered close to his as she extended a glass of lemonade to him. Her skin, damp from helping him wash the car, still smelled faintly of jasmine perfume. Bill took the glass and gulped the cool liquid, trying to wash the horrible taste from his mouth—a taste like he'd just burped up burnt flesh.

"It's okay," he said. "I must have lost myself in thought, that's all."

Her forehead wrinkled in concern beneath her thin blonde bangs. "It was the war, wasn't it? Your mother told me you were in 'Nam."

He looked at her. "When did my mother tell you that?"

"That time over at your house. I guess she thought it would help the relationship if I knew."

"Ah-huh."

"Do you want to talk about it?" Elaine asked.

"I don't think so, Elaine."

"Come on, honey. I sleep next to you; I know when you're having bad dreams. You yell in your sleep sometimes. You got out of the army six months ago—I'd think these things would have been sorted out. It might do you some good to talk about it. Your mom says you're awfully quiet about it all. You know you can trust me. I tell *you* everything."

He stepped away and began picking up wet towels. "No, you most certainly do not tell me everything. I'm gonna go in and hit the shower, okay?"

No, it just didn't help to mention to people that you had been in Vietnam. Too many people thought that they understood the war, because they had seen it unfold on the news night after night. Bill Hausman knew that unless you experienced it personally, up close—the sounds, the smells, the constant fear— there was no understanding, no common ground.

Elaine was just like Sandra and Helen—the other women who had occupied Bill's leisure time since he got out of the army. She was trying to close in on him, eke out a commitment, and move him into a more serious relationship than he wanted. These little tender moments were telltale signs that he should begin planning his egress.

Bill finished getting dressed as Elaine put breakfast on the table downstairs. He glanced at his six-foot frame in the mirror to see if any love handles were forming. He was concerned about losing his shape, becoming soft, and letting the easy civilian life consume him.

Being at Elaine's apartment had become all too convenient—part of female entrapment, he mused. He leaned briefly into her mirror, brushing his still unfashionably short brown hair. He didn't want to get too comfortable, and he didn't want complications. All he wanted from Elaine was some simple human connection, and he knew that talking about Vietnam would create a barrier between them.

Jogging down the stairs, he checked his watch. This was the third Sunday afternoon in a row he was going to have to lie to Elaine. He just couldn't tell her he was studying for the Foreign Service Exam. If he passed it and the final job interview in Washington, D.C., he had been assured that he would be put on the fast track and assigned overseas within several months. He knew Elaine would take that hard. He couldn't think of an easy way out of the situation, so he postponed the confrontation.

"Look at my man!" Elaine said, setting a plate on the table. "You look great, honey. How're the new slacks?"

"I love 'em. They're perfect. You're so sweet." He kissed her cheek and sat down. "What's the stuff in the omelet?"

"Fresh basil. You're an easy size to shop for . . . kind of standard."

He looked at her.

"Rock hard," she smiled, "but standard. You like it that way?"

"Um. Yeah. I like the way you put in the cheeses," Bill replied.

She watched him eat for a while before starting in herself. He could feel her big liquid green eyes mooning over him, making him feel a tinge of uneasiness. The early fun and games were over now. The meals were getting more elaborate. Little presents were appearing out of nowhere. There was definitely a crunch time coming when he would simply have to go.

"There's a ball game at home this afternoon. White Sox and the Tigers," she announced. "Want to drive downtown for it?"

"I can't, honey. I've got a big flight lesson this afternoon; probably take at least three hours. Tom is getting me ready for my first cross-country." He glanced at her to see if she knew he was lying.

"You know, I really wish you'd tell me these things ahead of time," she said petulantly. "You're gonna fly on a day this cold?"

"This is important to me, Elaine. Besides, cold weather is the best for flying. All the little air molecules are packed closer together, so you get better lift."

"Yeah, sure . . . whatever," she muttered, reaching for the Sunday Chicago Tribune. She brightened. "Well, can I come along?"

"Honey, it's a two-seater. What're you going to do, sit in the car and scan the skies for three or four hours? The moment I get back, we'll go out for dinner and a movie, okay?"

"Oh, all right."

Bill let himself into his parents' house through the back door that was never locked and went up to his old bedroom. On his desk there was a note from his mom to call Patrick, a friend from high school.

Looking for his college texts, Bill found the shoebox full of his childhood stored neatly on the top closet shelf. For a moment he shuffled through the photos, the sports ribbons, newspaper articles, and music awards. Bill wondered if he could still get through Chopin's Polonaise without the sheet music. Then he uncovered the Japanese yen that Uncle Vallie had given him.

"It's all your fault," Bill murmured. This fascination he held for things foreign. Uncle Vallie, who brought back Japanese yen among other souvenirs from Okinawa during World War II, had told his young nephew all about Japanese swords, their uniforms, their philosophy of life, and the mystery of their culture. It had all fascinated the impressionable ten-year-old boy. Bill now looked carefully at each yen note, feeling a familiar thrill of appreciation for their historical significance.

He put the shoebox back on the closet shelf and pulled down his old textbooks: *European History, A Survey of American Literature, The Political Development of South America.* He'd had months to cram old math books, *Newsweek, Time, U.S. News & World Report*—hectic months, considering the demands of his sales job—before the Foreign Service exam. He'd read every issue of the *New York Times* and *The Wall Street Journal* for the past six months, read the art book his mother had given him for Christmas two years ago, read anything that would help him pass that exam.

All he wanted to do was travel internationally. Uncle Vallie had planted the fascination years before, seeds that had grown into a full-blown determination to see and to learn about every corner of the world.

Of course, there was an ulterior motive as well. Bill sensed a strong need to keep moving at the core of his survival instincts. He just didn't feel comfortable in his old surroundings. Even though he loved his parents unconditionally, they had been hovering over him like he was mental patient who couldn't be trusted to be alone. Bill's mother wouldn't accept that Bill wanted some space and room to breathe. He knew that once he was truly out and on his own again, he would find some peace and become engaged in other diversions to keep his mind occupied and not thinking of Vietnam.

Once downstairs again, he decided to call Patrick back.

"Goddamn it, Bill! You're turning into a stone, a real drag," his friend complained into the telephone.

"Later, Patrick. In a few weeks I'll be free to hang out, but I've got other things on my plate right now," Bill answered.

"A woman, right? You've deserted your buddies for a woman! Are you slipping down the slippery slope?"

"No, no, no! It's not a woman. It's a test, an exam to end all exams."

"What the hell are you talking about? I swore when I finished *my* last college exam, I'd never take another test in my life."

Yeah, and you'll spend the rest of your life in Elmhurst, Illinois, too, Bill thought to himself.

"I know, I know. It's not fun for me at all," Bill bemoaned.

"Summer baseball leagues are forming. Sunday afternoons. You in?"

"Better not count me as a regular. Put me down as a sub, okay?"

After reviewing the latest on several high school friends, the conversation ended. Even though they were best friends, Patrick had nonetheless become a disappointment in Bill's mind, all because he chose to make his life at home.

Bill hung up the telephone and glanced out the kitchen window at the first signs of spring. Mr. Hershey, the elderly neighbor next door, was taking a walk with his wooden cane. In the apple tree in the front lawn, a robin and a cardinal argued noisily. Across the street, one of the Leahey twins was oiling the chain on his bike.

Bill grabbed a jock bag, threw in some *New Yorker* and *Atlantic Monthly* magazines, and decided to spend time catching up on current events at Wilder Park next to the library. He left his parents' house and headed down the street, glad to feel the warm sun on his shoulders and the cool breeze on his face.

"I understand you have a working knowledge of the Vietnamese language?"

"Yes," Bill replied simply. He sat across from three senior Foreign Service officers in a windowed office overlooking the diplomats' entrance to the State Department. He was enduring the final interview for a position as a Foreign Service officer entering into the career program to become an American diplomat. He had gotten through the qualifying written test three months before in good shape, and the two preliminary interviews as well. This was it.

"Mr. Hausman," the officer in the middle began, "this board is aware of your record as an army officer and, quite frankly, we're not convinced that your foreign experience and tour in Vietnam translates easily to a career with the State Department. Could you address your qualifications and why you are seeking a career in foreign service?"

Bill studied the three faces before him. They were bland on the surface, certainly, adept at not betraying the slightest inclination toward anything. He thought, *That's a fair question, but how does one answer it? Should I spout bullshit, saying what they want to hear, or just speak with true feeling?* He decided he had nothing to lose by being straightforward and honest.

"To answer your question, sir, whether you're talking about a job in foreign service, or any other, I guess what's really important is results. Once you have satisfied the basic requirements for a job, it's performance that counts. As a special forces officer, I was afforded experiences that few men ever have. I've worked with indigenous groups from many parts of the globe, overcoming differences and finding solutions to problems. All this was done in a foreign language, in a foreign land, and under difficult conditions. I'm not talking just about Vietnam. I also speak some Japanese and fluent Korean and have worked in both of those countries. Men in my detachment spoke a variety of other languages as well, from Spanish to Swahili. Through it all, I've gained a personal satisfaction that is rarely found in any other work environment, and I cherished those opportunities to contribute. I now seek to continue making a contribution to my country by working with other nations to overcome perplexing problems of our modern era. I see the mission of our Foreign Service as basically that, with the added responsibility of representing American interests abroad. Even though I think I've already had success in doing just that, I have no illusions, and I look forward to learning a lot about the Foreign Service from the professionals who have made it their careers as diplomats." His speech ended abruptly, totally unintended. Bill had nothing more to add. A long moment of silence followed.

"That's very interesting, Mr. Hausman," the middle interviewer offered. "I guess I never quite equated what *we do* with Special Forces. But thank you for your viewpoint."

After several circumstantial questions designed to judge the way he thought and problem-solved, the interview was over.

"Thank you for your interest in the Foreign Service, Mr. Hausman," the interviewer in the middle said without any emotion or zest. "We'll reconvene after lunch to make our final recommendations. You have an appointment with our personnel department this afternoon at three o'clock. Any questions?"

"No sir." The interview was over.

As Bill got up from the table, he had the feeling that he just didn't measure up to what they were looking for.

One of the interviewers, Ambassador Davila, tapped Bill on the shoulder as he was walking out of the interview room. "Do you have any plans for lunch, Mr. Hausman?" Without waiting for a reply, he said, "Why don't we go down to the cafeteria for something?"

Taken off guard, Bill responded with an "Okay," and they walked abreast down the long corridor.

In an attempt to break the tension of the interview, Ambassador Davila asked, "You're from Wisconsin, aren't you?"

Bill answered, "Not originally, but I went to school there."

"Have you ever been fishing up by Eagle River?"

Before Bill could answer, the ambassador continued, "I used to go up there with my father and my uncle—ice fishing—a long time ago. What a time we had—great fishing and good cooking. My wife is from Wisconsin, from Green Bay. Before you ask, yes, she's a Packer fan." The ambassador chuckled to himself.

Bill couldn't figure out where Davila was headed with this conversation, though he appreciated his effort to be friendly.

"How'd you get into foreign service, Mr. Ambassador?" Bill asked.

"Well, I went to school at Georgetown University, the School of Foreign Service, and I have a master's degree in international relations. It all sorta fell into place after I graduated. That and marriage. Are you married, Bill?"

"Not yet, sir."

"I feel so old when I think back to those days. You know, I was too young for the Korean War and too old for the Vietnam War. Never served in the military, though I always wanted to. I started out wanting to be a history teacher, too, and look where I ended up!"

"Have you enjoyed your career, Mr. Ambassador?" Bill asked.

Smiling at Bill, he responded, "All in all, it's been a hell of a ride! You know, what you said in the interview really hit home with me—your comment about personal satisfaction. Must admit, that's why I'm here today, but I don't want to talk about what I think, or about me, Bill. I'd rather talk about you, if you don't mind."

The two men had just reached the cafeteria, and agreed to meet up at a table near the courtyard windows where they could talk.

As he sat down at the table with Bill, the ambassador said, "You know, I've been in Africa and the Near East for most of my career, twenty-four of the last twenty-nine years, basically focused on regional political issues. I've heard and read so much about Vietnam, but rarely have I had a chance to sit down and talk with someone like you, who was there. Do you mind me asking?"

"No, not at all, sir," Bill responded.

"How was Vietnam? I mean, I know about the political considerations and how it got started and all that. What I haven't any appreciation for is what you young guys encountered over there."

"Vietnam is a topic that I generally don't talk much about, Mr. Ambassador. Do you mind if I just give you a quick overview?"

"Sure. I don't want to make you feel uncomfortable," he answered.

Bill took a deep breath and began, "I was a lieutenant when I arrived in Vietnam and was promoted to captain later on. I was a special forces officer and served a full tour there. Frankly, I'm not your poster child for Vietnam.

From my viewpoint, we were all asked to fight in a restrictive conflict that was politically motivated. From the beginning, there were no clear-cut objectives identified, and that made our presence in Vietnam all but meaningless. To be clear, we didn't fight the war to win it. As a result, all I wanted to do was survive another day."

The ambassador was hanging on to every word as Bill continued. "You want to know what the majority of us went through. As one veteran put it to me, it was simply mud, dirt, sweat, and tears covered with blood and guts. Too many Americans lost their lives, and too many Vietnamese are now dead because of our actions—not to mention the wounded and all those maimed for life. Vietnam is a national tragedy, sir. When it was written that war is hell, a truer statement cannot be made. Unless we change our course and commit ourselves to win this war, we would be best served to end it now and bring our guys home."

"Whoa, I guess I deserved that," the ambassador responded. "You should know that I have been against continuing the war in Vietnam since the Tet Offensive in 1968. Your testimony tells me that I'm right."

Bill nodded and the men lapsed into silence for a few minutes as they ate. Then Bill struck up a new strain of conversation, asking the ambassador about family life in the Foreign Service. Near the end of lunch, the ambassador asked Bill an unexpected question. "Would you ever consider a return to Southeast Asia as a Foreign Service officer, Bill?"

Intent on making a good impression, Bill answered, "I would accept whatever assignment was offered to me, wherever, whenever."

Little did he know what the consequence of that statement would be.

The decision was unanimous that Bill Hausman would be brought on with FSO class 125, and following training, would be assigned to Southeast Asia, to the American embassy, Saigon. He was going back to Vietnam.

CHAPTER 5

1973

Prior to John's arrival at Ukiah, the Reverend Jim Jones moved easily through the small crowd, an air of confidence surrounding him. People deferred to him, stopped their conversations when he approached to let him begin a new one, gave up their seats to him at the picnic bench, offered food to him—small, unmistakable signs of respect.

"Wherever I have a church, all people will be welcome," Jones had said during the service. "We are a family here, and I am the head of that family. Look to me to protect you, to care for you. I have the answers you are seeking."

Priscilla was mesmerized by Jones, held tight by his rich baritone voice, his glossy black hair and intense eyes. He had a movie-star handsomeness and glamour, and while part of her deemed his aviator glasses a silly affectation, the effect intrigued her nonetheless. Whenever he was nearby, her gaze never wavered from him. And when he spoke from the pulpit, she felt gripped by his message of tolerance and acceptance.

She had first heard of Jim Jones the previous December, at a Methodist church fund-raiser. Curious to find out more about the church that welcomed all races, Priscilla called the temple for information about their Sunday services. That weekend, she left Katrina at home with John and drove into downtown Los Angeles for an experience that would change her life forever.

On the drive home after hearing Jim Jones speak, her heart thrummed with the feeling that she had found someone who shared her social values and her outlook on life. As she pulled into the garage, she realized with a start that for the first time in years, she didn't feel completely alone.

John was a good husband, of course, and Katrina was a charming and obedient little girl, for the most part. But she was a child, not a confidante, and while John had once been Priscilla's closest companion, their relationship had changed over the past decade in ways she was only beginning to deconstruct.

John and Priscilla met at a bar in the Haight-Ashbury district of San Francisco. He was twenty-two years old and just starting his career as a salesman. At twenty, Priscilla had just finished her sophomore year in college and felt captivated by the counterculture movement that was sweeping the United States. She was wearing a T-shirt with a giant peace sign on it and made a point to explain to John that it was actually a symbol for nuclear disarmament that had originated in Great Britain. At the time, Priscilla espoused a love of nature, a passion for music, a desire for reflection, and a strongly marked independence. They married in February 1963, six months after meeting.

For the first time in her life, Priscilla felt the sincerity of a man's love in John. She'd never known her father, who died on Omaha Beach on D-Day, and when her mother remarried and had three more children, all boys, her stepfather's affection had seemed largely reserved for his sons. He never quite knew how to approach or connect with the little girl who shared none of his genes and bore so little resemblance to him or her brothers. As she grew up, he was always with his boys on weekends and hardly paid attention to Priscilla's academic achievements or her talents as a novice actress. In high school and in college, Priscilla grew apart from her parents. When she finally left home, only her mother really cared.

It was John's quiet self-assurance and dutifulness that attracted her to him at first. In a climate in which every young person seemed gripped by a fevered upheaval, John had spoken of his job and future with a security that made him seem older than his years. Her friends had regarded him skeptically at first, and a few were even hostile to him. But when he applied that same diligence to courting Priscilla, she fell for him. He doted on her and made her the center of his universe. She felt comforted by John, respected and honored by him. In turn, he became her world.

As the years passed, though, their differing views on life began to wedge them apart. As an avid businessman, John leaned toward conservative principles, insisting that the individual was responsible for earning his way. He rejected government encroachment on businesses through incessant taxation and the squandering of tax dollars on welfare giveaway programs that were rife with fraud and corruption. Priscilla, on the other hand, remained true to her political roots in the counterculture and relished the Civil Rights Movement's ideal of equality for the underclass of black people in the United States. She sought opportunities to reach out and help the poor in her daily life, volunteering at soup kitchens and church charities while her husband was at work. This part of her life was largely unknown to John, who concentrated on making a living for his family and enjoying the spoils that came with a successful business career. Over time, their relationship became characterized by heated arguments separated by long spells of silence and superficial conversation.

On her first morning at the Peoples Temple, Priscilla was reminded of what it was like to have someone speak to her heart's desire. She ruminated on this for some time that December morning, until the windows of the car became fogged with her breath. Then she went inside to her husband.

"The preacher was the best I've ever seen or heard, John," Priscilla had explained over dinner that night. "You have to come with me sometime to see for yourself. He's really something! It was so nice to hear some straight talk about equality and the fight for social justice in our lives."

"Sounds good to me," John responded. "Just let me know when."

And he did come. But only once, and his reaction was so negative, Priscilla wished she'd never shared this part of her life with him at all.

Now, months later, Priscilla sat in the bright Ukiah sunlight, watching Jim Jones work his way amicably through the picnicking crowd of Temple members. When he passed by, she stood up from her blanket and took the occasion to introduce Katrina.

"Reverend Jones, this is my daughter, Katrina. Katrina is eight years old and is getting ready to start third grade. Say hello to the reverend, sweetie," Priscilla directed.

"It's nice to meet you, reverend," Katrina said. She then turned to her mother and asked, "Is that enough?" When told "Yes, dear," ran off to join a group of children chasing bubbles in the air.

"That was nice," Jones commented. "If I remember right, you are Priscilla Olsen, correct?" Before Priscilla had a chance to respond, he added, "A relatively new member of our church, if I'm not mistaken."

Priscilla's heart fluttered at the discovery that he knew her by name. She felt like a schoolgirl talking to a rock star. "Yes, that's right. We've only been attending services for about eight months or so."

"Where's your husband?" Jones asked. "Doesn't he like picnics?"

"It's not that . . . it's just that he's coming later. At least I think so," Priscilla said, hoping that he wouldn't detect her lie.

"Well then, welcome. I hope you meet lots of people and have a great time," he said as he moved on.

Sitting back down on the ground, Priscilla could feel her heart beating at a record pace from her conversation with the Reverend Jim Jones himself. She'd never known what it was like to be in the presence of someone really special—until now.

CHAPTER 6

Early 1974

"Daddy, Daddy! I rode a horse!" Katrina Olsen tore through the red door of John's Ramada Inn hotel room.

As he held his arms wide for her, he couldn't help thinking that both Katrina and Priscilla seemed as comfortable here as at home. The other surprise was that his business was apparently flourishing without him. The same salesmen he had berated last week had just brought in the biggest order of his career.

Katrina flopped her skinny eight-year-old body in his lap, flung her arms around his neck, and demanded his attention with her continuing chatter, forcing his eyes away from the Sunday evening news. "Ukiah isn't as pretty as Santa Monica, but I like the ranch. I really like it."

He chuckled, "A ranch? I thought this was a church." John glanced at his wife, who stood leaning against the doorframe, her arms and ankles crossed.

"Oh," Katrina hastened to explain, her green eyes sparkling, "there was a church service when we first got there in the morning with lots of singing, but then there was a barbecue, and lots of room to run and play, and swimming. But mostly, I liked the horseback riding."

John smiled to see his child so happy. "I can tell you had a good time." He took her hands in his, turning them, examining them. "Look at the dust and dirt. I can smell the horse for sure!" He wrinkled his nose, and his little girl giggled. "Go take a bath. I'll be waiting to tuck you in, okay?"

Katrina nodded and darted for the bathroom. A moment later, John could hear the sound of the tub water running.

He looked toward his wife, but she turned away without a word. She didn't appear ready to talk to him yet, much less to put the day into words. Priscilla's coolness stung him even more here than at home. It made him feel unwelcome, like he was imposing on the place she had staked out for her and Katrina alone.

Sometime on the drive up, he had made up his mind that he wasn't just coming to retrieve Katrina; he wanted to bring Priscilla home, too. He'd always assumed she would lose interest in the Peoples Temple, just as she had in so many other projects and causes. But now he knew it was stealing her away from him, and he was determined to stop it. He wanted to reconcile his marriage.

Priscilla walked across the spacious hotel bedroom to the dressing table. She reached up, took the rubber band out of her ponytail, and shook her long, dark hair loose. Then she moved to the mirror on the wall and began working her fingers through her hair and talking to John without looking at him.

"They had said to dress casually, but I was surprised. Have you ever seen Bermuda shorts, sunglasses, flip-flops, and T-shirts in church before? Everyone had on picnic clothes, even Reverend Jones and his wife, Marceline. She told me that they encourage informality so no one will be intimidated by the wealth of another."

He certainly hadn't seen signs of wealth in or around the church grounds. The cars of the people spending the day were solid middle-class cars—Chevys, Fords, nothing flashy or ostentatious. The people who lived on the grounds, about twenty from what he could gather, lived in little more than summer camp cabins with cots—bare-floored wooden dwellings, stark and Spartan.

"What has impressed me more than anything is the racial mix—big-city blacks, Ukiah locals, and transplanted Midwesterners—people so committed to the Reverend Jones that they followed him from Indiana to California," Priscilla continued as she unbuttoned her denim blouse, her voice thoughtful and confiding.

She shot John a sharp look that he pretended not to see. He knew she wanted him to slip up and say something negative about the prominence of black parishioners. He didn't, so she went on, "One seventy-year-old black lady told me she came here because she was tired of struggling through life, and now the reverend takes care of her completely. Imagine that. If she were on her own, she might end up in a nursing home, or destitute, on the streets even. Who knows? But instead Reverend Jones lets her live here and work for the church and be an asset to others. He takes care of her medical needs. He even healed her bad hip. Can you believe it? Where else in this country can you find that kind of acceptance and kindness?"

John shrugged his shoulders. He couldn't deny that the Temple seemed to look after its own.

"I really feel a sense of belonging here, John," she added quietly. "I feel like I've found my purpose in life."

Two days later, John sat with his wife and little girl at the morning service, the muscles in his jaw clenching. It was the last service before they would all leave to return to Los Angeles. The Reverend Jim Jones stood behind a pulpit in the Butler building that served as a crude church on the Ukiah ranch.

The reverend's face dripped with sweat as he preached his message of "apostolic socialism," whatever that meant. John was hardly listening. All he knew was that it was hot, and Jones's armpits were wet. John wasn't at the service because he wanted to be. It was his attempt to demonstrate his understanding and openness to Priscilla. Maybe if he could communicate a desire to be a part of her world, he could bridge the chasm that had developed between them when he wasn't looking. Maybe he could convince her that she could have the church without abandoning him and their life together.

John glanced to his left. Beside him sat his daughter, and beside her was his wife. He shifted, putting his arm around the back of Katrina's chair, a protective, possessive move.

The day before, over morning coffee on the hotel balcony, Priscilla had dealt a harsh blow.

"You're what?" John had started, spilling his coffee onto the table. She had threatened to leave him before, but always in tears, during a fight. Now it was different. Now she was calm, dispassionate, as though she'd been rehearsing this for some time.

"I'm leaving. I'm taking Katrina and moving back here to Ukiah. You can come too, if you want, but I'm leaving." Priscilla sat at the table, her arms extended straight before her, her hands clasped as if in prayer.

"To this commune! Just like that, you've decided?"

"It isn't a commune," she protested, "and it isn't just like that. I've been thinking of this for weeks now, little else. I just know it's right."

"I thought you were over this. What the hell has happened to put you back on this collision course? What about us? What about our marriage? Doesn't any of that count?" He stood and began pacing the small balcony desperately.

"I want it to work, John, I really do. If you only understood how I feel. I just know we could be happy if you came with us and really tried."

"I couldn't be happy in Ukiah with that self-centered asshole Jones." He could hear himself blustering, and he couldn't stop. "I visited just like you wanted me to. I told you what I thought of him six months ago. For Christ's sake, Jim Jones is a screwball, a man with a religious gimmick, out for himself! Can't you see through all that?"

She shook her head, refusing to hear what he was saying. "No, he's not. He's a wonderful man, a kind man who thinks of everyone except himself."

"That's all crap!" Olsen shouted, not caring who heard him. "He's an egomaniac of the first order." He turned abruptly, pointing at her. "Money! I bet he expects you to bring money. He does, doesn't he?"

She paled and didn't answer, but her expression gave it away.

"Not my money," he screamed. "He's not going to get one cent."

"I thought it was our money," she countered angrily.

"It is our money, and it's our marriage, and it's our child, and Jim Jones doesn't play any part in any of it."

"If it's our money," she grew sarcastic, "why don't you share more of it? Or is it that money is everything to you?"

"Priscilla, we've had this conversation a hundred times before. For Christ's sake, there's nothing more to add, and you know it." John was running to the end of his patience.

"It's not just that, it's more. It's hard to explain." She looked at him, pleading for him to understand. "Dad Jones has given me answers and guidance that you never have. He knows what I'm thinking, feeling."

"Dad Jones, huh?" John's tone was scornful, scathing. "If I haven't given you answers, it's because I've treated you as an adult, not a child."

"You don't understand. I have solidarity with the community of friends here. I feel a sense of belonging and believing in something greater than you, or me. For the first time in my life, I feel that what I am doing is important. I feel human again."

John slapped his forehead with the heel of his hand. She was right. He didn't understand. He only knew he was angry, really angry. He whirled around, his face blanched with emotion.

"Have you already talked with Katrina about this decision of yours?"

Her silence told him she had not. He challenged her. "Let's wake Katrina up right now and ask her if this is what she wants."

Priscilla's chin went up. With tears in her eyes, she said, "This is what's best for her. She's coming back with me!"

"Since when have you known what's best for her? You've always acted like she was an imposition, like she got in the way of your more important affairs.

Remember last month, when I took her to the doctor so you wouldn't be late for that charity luncheon?" John bristled.

"You bastard! That's rotten! I was chairman and you know it! Besides, it doesn't kill you to be there for her once in a while, too. If I ever act like she's an imposition, it's only because I get no help from you, and when I do, you throw it back in my face months later! Of course you wouldn't prioritize a charity; you don't understand. Oh sure, you throw money at problems, but as far as your time goes, you're the least charitable person there is, especially when it comes to your family!"

John flagged a little under her words. His time spent at work and his lack of involvement in Priscilla's and Katrina's lives had become a familiar and painful accusation in recent years. It never did any good to defend himself by citing the demands of his job. He realized fleetingly that he should seize this opportunity to admit that she was right, and to promise to be more giving and supportive in the future. But his sullen rejoinder was already escaping his lips: "Still, your luncheon took precedence over your daughter's well-being."

"Her physical well-being is not as important as her spiritual well-being," Priscilla countered.

"That's more of his gobbledygook, isn't it?"

She glared at him. "This is what's best for her, and that's it, final!"

"No, it's what you think is best for her, and those are two very different things. You're not taking Katrina with you!"

"Oh yes, I am!" she shouted. She stood, yanked open the sliding glass door, and stalked back into the hotel room. John heard the door to the hallway slam and Katrina stir in bed. He wondered how much she'd overheard.

Now, as he sat listening to Jim Jones rant, John was determined to change Priscilla's mind. They would return home, and he would show her she didn't have to leave to fix her life. He'd spend less time at work on weekends. He'd make her see him as a husband for the man he was, and Jim Jones for the charlatan he was.

Gently, he extended the arm he'd wrapped around Katrina to lay his hand on his wife's shoulder. She smiled at him, and then lifted her hand to brush it off.

"It's too hot," she whispered before turning her eyes back to Jim Jones.

CHAPTER 7

1974

Three days later, John's office phone rang. He picked it up and heard his daughter's voice: "Daddy, you'd better come home. Mommy is packing and getting ready to leave. She got a call . . ."

Then John heard a clatter on the other end, and the line went dead.

John left for home like a shot. His thoughts ran wild as he tried to imagine what had spurred Katrina's phone call. Had he been wrong to believe that Priscilla wanted to leave him of her own accord? Was somebody else—some other man, perhaps—pressuring her to leave?

As he rounded the corner near their house, John saw Priscilla half-dragging a suitcase to her car. She looked up, saw him coming, dropped the suitcase, picked it up again, and struggled to get it into the trunk of her Volvo.

"What the hell is going on, Priscilla?" John exclaimed as he got out of his car. "Who called you? What's this about?"

She turned and walked at a brisk pace into the house. "Katrina! Katrina!" she shouted.

"Coming, Mommy," Katrina answered as she ran down the stairs with her stuffed bear in her arms.

"Get into the car. Did you hear me? Get into the damn car!" Her voice broke as she shouted.

John fought to keep his voice level. "Priscilla, what are you doing?"

"I've had it with you and with your stupid business. We're leaving, and don't try to stop me," Priscilla snapped as she picked up the last of the shopping bags full of clothes. Following Katrina to the car, she barked at her daughter, "Get in and shut up!"

Katrina's face crumpled and tears flooded her eyes.

"You owe me some explanation, damn it! What in God's name have I done?" John pleaded.

Priscilla turned and faced him, now standing by the front of her car. She shouted, "This is never going to work, you and me. We've grown too far apart. You're concerned with your business and with making money, ignoring us. I'm sick of it. Missed dinners, and you hardly have time enough to kiss your daughter good night. I just can't take it anymore. I'm through with you and all your bullshit! My counselor assures me that I don't have to continue with you anymore. We're through. I'm leaving! Believe me, divorce papers will be on their way."

"We can work things out. Let's go inside and talk, for Christ's sake. Leaving me is no solution!" John pleaded.

Priscilla took a step forward, her face close to his. "You make me sick! Do you hear me? You make me vomit! You've had your chance and you blew it. You don't respect my beliefs or me. All I hear you say is that Father Jones is a nut case, a con artist. Now that I am secure with my God and in my temple, I'm leaving, knowing that my temple brothers and sisters will care for me and look out for me and for Katrina. At least they are interested in—"

"Goddamn it, Priscilla! Don't give me that holy, holy crap," John interrupted. "I won't let you take Katrina! You can go and screw up your own life with that megalomaniac if you want to, but leave Katrina out of it."

"Just try to stop me, and I'll have you put in jail for abuse!" Priscilla threatened. "I have every right to raise Katrina as I see fit, and that's exactly what I'm going to do. After all, I am her mother. She's going with me, and that's it!"

With these words, Priscilla got in her car and locked the doors. Then, as John looked on helplessly, she pulled out of the driveway without so much as a glance back. Katrina leaned out of the passenger side window, crying and sniffling and waving a skinny arm in a frantic goodbye to her father. As the car rounded a bend in the cul-de-sac and groaned out of sight, John realized he should have run after it.

Chapter 8

1965

During the mid-1960s, the United States and the Soviet Union were locked in a seemingly unending cold war struggle, with the central feature the potential for a nuclear holocaust that would destroy the world. Schoolchildren practiced taking shelter under their desks when an alarm sounded, and communities stockpiled water and food in shelters judged safe enough to survive an initial nuclear attack.

In this climate of fear, Jim Jones was anxious about his safety and the future of his church. He paid close attention to the escalating internal strife in Vietnam and to the daily unfolding of world events. After reading an article in *Esquire* magazine that identified Ukiah, California, as one of the five places in the world that would most likely survive a nuclear attack, he made up his mind to move his church to Ukiah.

It took months to plan and prepare for the move, but finally, in 1965, Jim and about sixty-five church families relocated to Redwood Valley, a small town just north of Ukiah, in Mendocino County. In addition to Jim's desire to survive a nuclear holocaust, he judged that California would be more open to accepting an integrationist church than Indiana had been. In an effort to avoid criticism, he claimed publicly that the church moved to California because he and others associated with the church had received threats. He concluded that the racial unrest in the Midwest made it too risky for his church to stay in Indianapolis.

When he first began preaching in northern California in 1965, Jim used a mix of civil rights and social justice themes wrapped around some good old-fashioned revivalism and was an instant success. His message from the pulpit was new, unique, and powerful. Thousands of people, black and white alike, joined his church over time and listened to this handsome, charismatic man call for peace and justice. Jim was not some self-proclaimed wacko "prophet" or fringe religious leader. No, he was an ordained minister of the Disciples of Christ—a respected mainline denomination—who had captured the emptiness in the souls of thousands. At one point after arriving in Ukiah, his congregation numbered over eight thousand. It was composed largely of poor black Americans.

Wanting to appeal to a larger audience and possessing a keen understanding of human nature, Jim was canny enough to broaden his message by mixing new-left promises of economic equality with old-church rituals like faith healing. Just like any great performer on stage, he was a master of tone, innuendo, cadence, verbal emotion, and body language, with the charm and folksiness of an accomplished storyteller. He could mix the fervor of a Baptist preacher with the zeal of a maniacal dictator—all for a desired effect. As he spoke, his followers became enthralled by his words. They applauded, shouted, cheered, and shed tears of joy, fervently believing in his message.

Jim used staged skits for their impact on the faithful. He enraptured his followers with faith healings—actually laying hands on disabled or sick people who would miraculously be cured of any ailments. Though insiders subsequently revealed that these healings were faked, Jim's mastery of word and performance left few in attendance with any doubt about the legitimacy of his powers. He was astounded by his own success.

Once established in Redwood Valley, Jim soon expanded his reach into the San Francisco Bay area. Again, his priority was to establish homes for the elderly and the mentally ill. He also worked to set up halfway houses for drug addicts and foster children. The work done by the Peoples Temple was praised in the California newspapers and by local politicians. Largely due to these positive endorsements, Jim became a trusted leader within the community. Yet he was a much more complex man inside—a man who was more unbalanced than anyone ever suspected.

Jim's first step on his path to exploit political influence began in the spring of 1970. He created a fund for the families of slain police officers. This was the beginning of a viable process that he used to make valuable friends through charitable contributions. He gave money to the NAACP, the Ecumenical Peace Institute, and to a senior citizens' escort service. Even the then-governor of California could be seen at his church services, apparently wanting to identify himself with the Reverend Jones as a friend.

By mid-1970, Jim realized that San Francisco and Los Angeles were ripe for his ministry. Early in 1971, the Peoples Temple bought a building in downtown San Francisco and another in Los Angeles. Jim moved his headquarters to San Francisco. When the Temple arrived in San Francisco, Jim was preaching a message of revolutionary socialist change sprinkled with elements of Christianity. He never abandoned the Christian message, because it brought people to his church, but his focus became more and more political. He targeted young, idealistic, liberal white Americans with themes of racial equality and political activism, backing up his brand of socialism with passages from the bible. This made his left-wing ideas more palatable to those young adults coming from more conservative religious backgrounds. Membership continued to grow.

In addition to his work as the leader of the Peoples Temple, Jim was now an executive as well, managing large social programs, job fairs, and even healthcare programs for the poor. Eventually casting himself as a political progressive, he was embraced by liberal politicians throughout California. But there wasn't anything magical about his power. It was just raw politics. He was able to deliver what politicians wanted—votes. With Jim's encouragement, thousands of his followers could be mobilized to support any given political objective.

Following this period of incredible growth, Jim relished his newfound power more and more. Insidious changes began to occur in his conduct toward Temple members, starting with those who worked closest to him. The man full of beautiful ideals, whom many had come to call "Dad," was exhibiting a darker side now. He would resort to threats and play on peoples' fears to make a point or win allegiance. He began expressing a sexual interest in members of his congregation—women and men alike. Those who he felt had betrayed the Temple or strayed from his teachings were publicly humiliated and punished in front of the entire flock. Soon, a culture of intimidation, predatory sexual practices, and beatings had taken root.

Loyalty to Jim Jones and an absolute commitment to him became the standard for all employees who worked for the Temple. Though to skeptical outsiders and those in the know, Jim was a phony faith healer, his congregation was rife with true believers, and they pledged their loyalty to him in dollars. Money came in mail-order donations from desperate followers. Elderly members willingly handed over their social security checks to the Temple, and all working adults pledged twenty-five percent of their salary to the church. Some members even signed over all of their property. As the wealth of the

Temple swelled, Jim began experiencing delusions of grandeur, and with them, a growing paranoia.

Toward the end of 1975, in the company of the Temple planning commission, Jim staged the first "White Night"—a euphemism he coined for mass suicide. He locked the door to their conference room and, under an imperative pretext that suited the moment, required all of the members of the commission to drink with him wine they believed was poisoned. After a long moment, during which they sat quietly, waiting for death to overcome them, Jim rose and walked to the center of the room. "You are my strength, my friends," he said. "I now know that you believe in me."

At that point, the members of the planning commission realized that the wine had not been poisoned and that this had been a test of their loyalty. They stood and gravitated toward Jim, embracing him, some with tears in their eyes.

By the fall of 1976, Jim was at the pinnacle of his power. Celebrities, including California Assemblyman Willie Brown, Mayor George Moscone, activist Angela Davis, attorney Vincent Hallinan, California Lieutenant Governor Mervyn Dymally, and publisher Carlton Goodlett, among others, toasted him at a testimonial dinner. Shortly following that event, Mayor Moscone appointed him to a seat on the San Francisco Housing Authority Commission. Jim had brilliantly captured the attention and imagination of Californians in a span of less than five years.

From the outside, the Peoples Temple looked like an amazing success story. Yet on the inside, the church was transforming into a cult centered on Jim Jones. After the move to California, Jim changed the purpose of the Peoples Temple from religious to political. He became more of a communist than a staunch socialist. The members at the top of the Peoples Temple hierarchy were asked to pledge not only their devotion to him and the church, but all of their material possessions and money as well. Some members even signed over custody of their children to Jim.

Jim quickly became infatuated with power to the point of obsession. He required everyone to call him either "Father" or "Dad." Later, he began to describe himself as the "new age Christ" and then, in the two years before leaving for Guyana, claimed that he was himself God. To the concern of his inner circle, he was also taking a large quantity of drugs. At first, the drugs might have been to help him stay up longer, in order to accomplish more good works, but they took their toll. Those closest to him witnessed major mood swings, the deterioration of his health, and increased paranoia.

No longer was Jim just worried about nuclear attacks; he sincerely believed that the entire government, especially the CIA and FBI, was after him. This perception of reality framed Jim's decision to escape from the United States and take refuge in the South American country of Guyana, where the government would be sympathetic to his socialist ideals.

Chapter 9

1973 – 1975

A *shot rang out . . . then another. The gunshots sounded close.*

Picking himself up off of the floor, Bill moved carefully to the closet to retrieve his M-15 rifle. That feels better, *he thought.*

Slowly, he moved down the staircase and into the office spaces of the hotel. There, he saw two Vietnamese guards hiding behind a concrete guard post.

What in the hell is going on? *Bill wondered. He moved forward, trying to survey the area in front of the hotel.*

Another shot sounded, stopping Bill in his tracks. Whoever was shooting was in front of the hotel. After another long moment, he continued moving and finally took cover alongside the main door to the hotel.

There, standing in the street in front of the hotel was Bill's longtime girlfriend, Co Hoa, being confronted by a sergeant from South Vietnam's Tiger Division. He was obviously drunk. Minutes earlier, Co Hoa had left Bill's hotel room to return home. She insisted on taking a taxi to and from seeing Bill when he came to Saigon.

The sergeant had grabbed Co Hoa's ao dia *and was moving her about like a toy doll. He raised his rifle alongside Co Hoa's head and fired it into the air, shouting at her in a rage. He fired again and again, screaming, shaking her. The Vietnamese guards motioned for Bill to stay down . . .*

Bill opened his eyes and gasped for breath, his mind reeling. The dreams were coming to him night after night, and he was languishing under them. In spite of the army psychologists' predictions, they weren't going away.

———

"I'm not surprised, Mom," Bill explained over the phone when he was first told of his assignment. "Most of my classmates are academics with fresh advanced degrees, liberal ideas, and no experience," he sighed. "Combine that with all the flag-burning and anti-war sentiment, and State is having a hell of a time filling positions in Saigon."

His father, listening in on the phone extension, was quiet but intuitive. "Is this what you really want, William?"

Bill hesitated for an instant. His mind jumped to the smell of gunpowder; the piercing yell a human being can only make upon being shot; the image of a small body crumpled on a dirty street.

He cleared his throat. "Yeah, it is, Pops. They really need me there. There aren't many seasoned guys like me around. We'll have an early Thanksgiving before I leave. How does that sound? Okay?"

Bill left the States with the smell of his mother's turkey and dressing lingering in his mind and arrived in Saigon to equally familiar smells: rotting garbage, dust, and acrid fumes. No amount of mental preparation could ready him for the moment he stepped off of the aircraft and onto the tarmac at Phan Thiet. The city was new to him, but he'd have known he was in Vietnam if he were blindfolded. He was almost knocked off his feet by the rush of memories that overtook him. He pushed them down, steadied himself, and began the short walk to the jeep parked close by, where his new boss waited.

It was just as hot and humid as he remembered, but with one marked difference—not a U.S. military uniform in sight. The American troop pullout had been completed in January 1973, and now, just over eight months later, the country was in the hands of the South Vietnamese.

Bill was the embassy's new junior representative to the southern provinces of Military Region II, with its central office in Phan Thiet, the capital of Binh Thuan Province.

"It may look like just a little fishing village on the South China Sea," his boss explained as they drove from the airport to the province offices in the center of the city. "In fact, it *is* just a little fishing village, but—" He held up a finger for emphasis. "—it has great tactical importance. To get heavy tanks and artillery to Saigon from the coastal plain, you have to control the coastal highway, Route 1, which runs right through the center of Phan Thiet, then west to Saigon about 290 kilometers away, or 175 miles, if you'd like."

Bill nodded his head, listening carefully to his boss, Ryan "Mitch" Mitchell, the regional officer-in-charge and a senior-ranking USAID officer with over twenty-six years of experience.

"How many other Americans are in the area?" Bill asked.

"None, for all intents and purposes. It's you and me, pal, the only two Americans between Saigon and Nha Trang. There're two ex-army types here who have gone native and are married to Vietnamese, and one American missionary—a Jesuit Priest—but we hardly ever see them. Most of our work will be resettling refugees. We're also responsible for running a large rice distribution program and some other agricultural improvement programs, as well as coordinating several joint projects with the Vietnamese, including the construction of a shrimp processing and packing plant."

As Mitch spoke, Bill couldn't help but think that this was a lot for a two-man office, since he knew that they also had the normal responsibilities of economic trend reporting, political reporting, and keeping abreast of any military developments in the area—all with only twenty-six indigenous employees total.

"Could I ask what that smell is?" Bill's sickly impulse to curl his lips betrayed his opinion of the odor.

Mitch chuckled. "I wondered when you were going to ask. That's decayed fish, the stuff they make *nuoc-mam* out of. The words mean fish-oil seasoning. Phan Thiet is the world's capital for *nuoc-mam*." He sounded almost proud. "It's a liquid seasoning made from tiny fish and salt cured over a period of six to twelve months."

"The smell is tremendously foul," Bill said. "Does the odor ever go away?"

The older man grinned and shook his head. "Welcome to Phan Thiet."

After Bill had spent sixteen months in Phan Thiet, the North Vietnamese Army began making a big, successful push in the north and northwest in Da Nang, Hue, Pleiku, and Kon Tum.

The main road through Phan Thiet—Vietnam Route 1—was always busy, a main north-south thoroughfare that, only thirty-five kilometers farther south, turned west from the coast near Binh Tuy to Saigon. Bill noticed the increased traffic—people fleeing death and destruction. By the end of March, Nha Trang had fallen under the North Vietnamese offensive. Route 1 was now choked with people. Fear prevailed.

His boss, on leave to visit his family in the Philippines, was told by the Vietnam affairs office in Washington to stay in Manila until the military situation in Phan Thiet stabilized. Bill was left on his own.

"VC comes to Phan Thiet too soon, right, um Bill?" Bac Dang, his sixty-two-year-old cook asked.

Bill nodded. No reason to lie. The old man could handle anything after living through so many war years: first with the French, then with the Americans, and now among his own.

Bill and Colonel Phu were in close contact as the situation grew more and more precarious. Now complete cooperation was essential.

Colonel Ngo Tan Phu, Province Chief of Binh Tuan, was a courageous leader. At their first meeting, shortly after he had arrived in Phan Thiet, Bill had been immediately struck by the Colonel's command presence, his calm and confident manner. Over time, Bill and Phu had developed a personal bond.

For six weeks, the NVA advanced on South Vietnam, cutting off Phan Thiet from the rest of Vietnam. The military situation had worsened throughout the country in the face of a North Vietnamese rout. Phu kept Bill briefed on all bits of intelligence, which Bill reported dutifully to the embassy. Gradually, his role had changed to that of a military advisor.

It was an extraordinary time for Colonel Phu. When a crowd of mostly civilian refugees began looting the city for food, he ordered his military police to open fire on them. Over twenty looters were either killed or wounded. The looting stopped. So as not to lose control, Phu finally had to close Route 1, cutting off the main escape route to the south. Phu told Bill, "Time has come to fight the North Vietnamese."

The situation worsened throughout Vietnam. Asked to conduct a delaying action so the South Vietnamese Army could get a defensive ambush set up around Xuan Loc to the southwest of Phan Thiet, Phu judged the circumstances to be increasingly precarious.

Acting as a full-fledged military advisor, Bill met with Phu's staff and reviewed the plan to defend and hold Phan Thiet. All they had to work with were two regiments of Regular Forces and one local Peoples Self-Defense Force battalion, two thousand five hundred men in total—just about the size of a small infantry brigade. They were facing two North Vietnamese divisions.

Consolidating their forces around Phan Thiet, the Regional Force–Popular Force soldiers dug trenches and laid new mine fields specifically to stop the North Vietnamese T-34 and T-72 Russian tanks. Light anti-tank weapons were passed out among the units in the trenches. Within days of receiving orders, all basic preparations were well underway, and the work continued night and day to harden Phan Thiet's defensive shell.

Meanwhile, and in spite of regular Viet Cong rocket and North Vietnamese artillery attacks, Bill managed to get his employees out of Phan Thiet unscathed on a C-47 Air America flight. There were twenty-six of them and their families, and he shoved them into the plane, ignoring the protests of the pilot. This flight was the last one out of Phan Thiet. Bill shouted to the pilot, "When the door shuts, take off!"

The pilot didn't argue.

Bill's office became home for his five volunteers (two Vietnamese interpreters and three Nung guards) for the next twelve days. Even though he ordered Bac Dang to leave, his cook responded loyally, "When um Bill go, Bac Dang go too."

At least they were going to eat well, Bill thought to himself.

After eleven days of repeated assaults by the North Vietnamese to test Phan Thiet's defenses, the embassy was finally compelled to order Bill and his five volunteers out. The South Vietnamese Army had finished its defensive preparations at Xuan Loc, prepared for a major battle there, and withdrawn air support from the siege on Phan Thiet. Without the air support, it was a matter of hours before Phan Thiet would be overrun by North Vietnamese military forces.

Finally, Bill was ordered to leave Phan Thiet at 0600 hours on March 30th, 1975. He followed the pre-surveyed evacuation plan that called for an evacuation helicopter to arrive at 1600 hours that afternoon. At approximately 1400 hours, he made one last call by short wave radio to the embassy watch office in Saigon, reaffirming the plan for the evacuation; he planned to use the air-to-ground radio for direct communication with the chopper.

As he passed through the office one last time to ensure everything had been destroyed, Bill saw Bac Dang waiting patiently for him. "Time to go," Bill offered in Vietnamese.

Bac Dang waited until Bill came closer. "Need this?" he asked, pointing to his large suitcase.

"No, Bac Dang. Go ahead; use it for your things."

At that, Bac Dang held out his hand as a gesture of salutation.

"Where will you go?" Bill asked.

"I go to Da Lat. Go to live with my son." Then, in an honoring fashion, Bac Dang held Bill's hand, bowed, and said in Vietnamese, "Thank you so much. May Buddha hold you close to him." Bill looked back to see Bac Dang standing in the doorway as he scrambled to the jeep, which had a front-mounted M-60 machine gun ready to go.

Two hours later, Bill and Colonel Phu were hunkered down on the edge of the designated helicopter landing zone close to an abandoned airstrip. Still in broad daylight, Colonel Phu's men secured the bluff nearby and deployed two machine guns to protect their flanks.

After forty minutes of relative quiet, just as Bill was reassured that everything was going as planned, the North Vietnamese mortars began raining in on them, thankfully off-target.

After about an hour of the barrage, Bill heard the muffled sounds of two helicopters flying out of range roughly 4,000 feet above them. Bill tried to communicate with the choppers, but his radio had been damaged by a piece of shrapnel from the mortars and was inoperable. He popped green smoke, hoping that the pilot would know that it was him, an American on the ground. His smoke spent, he watched the choppers continue to circle in the air.

Time passed slowly. "They're not going to risk it," Bill commented to Colonel Phu.

Just then, one of the choppers began a steep descent over the ocean, leveled off, and skimmed the water toward the bluff. At the last moment, the pilot stood the helicopter on its tail to reach the altitude of the bluff, leveled off and landed all in the same motion in the center of the landing zone. The backup chopper stayed at altitude like an eagle watching her offspring fly.

When the helicopter touched ground, three mortar rounds hit close to it. Shrapnel from one of the rounds crippled the tail rotor, but the pilots, an American and a Vietnamese, made it out unscathed.

Another thirty minutes lapsed. Meanwhile, the damaged chopper sustained a direct hit and lay smoldering in flames on the ground.

"We've got to move to the alternate landing zone," Bill told Colonel Phu. "We don't have any choice."

With that, the group followed Bill. Using any available cover, they tried to shelter themselves from being hit by shrapnel—the North Vietnamese had already killed one of Phu's soldiers.

The mortar rounds were now more sporadic. As they moved farther south of the original landing zone, the American pilot was hit badly, wounding both his legs. After providing life-saving first-aid, the group continued its movement, finally reaching the secondary helicopter landing zone.

"It's coming in," yelled Phu as Bill tried to stabilize the American pilot.

When the chopper hit the ground, everyone rushed for it, at the same time that the North Vietnamese retrained its sight on the new target. As mortar rounds came in close to their position, Bill struggled with the pilot, trying to get him to the chopper. Phu and his men were taking cover.

Bill was half carrying, half dragging the pilot now, and his adrenaline rush was spent. With only ten yards to go, he collapsed forward, totally exhausted.

As he struggled to stand up, Bill's Nung guards jumped out of the chopper and grabbed him and the pilot, throwing both of them on board the helicopter. They barely made it out.

"Please come with me," requested the young political officer as Bill got off the helicopter at Tan Son Nhut Air Force Base in Saigon.

As the two men drove into the center of Saigon, Bill was struck by the lack of defensive preparations. Arriving at the embassy, he was whisked directly to the political counselor's office (one of the senior Foreign Service officers in Saigon). The top embassy intelligence analyst joined them.

Bill did most of the talking and briefed these senior officers on his personal observations of the military situation over past weeks in Phan Thiet and along Route 1 within Binh Thuan Province. The discussion lasted nearly two hours.

Leaving the embassy, the young political officer gave Bill a ride to a hotel used frequently for official visitors. On the way, the political officer told Bill that the embassy had formed an evacuation committee to plan for the drawdown of official dependents and other Americans in Saigon.

"Is President Ford going to back the Vietnamese in their fight for Saigon, or let the North Vietnamese Army have all of Vietnam for the asking?" Bill demanded. When the officer didn't respond, Bill cussed in frustration and exclaimed, "All I know is that this is a disgrace to all of the guys who lost their lives here! If we were taking this seriously, the dependents would have been gone two months ago, and there would be B-52s in the air all over Vietnam!"

The young political officer didn't want to argue the point.

Bill spent the next three days resting at the hotel. He found out that the American pilot had made it and was evacuated to the States.

"We've got a job for you, if you're interested," the administrative counselor said. Without waiting for a response, he continued, "We need one or two officers to work on putting together the pieces involved in a full scale evacuation of Saigon. You'll be working with the navy—the Seventh Fleet. There's a meeting this afternoon at 1500 hours with Admiral Bowlers and his staff to begin the coordination process and to work out the details of the evacuation plan."

The embassy's evacuation plan was simple and centered on getting the last of the American citizens out of Saigon prior to a North Vietnamese attack. For American citizens who could not leave early, there were eleven buildings in Saigon designated as final rooftop helicopter evacuation points.

The North Vietnamese attack on Saigon began at 0400 hours on April 29th, 1975, with the explosion of rockets and artillery shells at Tan Son Nhut Air Force Base. After four hours of shelling, Ambassador Martin finally ordered the evacuation of all Americans in Saigon.

As soon as the decision was made, the American Radio Network began playing "White Christmas" by Bing Crosby, the signal for the evacuation. Bill was already at the embassy with his passport and checkbook, ready to leave.

The evacuation plan ran on its own impetus. Seventh Fleet heavy lift helicopters were coming and going from the embassy without incident, flying more than 650 sorties and taking the remaining embassy staff to ships sitting twenty-five miles offshore.

The final evacuation of Saigon took about twenty hours. After doing what he could to ensure that all Americans had been collected at the eleven evacuation sites and safely taken to the ships, Bill was one of the last embassy officers to leave Saigon. He departed from the embassy's rooftop aboard an Air America chopper and was taken to the USS *Denver* (LPD-9), an amphibious transport vessel with a helicopter landing platform on the stern.

Regardless of how well the evacuation had turned out, Bill's emotional fabric had been torn. As he sat in the chopper watching the jungle landscape give way to ocean, the anxiety of his experiences there washed over him anew. He felt depressed by the inaction of the U.S. government when it came to brokering a political solution in Vietnam. He thought of the close friends he'd left behind—Vietnamese whom he knew would die, men he would never forget. At last, nearly two years after returning to this war-riddled land, he realized that his role in Vietnam was over. He would go home, recuperate, and receive a new assignment to a more peaceful region, where he could fill out his duties as a Foreign Service officer from behind a desk. He'd finally get the chance to experience a new culture as a civilian would—without guns and destruction and slogging through the mud in pursuit of a target. At thirty-two, he was ready to leave the combat and violence and nightmares behind him and move on with his life.

It was April 30th, 1975.

Chapter 10

1976

Bill eased the pillow from his burrowed head and sleepily opened one eye. Rising on his elbow, he looked about the darkened room, searching for the luminous dial on the clock radio.

Ten o'clock! He groaned inwardly. Last night when he had discovered the alarm wasn't working, his mother had promised to wake him early so he could begin packing.

Lying back on the soft feather pillows, Bill sighed. His parents were probably downstairs discussing how they might persuade him to remain at home a few more days, even though they, and he, knew it was impossible. He had to leave tomorrow at the latest to drive from Chicago to Mexico.

Mexico! Whenever he thought of it, Bill became excited, anxious to be on his way again. It would be a different experience from Vietnam, with a culture he wanted to learn about and rich archaeological treasures to explore.

Since receiving his assignment, he'd spent six months studying Spanish at the Foreign Service Institute and attending the consular officer's Basic Course, and five months working on Mexican affairs. Bill was ready for his assignment to Mexico as a vice-consul. He hoped to be assigned to one of the consulates outside of Mexico City, where he would have the responsibility of managing an office rather than merely issuing visas and performing other routine consular duties.

He sat up in bed and stretched, letting the covers slip from his broad, tanned chest, then swung his feet onto the multicolored hook rug of his longtime bedroom.

"Let's get to it," he said to himself as he stood and began doing jumping jacks—the start of his daily dozen exercises, a holdover from his army days.

Normally these would be followed by a five-kilometer run, but not today. He had too much to do.

A 1976 Dodge Dart, brand new, fully equipped, and plush, sat waiting outside his parents' home. At the end of his Mexico tour, he would sell the car for about the same price it had cost new. Used cars were far more valuable in Mexico than in the States. The only catch was that the same model of car had to be produced in Mexico. His Dart fit the bill.

Before leaving the Washington area, he had supervised the packing of his household effects and had them sent on their way. He had canceled the lease on his one-bedroom garden apartment in Falls Church, Virginia. He would spend the last day and night of his leave with his parents, and early tomorrow morning, be on his way across the border to Mexico City.

Completing his calisthenics, Bill breathed deeply, gazing about his childhood room. He realized with a twinge of surprise that he would miss home when he was finally gone. Not his apartment—that had never felt like home—but rather, the house he'd grown up in and the people in it. His parents, both in their late sixties, had lived in this house for twenty-six years. Both were retired, and his mother, in excellent health, was devoted to nursing his father back to health after he had suffered a mild stroke just two months earlier. His brothers and sister had all moved away, and though they each visited often, it was rarely at the same time. Of course, they'd all come when his father had gone to the hospital.

The stroke should have made Bill want to stay. After all, it drew some of his mother's incessant concern and attention away from him and was a reminder of how suddenly one's parents could succumb to old age and disappear. But strangely, it had only spurred his desire to get going. Seeing his father like he'd been in the days immediately following the stroke—slow-moving, partially paralyzed—had been horrifying. This contrasted sharply with Bill's childhood memories of the man: a strict, strop-wielding disciplinarian hardened by his service in World War II. He saw in his pale, weakened father a reflection of himself—the way he must look upon waking up from a nightmare, shaking and in a cold sweat. He'd thought that the two-year tour in Vietnam would help him lay those demons to rest, but they'd kept at him. Some nights he'd even dream of Phan Thiet or Saigon and the faces of men who had died there—fresh shadows to haunt his battered brain. He relied on drink to calm himself more often than he liked to admit. He needed to keep moving and prove to himself that he wasn't disintegrating at the age of thirty-two.

"Are you coming?" asked Bill's mother, as he hurriedly finished dressing. "Brunch is already on the table!"

Starting down the stairs, he heard the ring of the telephone. "Good morning, William," Bill's mother said softly as she met him close to the yellow telephone hanging in the kitchen. She lifted the receiver to her ear. "Hello," she said. "Yes, please hold on for a second." Turning to her son, she whispered, "It's for you, the Department of State."

"Thanks, Mom. I'll take it in the den." Slipping into the room opposite the stairs, Bill picked up the receiver. "Hello, this is Bill Hausman." As he listened, his smile fell, and he suddenly felt sick with disappointment. "I can't believe you've waited until the last minute to call me, after all the preparation, after my travel orders were issued!" he growled. "I don't care if there's been a reduction in staff! This should have been known weeks or even months ago!"

Reminding himself that the person calling was not to blame, Bill said more calmly, "Okay, okay, I know you're only relaying the message. Anything else I should know? Okay, I'll give Dan a call right away. I appreciate that. Thanks for the call. Goodbye."

Stunned, Bill sat motionless in the den's leather chair. The room suddenly seemed too small and too warm, just like the rest of the house. It felt stifling. He couldn't believe that a few minutes ago he'd been thinking about how he'd miss it. Now his apartment was gone and he was going to be stuck here at home for God knows how long.

His mother came into the room, her forehead creased with concern. "What's wrong?"

"You'll never believe this. They've just canceled my assignment to Mexico! Some crap about reduction of staff at the embassy and assignments canceled as a result. Damn it! I can't believe this is happening."

"Take is easy. I'm sure it will all work out," his mother said.

"Let me call Dan to find out what's going on."

Dialing brusquely, Bill asked for his immediate supervisor. "Dan," he snapped, "what's going on with my assignment?"

"Bill, these things happen. As you know, next year's budget projections call for a reduction of four positions in Mexico City, two in consular affairs. The undersecretary decided yesterday that the cuts should be made now, so that we can avoid over-staffing next year when the reductions actually occur. As a result, your assignment has been canceled, as well as two others. The guys in Mexico have been asked to extend for a year. That's all I know."

"This is bullshit, Dan, and you know it! What the hell am I supposed to do now?" Bill answered.

"I can only say how sorry I am that this is happening. I've already contacted personnel and they're looking for another assignment for you. That's about all we can do." Dan offered.

"Yeah, no problem, Dan . . . thanks." Bill's voice was draining of energy, out of a sense of defeat.

"Come on back and we'll work this out together," Dan said.

"No way, José! You've got this number. Why don't I just stay put until you work out a new assignment for me? I have nowhere to go and I should at least be given some time to adjust to this door being slammed in my face."

"Okay, stay where you are and I'll get back to you," Dan agreed. "Frankly, I'd feel the same way, and I think I can get you some admin leave time. At least I'll try, okay?"

Bill joined his parents in the kitchen, which was still decorated in a 1950s motif. "My God, Mom, what did you do, prepare a Sunday meal?" He sat down and poured a cup of coffee.

"Eggs, Bill?" his father asked, slurring his words, still showing the effects of the stroke.

"No thanks, Dad. I'll be satisfied with coffee cake and some fruit."

After explaining what had happened, Bill asked, "Well, do you think you can put up with me for another couple of days or so?" He couldn't voice aloud the possibility that it might be longer than that.

"Of course we can," his mother said, beaming.

"I'll go somewhere, eventually, just not to Mexico, that's all."

One week later, Bill still didn't have an assignment. Dan had asked him to return to Washington; it wouldn't be delayed any longer.

"Dan? Well, I'm back, staying at the Marriott in Rosslyn, Room 1006. Any news?"

"Bill," he shouted, "we have a great assignment for you! You're going to Guyana!"

Bill racked his brain to locate the name on a map, and then cried, "Are you guys nuts? Why send me to Africa?"

"Not Ghana," Dan corrected with a laugh. "Guyana, you know, in South

America. It used to be called British Guiana." Reacting to the deafening silence on the phone, Dan said, "Hello?"

"I'm still here, Dan. What else?" Bill sounded disappointed.

"Guyana is a really challenging assignment," Dan assured him. "They received their independence from Great Britain in 1966 and changed their name to Guyana. That's an Amerindian word meaning 'Land of Many Waters.'"

When he paused for a breath, Bill said, "Got it. Thanks, Dan, now I know exactly where you're talking about. But why me? Isn't there any Latino country out there looking for a freshly trained, *Spanish-speaking* vice-consul?"

"Why not you? It's a chance to see new territory and to advance your career. I've heard that the consular jobs in Guyana are really challenging, just like in Mexico. Plus, there's a twenty-five percent differential and an R&R to Cancún." The job was getting more interesting as Dan spoke. "You'll be going to the embassy in Georgetown, the capital. Take the next day or two to read up on some background on the country. Then we'll talk."

"Will do, Dan. Thanks. I'll get back to you."

At the library, Bill found information in several reference books and began to take notes. Guyana had an estimated population of 783,000. Georgetown was the capital, a port city of 170,000, and the largest city in the country. Its main exports were bauxite, rice, sugar, timber, gold, and diamonds. Guyana's weather was tropical, hot and humid most of the time. The official language was English, although the rural population spoke only the dialects of the Amerindian tribes. The Portuguese language was commonly used along the Brazil–Guyana border to the south. Finally, Guyana bordered Surinam to the east and Venezuela to the west.

Bill copied this all down painstakingly in a composition notebook, feeling vaguely like he was back in grammar school, writing a report. But this was the only way he could think of to prepare for this unexpected change in plans. He wanted to know what he was getting into.

Next, Bill obtained a copy of the Post Report for Georgetown. *Okay! It's a furnished post,* he thought to himself. All he had to do was get his household effects shipped from Mexico City to Georgetown.

Aside from that chore, his main concern was his car. Everyone in Guyana drove on the left side of the street, a holdover from British colonization. Only right-side-drive vehicles were allowed to be imported, and his new Dart didn't qualify. He would have to part with that vehicle right away. Luckily, due to the circumstances involved, Bill would be reimbursed for the loss incurred. He learned that a small car was best for Georgetown, and decided on a new Honda Civic, which he ordered directly from Japan, right-side-drive and all.

After making the decision on the Honda, Bill planned his departure. He would leave Washington, D.C. at 7:00 A.M. on September 26th and fly to New York, a day before his connecting flight to Guyana on Pan American Airlines. While in New York, Bill would spend the day with the Immigration Office at Kennedy International Airport to learn the ropes of detecting visa fraud and spotting phony passports. The Department of State considered Guyana a "high crime and fraud" country. The challenge of this assignment was beginning to grow more and more interesting to the young vice-consul.

CHAPTER 11

September 1976

Early on the 27th, Bill arrived at Kennedy Airport two hours before his flight's scheduled departure, got his boarding pass, and waited. When the plane began boarding, he realized it was a small flight. He got on and found his seat by a window, stored his carry-on, and buckled his belt. Then he rested his head back and shut his eyes.

Periodically he'd open them to scan the plane. It was only about half full. He'd have room to stretch out and relax, most likely. He could hear the flight attendant passing back and forth, making small talk with passengers and instructing a few how to work the seat belts. Then he heard a soft thud overhead and felt the plane jostle a little. He opened his eyes to see a woman in a peach-colored suit struggling to lift a large bag into the overhead compartment. A brass buckle on the bag had gotten stuck on the rim of the bin, and she was trying to shove it in anyway.

Instinctively, he sprung up to help her, hoisting the bag out of her arms and over the ledge. She beamed at him gratefully and smoothed the front of her suit as he slid back into his seat. Then she sat down in the aisle seat next to him.

"Thanks," she said.

"No problem," he answered, trying not to stare too conspicuously. She was well dressed and attractive, with a ruffled blouse and thin gold necklace peeking out from her jacket lapels. She had a narrow neck and pretty face. Her dark hair was tied behind her head in a blue bow that looked almost girlish in contrast with her business attire.

She buckled up, then angled toward him, her hands clasped around her knees in an intimate way, as though they were already friends in mid-conversation.

"I guess we won't have to worry about someone sitting in the middle," Bill said, just to break the ice. "There aren't many people on this flight."

"You won't encounter any problem with crowded flights *going to* Georgetown. Only coming from Georgetown. That's when you find the crowd," the woman responded in a strong British accent.

Their nascent conversation was interrupted briefly by the flight attendant's safety instructions, and then by the takeoff.

"It always amazes me that this heavy bird can actually fly," Bill commented. "Do you travel often to Georgetown?" he asked.

"Actually, I live and work in Georgetown," the woman answered. "On this trip, I attended a four-day seminar at American University in Washington, D.C. on 'Breakthroughs in Biochemistry.' It was really interesting."

Bill raised his eyebrows in appreciation. "Did you get to see anything of Washington?" he asked.

"I would have enjoyed that, but there wasn't time this trip. Maybe on the next."

Then, after an awkward pause in the conversation during which he feared that she might not want to continue talking with him, he hastened the offering. "I'm Bill Hausman," he said, holding out his hand.

"A pleasure to meet you. I am Celeste Campalena," she answered, accepting his handshake. Then, giving attention to a family of Guyanese with five children seated in a group of seats immediately in front of them, she said, "They have rather large families in Guyana. I'm not sure if it's the same in the States."

"In some parts it's probably still true, especially in the heartland of the United States. My parents had four kids, a girl and three boys, but we lived in the suburbs of Chicago. I'm the second youngest one." Bill turned the subject back to her: "Why the seminar on Biochemistry?"

"That's easy. You see, it's my field. I'm doing cancer research in Guyana under contract with a private organization, the London Institute of Biological Studies. I work primarily with live animals of the marsupial class. We're trying to determine if there's a connection between an extremely low incidence of cancerous tumors in opossums and other marsupials, and their total immunity to the effects of snake venom."

Bill was captivated by his new acquaintance. He realized her poise and confidence weren't learned affectations, but rather the natural result of being in possession of good looks, high education, and native intelligence.

He asked, "That's fascinating, but where do you get snake venom these days to do your research?"

Apparently a bit intolerant of superficial remarks, Celeste answered, "From snakes, primarily." Then, seeing that Bill didn't know quite how to react to her subtly insulting remark, she smiled and backed off. "We crystallize venom from the labaria snake, a species commonly found in the Amazon River basin, and then use it in our experiments. The labaria's venom is both hemolytic as well as neurotoxic. In other words, if you were to be bitten by a labaria, it would be comparable to being bitten by both a western rattlesnake, with its hemolytic venom, and a cobra, with its neurotoxic venom, at the same time. It's really amazing, but some marsupials are virtually immune to its venom."

Bill nodded agreeably, trying to process the information and missing a good deal of it out of sheer unfamiliarity. Realizing he couldn't comment on that particular subject, he changed it. "How did you get involved in cancer research, Celeste?"

"Actually, it was by accident. I'm Portuguese. Grew up in Lisbon, but took my university studies in London." Reacting to Bill's expression, she asked, "Is this confusing?"

"No, no. I've just never met anyone from Portugal before," Bill admitted.

"Anyway," Celeste continued, "after graduation, I interviewed for the research position, got it, lived in wonderful London for four years, and then decided to do the field end of the work. It's been a great experience. I've been in Guyana now for over a year."

"That sounds great," Bill responded. "This is my first trip to Guyana. I'll be the new vice-consul at the American embassy in Georgetown, but frankly, it all came about so quickly, I really know very little about Guyana. What should I expect?"

Handling the question in a matter-of-fact manner, Celeste answered, "If you don't mind mixed races, you'll be fine."

Bill shook his head and assured her, "Fine by me." He'd been just a kid when he heard his father and mother talking about how blacks in Alabama had managed to get the busses desegregated by staging a boycott. His father had said, "Well, it's about time," and his mother had nodded her agreement. He figured that even if he'd been raised otherwise, serving alongside black soldiers in Vietnam would have quelled any racial antagonism he might have harbored.

Then, as if intuiting that he was thinking only in black and white, Celeste clarified the issue: "Actually, the Guyanese are made up of a mix of five races: northern Europeans, mostly from Holland; Indians from India; Chinese;

Portuguese; and Africans. There are also the Amerindians in the rain forests, but they remained isolated from the colonial settlers and did not mix racially. They're still rather isolated, even today."

"I can understand the Dutch and Portuguese settlers being in Guyana, but the Indians, Africans, and Chinese puzzle me," Bill commented. "How did that happen?"

Celeste hesitated before answering. "I'm not up on Guyana's history, but I do know that most outsiders came to Guyana either as colonial masters or as people being exploited—that's right, mostly as slaves or indentured servants, to work on plantations along the coast. It has been basically a racial mixing bowl for some three hundred years, much like the U.S."

Bill listened intently, while his eyes took in Celeste's natural beauty. A straight, narrow nose and flawless complexion accented her high cheekbones. He felt certain that Celeste could be a cover girl for a fashion magazine, if she wished.

"The trouble with Guyana is that the two main racial groups, the Indian and African descendants, are divided. The majority of Indians live in rural Guyana and still provide the core of the agriculture work force. The African descendants, on the other hand, have taken over the cities in Guyana and occupy just about all of the civil servant positions. The merchants and landowners of Guyana are mostly Indian descendants. They really control the wealth of the country, truth be told."

"What happened to the Dutch, Chinese, and Portuguese?" Bill inquired.

"Most of the Guyanese of Chinese and Portuguese extraction left just after independence, when the British left. It was a mess politically, and it was a violent period in Guyana's history."

"From what I've read, there are only two major political parties, right? The Peoples Progressive Party, a leftist political philosophy, and the Peoples National Congress Party, the democratic socialists," Bill volunteered. "I understand that they divide the country along racial lines. The Indian population primarily supports the PPP, and the Africans support the PNC."

She nodded and smiled easily, enjoying his attempt to explain the political landscape of Guyana. She appeared impressed that he had most of it correct.

Bill asked, "If Guyana is such a racial mix of people, why are they having racial divisions along political lines?"

She pursed her lips and shrugged. "The Guyanese would never admit it, but the shame of it all is that the mixed races are a constant reminder of their history, that's all—the too-well-known tale of colonization, slavery, and indentured servants. Both of the political parties love it. It gives them the right to wallow in the past misery of the country. They try to make the colonial powers to blame for all of Guyana's current woes."

"That's an interesting perspective . . . but why wallow in the past?" Bill asked.

"It's supposed to make the people feel good! It's just a shame. They forget that they owe the colonists for their own rich culture and diversity. Guyana is an intriguing country with great natural resources, if only they would put their energies into the right things." Celeste stopped short of drawing a conclusion. Then she added, "Don't worry, you'll see, and I hope you enjoy it *all*."

"I've seen some Asian countries, but this is my first trip to South America. I guess Guyana is unique in a lot of ways. It's probably the only South American country where English is the principal language . . . Interesting, really interesting. How long to you plan on staying in Guyana, if I may ask?" Bill said.

"That's hard to say," Celeste answered. "I guess it all depends upon the success of our research and continued funding. I'll be in Guyana for at least another year, though. How about you?"

"This will be a two-year tour for me, with a third year if I want," Bill replied. "Do you like Guyana and its culture?"

"There are some fascinating aspects to it, I suppose," Celeste said thoughtfully. "In Guyana, ethnic traditions and religions are still alive and well. You will see the cupolas of Hindu temples, the minarets of Moslem mosques, the steeples of Christian churches—all monuments to Guyana's diverse beliefs. Religious festivals will fascinate you. There's Phagwah, Deepavali, Eid-ul-Adha, Youman Nabi, Easter, and Christmas. It's really quite unique."

Bill was truly enjoying Celeste's insights, none of which had jumped out from the library books that he had read. He responded, "Fascinating, absolutely fascinating! In some ways, Guyana's development paralleled ours. We were colonized in the beginning, then freed the slaves, and we became a country of immigrants. But why is there so much pressure on the Guyanese to leave their country?"

"It's simple, really: There's a very high level of unemployment. Officially, it's about fifteen percent. Actually, it's probably double that," she commented.

Bill nodded. "From what I've been reading, the new wave of so-called 'cooperative socialism' being pushed by Linden Forbes Sampson Burnham—"

He frowned, carefully pronouncing the name of the Guyanese Prime Minister. "—has the business sector concerned for the future. Just how serious is this socialist movement?"

"Burnham hopes to strike some kind of a balance between democracy and socialism. You know, there's quite a worldwide movement these days, led by the European Social Democrats. I'm not sure Guyana is that well served by it all," Celeste answered. "We'll see how things go, won't we?"

"I guess you're right. I'm sorta looking forward to it all," Bill remarked.

The rest of the flight was nothing short of fantastic. Celeste was a delight to talk with, and Bill enjoyed every moment of their conversation. Soon the "fasten seat belts" announcement signaled their approach to Timehri International Airport, about forty-four kilometers outside of Georgetown. Meeting Celeste had been a welcomed encounter that made the flight time pass quickly. Plus, Bill had learned something about Guyana.

Upon arrival, Bill handed down Celeste's carry-on and then followed her into the airport's immigration and customs area, where they turned to each other. He gave her one of his cards and said, "Stop by the embassy. You have a standing invitation to lunch, anytime."

"Thank you." She took the card and they began to drift apart. "It was nice talking with you. Hope we have another opportunity," she added. As Bill moved away and into the "diplomats only" immigration line, Celeste waved her arm and called out, "Bye!"

Only when he had climbed into the embassy sedan did Bill realize that he had not asked Celeste for her telephone number. *That's another one that got away,* he thought.

He had little time to dwell on it. For the rest of the drive, Bill's attention focused on the new world he was entering. Off in the distance, he spotted what he guessed to be deserted hangars left over from World War II, when Timehri had been used as a refueling stop for U.S. bombers flying to Africa in support of Allied offensives against the Germans. He saw huge slabs of concrete leading from the hangars, and figured these must have been aircraft parking and maintenance areas.

Bill was still on the edge of his seat after the driver steered the embassy car onto the paved, two-lane highway leading to Georgetown. For a time, his impression of Guyana was nothing but swamp water and sparse trees. Finally, nearer to Georgetown, he began to notice rice and sugar cane fields, small huts of various sizes, and construction that dotted the landscape.

The ride from the airport in an air-conditioned embassy car did nothing to prepare Bill for the oppressive heat. From the moment he arrived at the Tower Hotel, he was soaked with sticky perspiration. An ancient ceiling fan turned lazily overhead as he entered his small hotel room. The slatted wooden windows let in only more sultry air. Looking about, Bill was nevertheless satisfied. He had known much worse accommodations in Vietnam.

He stashed his bags in one corner of the room, resolving to unpack later that afternoon. Then he collapsed down on the bed, fully clothed and weary from the trip. As he drifted off, his last conscious thought was of the blue satin bow in Celeste's hair.

CHAPTER 12

1976

The next day, refreshed and rested after a shower and a change of clothes, Bill decided to walk the one block to the embassy at 31 Main Street. As he walked, he noted mostly buildings of Victorian-style architecture—many of them wood structures.

The administrative officer greeted Bill at the embassy and led him almost immediately to the office of Andrew Blacken, chargé d'affaires.

"Welcome to Guyana, Bill," Blacken greeted him enthusiastically, extending his hand. "Glad to have you aboard."

"Thank you, sir. I'm looking forward to working with you."

"Good. Have a seat, Bill. You've no doubt had a tiring trip. Would you like coffee?"

"No thank you, sir. I had coffee at the hotel."

"The Tower and the Pegasus Hotels are the safest places to eat right now. I guess I should tell you to be careful and always alert on the street. Crime is a serious problem here. They have coined the expression 'choke and rob' for street muggings. Well, enough on that."

"I already got the same warning at the Hotel," Bill responded.

"Good. Now, I'll try to give you a general overview of Guyana and the U.S. Mission in Georgetown. We are basically an embassy with USIS and USAID offices," Blacken said, "Right now we have only four officers in the USAID office, but as we implement additional programs aimed at long-range developmental goals here, our staff will grow. Fifteen officers make up the total embassy complement. You are one of four consular officers. Because we are so small, I must rely upon everyone to do his job well, and then do more."

Bill nodded. The same was true of other posts. Not enough manpower to fill all jobs was a common issue.

As he listened to Blacken, Bill liked what he heard. Blacken appeared to be businesslike, decisive, engaging, and persuasive, all qualities that combined to make a strong leader and a likable boss.

"We do have our problems," Blacken continued. "The mission has been without an ambassador for months, but we're hoping one will be named soon. With no ambassador at post, it's difficult to deal effectively with the Guyanese."

After relating to Bill a few personal anecdotes about Guyana, Blacken seemed to relax a bit. "Do you have any questions?"

"I'm certain I'll have plenty once I begin work," Bill answered with a smile. "Right now, I suppose the big one is how long I'll be at the Tower?"

Blacken nodded as he stood. "We'll work on that. It shouldn't be too long. I'd like to have you over for dinner tonight to meet my wife and children, say at seven? I'll send my driver to pick you up."

"Thank you. That'll be great," Bill replied, standing also.

"Your boss at the consulate is Alex Manus," Blacken informed him as they walked together down the stairway to the embassy's reception room. "He hasn't been here long either, but he's a ten-year veteran with some great experience. I think you'll find him well versed and able to point you in the right direction."

Extending his hand, Bill thanked Blacken and promised to be ready for dinner at seven. Then, leaving the three-story wooden embassy—one of the few in the world—he walked three blocks down Main Street to Bentrick Street to meet his new boss. The consulate was a modern, single-level concrete structure on the corner.

Bill and Alex Manus seemed to have instant rapport, and before long, Bill had learned a good deal about him. Besides speaking French, Manus was also fluent in Mandarin Chinese, having served a tour as a consular officer in Taipei, Taiwan. He married there, and had a beautiful one-year-old daughter. His claim to fame was that his paternal great-grandfather was a famous British explorer. Alex said that Manus Island, located just north of New Guinea in the South Pacific, and part of the Bismarck Archipelago, had been named for his great-grandfather.

Manus had been looking forward to having another officer on board, someone with some life experience. As it happened, Bill would be the senior consular officer next to Manus, a deputy of sorts.

Bill spent the next few hours with Manus, going over the full scope of consular operations in Guyana. By the time he joined Andrew Blacken that evening, Bill felt well versed in the inner workings of the consulate. Blacken was pleased that Manus had taken Bill into his confidence.

The first days on the job were all-encompassing, as Bill learned the procedures followed in conducting consular business in Guyana. Bill and Manus spent hours reviewing the strengths and weaknesses of the consular staff, including two first-tour vice-consuls and ten Guyanese employees.

Within weeks, Bill was supervising the entire visa processing operation for both immigrant and non-immigrant visas. His days were busy and he enjoyed the work. It wasn't long, though, before political turmoil made his job more complicated.

On October 19, 1976, a Cubana Airlines flight from Georgetown to Havana with a stop in Bridgetown, Barbados, was sabotaged as it took off from Bridgetown. A bomb had apparently been placed aboard the flight. Seventy-eight lives were lost in the bombing, including eleven Guyanese students traveling to Cuba on scholarships offered by the Cuban government. An extremist anti-Cuban group headquartered in Miami, Florida, claimed responsibility for the bombing.

The initial Guyanese reaction to the bombing was hostile. Andrew Blacken was summoned by phone to meet with Prime Minister Burnham. During their meeting, Burnham lashed out, angrily accusing the United States Government of harboring terrorists in Miami. He would not listen to any reasonable response. It appeared the reason for calling the meeting was to give the prime minister the opportunity to vent his anger and frustration.

The next day Burnham and his Peoples National Congress Party organized a rally protesting the bombing and publicly expressing the anger of the Guyanese people over the loss of their eleven Guyanese "comrades." The prime minister gave a blistering speech to tens of thousands of Guyanese at an open park close to his official residence. In a highly emotional tone, Burnham directly accused the U.S. government of complicity in the bombing.

Secretary of State Henry Kissinger responded decisively to Burnham's remarks. He immediately recalled Chargé Blacken to Washington. Kissinger insisted that a formal apology come from the Guyana government before the chargé would return.

The apology was not forthcoming, forcing changes in the lineup at the embassy. Alex Manus was named interim chargé. Bill was left in charge of the consulate, and one man short. He welcomed the challenge.

To take his mind off work, Bill decided to see if he couldn't get in some flying time. He had already received his private pilot's license for single engine, land-based, fixed-wing aircraft, and didn't want to let his skills lie dormant. But despite his experience, his license, and his enthusiasm, Bill found that he could not pilot a plane in Guyana until he had obtained a Guyanese commercial pilot's license.

In the aftermath of the Cuban Airline bombing, however, the Guyanese were not particularly cooperative with the American embassy. Just trying to find out the requirements for a pilot's license brought him face to face with a stone wall.

Not one to give up easily, Bill related his troubles to a couple of American pilots he had met at the Tower Hotel during his stay there. They were under contract with the government of Guyana to fly a C-46 cargo plane into Guyana's interior in support of several government projects. Over drinks, they recommended that Bill get in contact with Roland DaLuz, the chief pilot for Guyana Airlines, who had helped them get familiar with Guyana. They passed him DaLuz's telephone number.

As Bill drove home that night, his thoughts turned to flying and to the moments of sheer fear that were part of that realm.

CHAPTER 13

1974 – 1975

"I don't give a damn! Find out what legal recourse I have. I just can't accept that she can take Katrina like that," John Olsen insisted to his attorney on the other end of the line. "Okay, okay, we'll take it step by step, but damn it, there must be a solution to this, something that I can use to get my daughter back. Whatever it is, we've got to find it. I expect the law to work for me, not against me. Just do your best and keep me advised, okay? Thanks. I'll be home for the rest of the afternoon. Bye." He hung up the telephone slowly, numb from what had just happened.

After years of pain, it was done. Priscilla had taken the step.

Lonely weeks passed, then months. Priscilla's lawyer was the only contact he had with his wife and daughter. She had gone to Ukiah to become a working member of the Peoples Temple. A preliminary injunction had given Priscilla custody of Katrina until terms could be worked out in the final divorce settlement. His attorney assured John that he would get joint custody and have his daughter on some weekends and split holidays. Of course, he would have to pay child support and alimony, standard for California.

It took six months for the divorce to be finalized—an eternity for John. Even knowing that it was over, John was terribly uncomfortable with it all. Being separated from his daughter was the worst feeling of emptiness he had ever known. He wondered how anyone could ever tolerate these legal arrangements.

As he sat at the kitchen table reading the final sentences of the divorce settlement, John began to weep uncontrollably. It was April 30, 1975.

———

As time passed, Katrina seemed to adjust to her new living arrangements. Priscilla moved them into a two-bedroom apartment a short drive from Ukiah and the Peoples Temple complex. Katrina attended the local grade school and had made a few new friends.

" . . . I'm coming right after work and probably won't get in until late," John said when calling Priscilla late on a Friday afternoon to arrange a visit over the weekend.

"Why don't you stop by for breakfast in the morning around 9:00 A.M. and you can go from there? Katrina is really looking forward to this weekend. She's had mid-year tests this week and it's been stressful for her. Do you have anything special planned?" Priscilla asked.

"As a matter of fact, I've found a really neat farm that doubles as a petting zoo fairly close to Ukiah. It should be fun." John spoke lightly, marveling at his ability to be so calm. A few months ago he would have been screaming into the receiver at the woman who had taken his daughter away. "I'll let you know how it goes and maybe you could organize a weekend trip for a group of the children at the church."

"That would be great. I hope you guys have a good time together. See you around nine. Bye."

For all outward appearances, John and Priscilla had reconciled their relationship and were learning to work together for Katrina's sake. He visited every other week. In between visits, he called Katrina almost daily. Even though the divorce agreement called for sharing holidays, he learned that it worked best for him to just plan out the holiday. As a result, Priscilla and Katrina even spent a four-day break over Thanksgiving with John. They slept separately, of course, but it seemed to work. Priscilla had become less defensive about her newfound religion and was generally careful about what she said. While a truce was never declared, their interactions became more cordial.

Priscilla considered herself lucky to find work right at the church complex in Ukiah. Her hours were flexible so she could be home when Katrina returned from school. She worked six days a week and was considered a full-time employee—thereby giving her employment benefits. She relied upon a local woman who came on Saturdays twice a month to keep an eye on Katrina when John wasn't there. This routine established, it all seemed to be working out for the best.

CHAPTER 14

1976

"The right engine—check the oil pressure," Roland DaLuz yelled to his copilot over the whine of the aged Caribou aircraft carrying a full load of passengers and cargo from Lethem, a border town in the southwest part of Guyana near Brazil, to Georgetown.

"Oil pressure is dropping fast!" the copilot reported.

"We must have a blown gasket," Roland said as he feathered the right prop and cut off fuel to the right engine, shutting it down. "Get back there and throw out all extra cargo, baggage included, now! Move it! We're losing altitude." As his copilot hurriedly got up from his seat, Roland fine-tuned the left engine to milk the most power out of it.

The copilot returned to the cockpit with a thumbs-up and said, "All done."

"That's super! At least we'll be able to maintain our altitude. What did you have to throw out?" Roland asked.

"All of the tires, spare parts, the beef…"

"What about my boxes of fertilized eggs?" Roland asked.

"They're gone too, sorry!"

Looking at Roland's face, the copilot knew he had screwed up badly.

"God damn it! They cost me G$200 a box! I said 'extra cargo' and 'baggage.' I wasn't talking about my eggs, for Christ's sake," Roland shouted. His investment of G$1,200 for fertilized chicken eggs would normally earn him G$5,000 in Georgetown. While not a great business, it was what Roland did to supplement his airline pilot's salary.

After landing the Caribou safely at Timehri Airport, Roland turned to his copilot and said, "You owe me G$1,200 for this flying lesson, man."

The copilot knew he wasn't joking.

The morning's fiasco was an annoyance, but it was nothing compared to some of the spots Roland had been in during his career. Hired at nineteen by Guyana Airlines' predecessor, British Guiana Air, Roland had been the first Guyanese captain for the airline. In the years since, he'd weathered all manner of catastrophes—storms, failed engines, even gunfire. In 1972, he had been commissioned by the Guyana Defense Force to lead an aerial assault when the Surinamese Army established an encampment on a contested area of land. The mission was a success, and Prime Minister Burnham recognized Roland in a public ceremony months later, awarding him the Cacique Medal of Gallantry, the Guyanese equivalent to the Distinguished Service Cross in the U.S. Armed Forces.

All things considered, a blown oil gasket and a few lost eggs were just par for the course.

Given that he was a national hero and the senior captain for Guyana Airlines, Bill wondered whether Roland DaLuz would even give him the time of day to talk about getting a Guyana pilot's license. Nonetheless, he decided to make the call.

"I'd like to talk with Captain DaLuz, if he's in, please," Bill said to the woman who answered the telephone.

After a long moment, Roland came to the phone. "DaLuz," he said.

"Good evening. I'm Bill Hausman. I'm newly arrived here in Guyana and I'm interested in getting a pilot's license. I was told that you might be able to help me out."

The phone crackled and the voice on the other end boomed cheerfully. "Oh yes, you're the chap from the embassy, right? Your friends from the Tower Hotel told me you might call. How do you like Guyana?"

"It's been great so far. I've had lots of work, but I guess I'll get used to it. I'm really interested in flying here in Guyana to see some of the country. I already have a U.S. pilot's license and understand that I need to get a Guyanese license to fly here. Is that right? They're giving me a run-around at the Office of the Director of Civil Aviation, so that's why I'm calling you. Do you think there's any hope here?" Bill was trying not to be too critical of the Guyanese bureaucracy.

"Basically, that's correct, but those guys downtown aren't going to be much help to you. Look, let's get together over a drink and talk about it. Are you still at the Tower?" Roland asked.

"Yeah, but I'm at work right now," Bill responded.

"Why don't we meet and talk at the Tower Hotel bar after work, say at six?" Roland asked.

"Done! I'll be waiting; the American in a light blue shirt-jac. Hey, thanks a lot," Bill offered.

"My pleasure. See you at six."

Bill had to hurry down the street to make it to the Tower Hotel on time. When he entered the bar, he gazed about and saw a couple seated at a table near the back. The man was tall, tanned, and well built, with short curly black hair. As Bill approached, he noticed a heavy, silver identification bracelet on the man's right wrist, with the bold letters of his first name engraved on it. Seated next to him was a gorgeous, bronzed woman with long dark hair, lipstick-red lips, and an attractive figure, dressed to show it all off.

As Bill reached the table, the man stepped forward and introduced himself. "Roland DaLuz. You must be Bill Hausman."

"Yes. Nice to meet you."

Roland turned to introduce the woman seated at the table. "Bill, I'd like you to meet my fiancée, Jenny."

"It's a pleasure." Bill took a seat next to Jenny, facing Roland.

"We're already ahead of you. Would you like a rum and Coke?" Roland asked.

"That'll be great, thanks."

Roland snapped his fingers to get the bartender's attention. He came right over to the table. "Another rum and Coke, man—let's use the five-year-old Demerara rum." Then he turned to address Bill. "How long have you been in Guyana?"

"Not very long. I arrived in late September," Bill responded.

Jenny asked, "Has the embassy found a house for you yet? It must be awful living out of a suitcase and staying here."

"It's not that bad, really," Bill commented. "I'm told that they're fixing up and painting a house for me in Bel Air Springs. Do you know where that is?"

Roland answered, "Oh yes, north on the seacoast road about five kilometers. I have friends living there. You'll be right on the coast."

"We live in Bel Air, not far from here," Jenny added. "Have you had a chance to get familiar with Georgetown?"

"Not really. My car hasn't arrived yet."

Looking at Roland, Jenny offered, "Maybe we can show you around."

Bill's drink arrived then, and Roland raised his glass in a toast. "Cheers! Welcome to Guyana."

Bill did the same and replied, "Nice to be here."

"Now, tell me, what kind of problem are you having with our Director of Civil Aviation?" Roland asked in a mocking tone. It was obvious that he had no respect for the office.

Bill tried to be brief, ending with, "It seems impossible to even find out what the requirements are for a Guyanese pilot's license."

Roland smiled. "You take a written test similar to the one you took when you got your original pilot's license. You also need to log five hours of instruction with a flight instructor qualified here in Guyana. Then you'll take a check ride with the Director of Civil Aviation himself, who decides whether or not to issue you a Guyanese commercial pilot's license."

"That doesn't seem too complicated. Why such a fuss over pilot's licenses?"

Roland's expression turned serious as he answered, "You see, there have been a lot of pilots who have come to Guyana with their airplanes—missionaries, adventurers, even smugglers. Most of them don't live very long. One mistake, one oversight, and you're dead. The jungle will swallow you up and you'll never be found. We see it happen time after time. That's why."

"Roland, stop it," Jenny protested. "You're going to bully Bill into changing his mind."

"No, that's okay," Bill assured her. "I've seen pilots in other parts of the world as well who don't take this business seriously. They end up just as dead. Look, I know about the risks, the short dirt airstrips, the weather here, problems with water in aviation fuel, and the lack of navigational aids. I've talked with other pilots and understand what I'm getting into, believe me. What I need is some guidance and direction."

In response Roland asked, "How many hours do you have, Bill?"

"Not very many. Maybe one hundred hours, of which forty or so are solo hours on cross-country flights. I've flown mostly in Cessna 172s. I can bring you my log book if you want."

"Look," Roland began. "This is no place for a novice pilot to cut his teeth." Glancing at Jenny, he added, "I have to be honest with you. Besides having to learn the ropes here in Guyana, you'll also have to learn how to fly a high-performance airplane. All the single engine aircraft are either Cessna 182s, 206s or 210s. There aren't any others. It'll take considerably more time to learn what you need to know than just five hours of instruction. Are you still interested?"

"I've got nothing better to do with my time and money. Besides, I look at this as a challenge, one that you don't come across very often. Call it my adventuresome spirit. Yes, I'm very interested."

Roland smiled and said, "Right you are! I'll work with you, give you the flight instruction, so forth, and so fifth." He laughed.

"When do you want to begin?" Bill asked.

"How's Saturday morning sound to you?"

"Great! Do you have an airplane or will we have to rent one?"

"All you have to do is show up at Ogle Airport," Roland said with a smile. "We'll work out the details then, okay?"

"Sounds good to me," Bill said as the two men shook hands. Noticing his companions' glasses were getting low, Bill signaled the waiter to bring another round of drinks.

As the conversation paused, Jenny spoke up. "Tell us about your family, Bill."

"Well, there's not much to tell," Bill said. "I'm not married yet, so my family is basically my parents, two brothers, and a sister."

"Are you serious?" Jenny responded. "You're still single? You better watch out. Some Guyanese girl is going to put you in her sights. Tell you what. I'll work on fixing you up, okay? At least you'll be saved from the regular vultures that prey on diplomats assigned here."

"It's that bad, huh?" Bill said. "Thanks for the warning, and I'll be looking forward to meeting one of your friends."

Over the course of the next hour and two more drinks, Jenny became more and more interactive. Born in Brazil, Jenny had come to Guyana at the age of ten, having been sent to live with an aunt and get an education. She was the eldest of eleven children, and her parents wanted her to have more than they could provide. By the end of the evening, Bill suspected he'd gained not only a flight instructor, but two new friends as well.

After Roland began giving him flight lessons, Bill realized that flying in Guyana was totally different from flying in the States. The Cessna 182 that Roland "borrowed" from the owner at Ogle Airfield was much more powerful and more complicated than anything Bill had flown before. He had already taken the written test and scored ninety-seven out of a possible one hundred points. The next step was the flying and practice to master landings and takeoffs from short, grassy airstrips.

Occasionally Bill would make mistakes and judgment errors, but Roland never let them pass. He emphasized that flying in Guyana was absolutely unforgiving. They practiced emergency procedures over and over, pushing the Cessna to its limits. Bill was getting a complete, personalized course in becoming a bush pilot.

"When I started flying for Guyana Air," Roland commented after one lesson, "the company had only two types of aircraft, C-46s and Grumman amphibians. Because I was a new pilot, I flew the less desirable amphibians, landing on the rivers that cut through the jungle, resupplying missionaries and the growing settlements of gold miners, or *pork knockers* as we called them, and flying out emergency medical cases. Believe me, those were the times. As the settlements expanded, they were able to construct landing strips. Newer, land-based aircraft gradually replaced the Grumman airplanes. By the time I was twenty-eight, the last of the Grumman aircraft had been sold off, and we entered a new era of flying."

"Sounds like you miss them," Bill observed, as the two men got into Roland's Elan Sprint Sports Car.

"Miss the excitement is more like it—the pioneering part of it. But hell, it has by no means become routine to fly anywhere in Guyana, even today. That's why I'm on you to learn it right, from the beginning."

"Can a pilot earn a living wage here?" Bill asked.

"That's a tricky one, it is. If all you do is fly professionally, you'll starve, most likely. On the other hand, if you're willing to 'do favors' for folks, you can make a decent living."

"Are you including illegal stuff—the favors, I mean?"

"I'll do a lot of things, but I won't break any laws. I'm into my lifestyle here and don't want to ever lose it. If I'm flying a passenger/cargo load out of Lethem, for example, I'll purchase whatever I think I can sell here in Georgetown and top off the weight on the aircraft. Guyana Airways doesn't mind us doing that. They don't charge the pilots for any 'personal baggage' that a pilot may want to carry. Packaged meat is always a good bet—and really cheap to get in those areas."

Roland flashed a grin, and Bill was instantly reminded of cartoon depictions of wily, street-wise tomcats. He guessed trying to eke out a living in a place like Guyana could turn anyone into a wheeler and dealer.

CHAPTER 15

1974

"Our plan is to establish a settlement for about twelve hundred people, all members of the Peoples Temple, here in Guyana near Port Kaituma," Sharon Amos announced during her initial visit to the American embassy in Georgetown. She led a group of three Temple representatives sent to Guyana to begin making arrangements for taking possession of the land the government had offered the Peoples Temple. "We are also looking for office space here in Georgetown to support our plans."

"That sounds terrific. Do you know when your main group will be arriving?" the consul asked. "And can you give us a general idea of the make-up of your group by age? That will give us some measure of the consular services you may require."

"That's a good question. So much depends upon how quickly we can get established here in Guyana. As for our members, we are all shapes, sizes, and ages," Amos said, smiling broadly. "I'd say that about a fourth of the group is retired and over sixty. The remainder is divided into two-thirds adults over eighteen, and one-third children."

Following cordial discussion to clarify a few other questions, Amos and the two other representatives from the Peoples Temple departed.

After this initial meeting, the consul drafted a telegram to the Department of State alerting Consular Affairs that in the near future there would be an influx of American citizens to Guyana. While he identified the group, he made no comment as to the nature of the group or the purpose of their relocation to Guyana. The consul focused exclusively on issues related to issuing new passports, birth and death registrations, supporting U.S. citizen social security benefits, veteran benefits, et cetera. When viewed from the consul's perspective, this was simply a manpower question. In his telegram, the consul requested that the Department consider opening a new consular slot in Georgetown.

Shortly after Amos' visit, the advance team from the Peoples Temple arrived in Guyana and flew down to Port Kaituma to start its initial survey of the leased land that would be their settlement, and to draw up plans to develop it. By then, Amos had rented a house in Georgetown as the Peoples Temple's official office, which doubled as a communal living space.

Sharon Amos, as it turned out, was one of Jim Jones' most faithful followers, a trusted senior personal assistant. Amos notified Guyanese officials that the office in Georgetown would interface with them on all issues on behalf of the Peoples Temple and coordinate settlement-related activities with its California base as well. She told them that the settlement would be named after the Reverend Jim Jones and called *Jonestown*.

By the early summer of 1977, the majority of visa applicants wanted to escape Guyana to seek their fortunes in the United States any way they could. As a result, fraud was rampant. About 75% of applicants were refused visas.

By June 1977, Chargé Andrew Blacken had returned to Guyana after nine long months and was reinstated as chargé d'affaires. The Guyanese had finally expressed regret over Burnham's remarks concerning the Cubana Airlines bombing in October 1976. But they weakened it by saying that the prime minister had spoken in a moment of great grief and emotion. Everyone at the embassy grumbled over this, but they were only too happy to have the chargé back.

At the beginning of the summer, the Peoples Temple group from California was beginning its move to Guyana. According to newspaper reports, the group was trying "to escape the yoke of prejudice prevalent in the United States." Newspaper articles listed their goals: to erase oppression of the poor; to eradicate class distinctions; and to prove that people from diverse backgrounds and experiences could live together in harmony and peace. Another prevalent theme was that the leader of the group, the Reverend Jim Jones, believed in socialism and wanted to assist in Guyana's progressive socialist movement. This last goal was never stated officially, but was circulated via the Georgetown gossip train.

Not long after, the embassy staff learned officially from the Guyana government that Deputy Prime Minister Ptolemy Reid had arranged a lease agreement with the Peoples Temple for a tract of three thousand acres near Port Kaituma, located approximately 210 kilometers northwest of Georgetown, in the center of Guyana's magnificent tropical rain forest.

The Guyanese Foreign Minister briefed Chargé Blacken that the land in question was to be used to build a settlement for the development of otherwise unproductive acreage. From Blacken's viewpoint, the Burnham government was discounting the importance of its rain forests in the larger picture of global ecological balance, but he realized that the decision was the government's alone. It seemed that the government was more interested in the political gravitas its support of the Peoples Temple would bring internationally.

Soon after the members of the Peoples Temple arrived in Guyana and moved to Jonestown during the second half of 1977, a new radio station hit the airwaves, making three FM stations total receivable in Georgetown. The new station played current pop music from the United States and was sponsored by the Peoples Temple. The station's programs would be interrupted at various opportune times throughout the day with fervent religious messages.

Taking the opportunity to stop by the consulate on occasion, Sharon Amos appeared interested in keeping her lines of communication open with Alex. "It's really been hectic getting everyone moved down here, as you can imagine," she commented during one of her visits.

"I can appreciate all of the work that you have done over the past year to get things ready. It looks like a massive undertaking," Alex responded.

"Just so that you know, we have radio communications with Jonestown over a single-side-band radio—the same one we use for contact with the Peoples Temple offices back in California. It really was an essential tool in coordinating all of the travel for our group to come to Guyana," she explained. "The radio also made arranging shipments of machinery and other goods from California to Guyana easier."

Alex responded kindly to Amos, wanting to cement confidence between her and the consulate. After all, she represented the needs of a lot of American citizens living in Guyana.

CHAPTER 16

1977

A t the same time, personal changes were taking place in Bill Hausman's life. The activity of the past year, both the long hours at the consulate and an active social calendar—dating some of Jenny's friends as well as keeping up on the events offered within the diplomatic community—had somewhat drained him. Bill began spending more time relaxing at home during his off-hours, reading and listening to taped classical music on his new stereo system, which included a turntable for records. He also acquired a street dog puppy named Hutch, a kitten named Josephine, and an Amazon parrot chick he dubbed Henrietta.

A full-time housekeeper and cook, Serita, rounded out his household staff. A rather large Indian woman who worked barefoot, Serita ran a tight ship, was impeccably neat and clean, and introduced Bill to superbly prepared Guyanese dishes such as *cook-up, pepperpot* and curry, among others.

One night after work, Bill was sharing a drink with the other consular officers at the Pegasus Hotel bar when two hands appeared suddenly before his face and covered up his eyes. From behind his head, a woman's voice said in a British accent, "I'll give you two guesses. Who am I?"

"Is it Auntie Silvia?" Bill answered, being foolish.

"No, try again."

"No, no, no. Who is it?" Bill said, prying the hands from his eyes and turning around. A dark-haired woman in a blue blouse stood before him, grinning broadly. "Celeste! My God, it's been a long time. How are you? Please join us."

"I spotted you when you came in. How are you doing? How do you find Guyana?" she asked.

"Everything is fine," Bill said, looking at Celeste in wonderment. He'd almost forgotten how beautiful she was. Then he introduced the two other consular officers to her.

"I came to the consulate to see you, but you were out," Celeste commented. "Wanted to collect on your lunch invitation, remember?"

"Of course! Can we get you something to drink?" Bill offered.

"Thanks, but I really can't stay. My friend and his wife are meeting me here for dinner." Leaning toward Bill, Celeste teased, "Have you linked up with any of the local women yet? Gotta be careful of these Guyanese girls, you know. They'll steal your heart away!" She straightened and glanced at the door where a young couple had just entered. "Sorry, there they are. Got to go."

"Wait a minute!" Bill implored. "I didn't get your phone number the last time. I can't let you escape without that!"

"I'm sorry. Of course," Celeste said as she took her card from her purse and gave it to Bill.

"It's great to see you again," Bill said, placing a hand on her shoulder.

Then Celeste leaned forward and gave Bill an embrace. "Really nice seeing you too." She nodded to the other officers. "Nice to meet you both. Bye." And she was gone.

In response to this encounter with what was arguably the best-looking woman in Guyana, Bill had earned some major barbs from his younger colleagues, all bachelors. Of course, they didn't believe his innocent story.

The next day, Bill called Celeste at her laboratory. "It's so nice to talk with you," Bill began. "Is this a good time?"

"Oh yes, no problem. I just finished a report and am getting it ready to mail to London. This is a good time to catch up. How are you?"

"I'm doin' fine, thanks. Guyana—or should I say Georgetown—is really a fascinating place. Too much work, but that goes with the territory, I suppose. Everyone seems to want a visa." Bill realized that this was a boring start to the conversation. "I've come up with an idea for something to do this Saturday, if you're willing. Are you game?" Bill asked.

"I don't know," Celeste answered coyly. "What sort of an idea is it?"

"Oh, come on, don't you trust me? Where's your sense of adventure, striking out into the unknown?" Bill knew he wasn't handling this conversation well at all. When he heard a long moment of silence, he quickly tried to fill the void. "How would you like to go on a picnic with me, Saturday afternoon? I'll pick you up around 1:00 P.M."

"Okay, that sort of an idea. I haven't been on a picnic in years. Actually, the last time was with my family when I was a teen. What a pleasant idea! Very proper for a first date, you know. I'd love to go," she exclaimed.

Thinking that he finally was on track, Bill added, "I've already checked the weather and it will be a nice sunny day, so wear comfortable clothing and a hat that protects you from the sun, okay?"

"Yes, Father," Celeste said sarcastically. "Do you want me to bring anything?"

"I don't think so. I'll throw some things together. Are you a white or red wine person?" Bill asked. "My instinct tells me red, but I may be wrong."

"No, you're right on the mark, sir. Red wine is just perfect for a picnic. This is really a nice surprise. I can't believe that I'm going on a picnic in Guyana. Thank you for calling." She gave Bill directions to her apartment and they said their good byes.

Bill arrived only fifteen minutes late, with a small bouquet of freshly cut flowers in his hand. For the first time in many dates, he felt nervous.

Celeste invited Bill inside while she placed the flowers in water. As she moved about, he noticed that her apartment was sparsely decorated but neat as could be. Photographs were on display around the sitting room. Bill gestured to one. "Is this your family portrait?" he asked.

Celeste had wandered up beside him. "Yes. That one was taken when I was only sixteen. This is my father, mother, older brother Gustavo, and my two younger sisters, Rose Marie and Veronica."

"What a wonderful family," Bill remarked sincerely.

"We are who we are, I guess. It's a blessing that my parents are still enjoying good health. Are we ready?" she asked.

In response, Bill said, "*Vamanos, muchachos,*"—*Let's go, boys* in Spanish—which tickled Celeste. Bill explained, "I went to Spanish language school before coming to Guyana, for all the good that did me."

"Learning a foreign language is always a good thing, Bill, and not an easy thing to do, I might add," Celeste commented.

As they made the short drive to the picnic destination, the conversation ebbed and flowed. Bill found it harder to talk to Celeste easily now that they were on a date. He was suddenly acutely aware of her intelligence and class and was wary of slipping up and saying something dull, or worse, downright stupid. After a slightly awkward silence, Celeste piped up, "So, where exactly are you taking me?"

"The ambassador's residence," Bill replied, just as he turned the car off the road and onto the driveway. The embassy security guards recognized Bill and immediately opened the gates.

Celeste peered through the windshield at the grounds and exhaled in appreciation, "Oh, wow."

Because there was no American ambassador named to Guyana, the official residence in Georgetown was not occupied but continued to be maintained by the embassy. Official receptions were often held at the residence, a large wooden structure with a sensational view of the port of Georgetown. Open to embassy staff, the grounds around the residence were impeccably maintained as well, including a tennis court, pool, and a shaded area with several old-style picnic tables.

Upon exiting the car, Celeste stood gazing at the grounds of the residence. "This is absolutely beautiful. What a lovely garden design . . . I love the flowers and the stone walking paths."

Bill was unloading the car, and carried two baskets to a picnic table. He immediately began unpacking the lunch that Serita had prepared for them.

Without asking, Celeste pitched in to set things up. "Here are the wine glasses, hurrah," Celeste exclaimed. "And here's the wine—wonderful."

After setting everything up, Bill opened the wine, being careful to demonstrate to Celeste that he knew how to let wine breathe before filling their glasses. Then he raised his glass in a toast: "Here's to 'America's Airline to the World'—Pan Am. If it weren't for Pan Am, we never would have met. Cheers!"

Celeste's cheeks flushed with pleasure. "Cheers!" she chimed back.

They took their time eating and let the conversation lapse at intervals to enjoy the food and wine. Now that they were outside, these silences seemed pleasant, and occasionally Bill would catch Celeste's gaze while she was chewing and smile. An embassy officer and his family, including two youngsters under six years of age, stopped by the residence to enjoy the pool. Bill and Celeste watched the bunch splashing and playing, and made small talk with the parents.

After having lunch and packing up, Bill took Celeste on a leisurely walk along the seawall that protected Georgetown from flooding at high tide. The afternoon ocean breeze was refreshing, and both enjoyed the view of local fishing trawlers moving about close to shore.

Just as dusk was falling, Bill returned Celeste to her apartment. "I really enjoyed your company . . . and I hope we can get together again soon," he said.

Celeste smiled at him. "I hope so, too. I'm becoming more and more impressed with you, young Mr. Vice-Consul. This was great. Thank you for a wonderful afternoon."

"You've just stolen my thoughts, Senorita Campalena." He leaned forward as he said it, dipping his head to kiss her, but hesitated and stopped just short of the mark. She instinctively closed the gap and their lips met and held for a long moment. At last, she pulled back and met his gaze, her lips spreading into a smile.

"That was really nice, Bill. I hope I see you soon."

Bill grinned and shook his head. "Nice doesn't quite get there. Spectacular maybe; stupendous for sure! I'll call and we can make plans." He stepped back from her door and descended the steps to his car. As he drove away, he glanced in the rearview mirror to see Celeste, pale white in the gray light, still standing where he'd left her.

———————

That night, Bill lay awake, replaying moments from the day in his head: the way Celeste looked, the sound of her laugh, the feel of her lips on his. It was more than an hour before his brain settled down and he drifted off to sleep . . .

With the sound of explosions detonating behind them, Bill and the others ran for their lives in the direction of the landing zone. Val kept pace with him, but after the first glance, Bill kept his eyes glued to the jungle ahead.

Now that contact was broken, as part of its standard operating procedures, the recon team knew to disperse tear gas grenades to discourage the North Vietnamese from following them. It was now a run-for-your-life attempt to escape.

The team was staying together, following Bill, when the F-4s made their run on their previous location, now overrun with North Vietnamese. First came the roar of the jets directly overhead, then the shock wave from the deafening explosions. That was almost too close, Bill thought as he continued to run.

Reaching the landing zone, he set up a defensive perimeter and then heard the call from the evacuation chopper: "Lightning Four, this is Red Rover on station, over."

Bill responded, "Roger, Red Rover; this is Lightning Four, throwing smoke."

At that moment, Val threw a red smoke grenade onto the landing zone.

"This is Red Rover, I have red smoke, over," the pilot reported.

"Roger, Red Rover; Lightning Four confirms red smoke."

With that, the chopper began its descent as two Cobra gunship helicopters circled the area, looking for enemy targets.

As the team closed in on the helicopter, Bill stayed alert to cover everyone until they were on board. He planned to be the last man to go.

It turned out Val had the same idea. Catching Bill's attention, Val signaled for him to move out. With no time to argue, Bill turned and ran in low profile to the chopper.

Not quite there, he felt a blow to his left arm. He launched himself through the chopper door before looking down to see that a round had gone through the fleshy part of his arm, just above the elbow. Outside, he could see Val sending magazine after magazine of fire into the enemy, while the helicopter door gunner returned fire.

As if in slow motion, Val turned and started to run toward the helicopter. He was halfway there when he caught two North Vietnamese rounds in his back and one in his right leg.

He crumpled, and as he fell, the Cobra gunships swooped down and raked the enemy troops. Leaping to the ground, Bill and Captain Phuoc retrieved Val, dragging him onto the chopper.

As soon as they'd made it, the pilot pulled up and away, with both door gunners firing.

Bill's attention was locked on Val. The bullets had torn clean through him, and blood seeped out onto the chopper floor.

Captain Phuoc grappled for a first-aid kit while Bill tried to stanch the bleeding with his hands. Val reached out to him, clutching his arm and struggling to breathe.

"Stay with me, Val," Bill said, looking into his eyes, wild with pain.

But it was no use. The gunmen had scarcely stopped firing when Val took his last breath, and was still...

When Bill awoke, his bed was damp, and the happy thoughts that had lulled him to sleep felt like distant memories. Turning onto his side, he drew his knees to his chest and waited for the dream to leave him. The knowledge that it was Val's decision made no difference to him. On nights like this, he could hardly live with the feeling of guilt.

The dreams went on, but life did as well. Over the next few weeks, Bill and Celeste continued to see each other, attending parties and diplomatic functions, having cocktails with Roland and Jenny, going out to dinner and taking walks around town. Bill kept waiting for the sense of constriction and irritation that normally accompanied his budding relationships, but it didn't come. Celeste was impeccable. And perhaps because of this, Bill found himself moving more slowly with her than he had with other women. She seemed to sense his hesitation, and was cautious in return, never pushing, not wanting to scare him off.

Being with Celeste was magical, almost medicinal for Bill. He suspected that he was falling in love with her, and the idea tantalized and scared him simultaneously. He hadn't felt this way since his army days in Vietnam, when he would take leave from the fighting and retreat to the salvation of Co Hoa's arms.

Amid all the chaos, those arms had been his world. Now, the more time he spent in Celeste's company, the harder it was to keep memories of Co Hoa from surfacing.

The Vietnamese hotel guards motioned for Bill to stay down. He nodded to show that he understood, but complying was harder.

The sergeant was yelling at Co Hoa in words Bill couldn't understand. My God, what does he think he's doing? *Bill wondered. Could he have mistaken Co Hoa for a prostitute, since she was exiting a hotel where only Americans stayed?*

Holding his M-15 in front of him, Bill contemplated shooting the soldier— but in doing so, he'd run the risk of hitting Co Hoa, not to mention disciplinary retribution.

Then another shot rang out, and Co Hoa screamed for her life.

Bill had seen enough. He set his weapon down, readied himself, and charged the soldier like a linebacker—his only thought was to knock the guy to the ground.

He had fifteen yards to cover and was almost there when the sergeant noticed him and turned in his direction. But he was drunk and slow and barely had time to look surprised before Bill slammed into him, sending the man, Co Hoa, and the M-16 rifle flying.

The sergeant crumpled easily under Bill's superior weight, and they both hit the ground hard. Out of the corner of his eye, Bill caught the falling motion of the rifle. It hit the street flat on its side, and the impact was enough to trigger the weapon to fire.

A shot rang out. Scrambling upright, Bill turned to Co Hoa. She was lying still, not five feet from him.

"No!" he cried out, rushing to her side.

The errant round had hit her just under her left ear, blowing apart her skull. Her black hair lay soaking in a pool of blood. Bill picked her up and held her to him and began to call for help, knowing that it was hopeless. The woman he loved had died instantly. No one could help her now.

Bill's eyes opened to the dim light of his room, his vision blurred with tears that had welled up in his sleep. His heart felt hollow, empty. *Two deaths in Vietnam.* Put that way, it sounded so insignificant, compared to the thousands of lives lost in the war. And how many of those casualties had Bill been responsible for? Dozens? Hundreds? Would he ever know for sure? Some would call him a war hero for taking out so many Viet Cong, but he would never look at it that way. And even if he could, how could he ever reconcile himself to the two deaths—of Val and Co Hoa—that continued to haunt him to this day? He hadn't pulled the trigger, but in his heart, Bill knew he'd killed them just the same.

CHAPTER 17

Summer 1977

Late one afternoon, after Serita had gone out shopping, Bill was just getting settled on his front porch when he noticed a young couple approaching a house several doors down from his. He assumed they were residents of the housing development. In the course of an hour, as he sat listening to taped music, the young man and woman systematically moved from house to house, drawing closer to his own. His curiosity was aroused.

American in appearance, the young man had short, dark hair and a tall, trim, athletic build, and his tanned face was clean-shaven. His companion, a young woman of about twenty, was petite, her sandy hair almost blonde. She was a blue-eyed bundle of energy, evident in the way she walked and talked. Wearing jeans and colorful shirts, both seemed to Bill the epitome of all-American youth. When they reached Bill's yard, he called out a cordial welcome.

"My name is Robert, and this is my fiancée, Carol," the man responded, smiling and extending his hand to Bill for a firm handshake as they joined him. "We're in the area today to talk with people about our new settlement near Port Kaituma. Perhaps you've heard of Jonestown?"

"Yes, I have," Bill replied. "Come on inside where it's more comfortable."

"Good," Carol said, "and after we've shared our story with you, we hope you'll give us a donation. That's part of our purpose, too, you know. We can always use funds to help carry out our exciting plans for Jonestown."

"I guess all of us could use more money," Bill said with a smile. "I'm goin' to get a soft drink. Can I offer you one?"

He almost missed Robert's nod to Carol, who answered, "We'd love something to drink." Bill excused himself and returned moments later with a tall glass for each, which they eagerly accepted.

"It must be extremely difficult living in such a remote area," Bill commented, as they all sipped their sodas. "You and the others who came must literally be carving your home sites out of the jungle."

"Oh, much of the work had already been completed when we arrived," Carol answered quickly. "We have adequate quarters to live in, and we have already begun growing some of our own food. We do work hard, but what small inconveniences we have are well worth it. We are blessed to be a part of the wonderful ministry that our founder, the Reverend Jones, has struggled and sacrificed to bring about." Carol's speech was fervent, her blue eyes sparkling.

"Yes," Robert agreed, his own face shining. "We're part of a special, select family in Jonestown. Like the children's song says, 'Red and yellow, black and white, they are precious in His sight.' Father Jones teaches us to love everyone and that we are all equal. We may have to toil right now, but we are building a city that will be all we've ever wanted when it is completed. All of us will find peace and live in harmony together."

"But why come so far to build in such a remote place?" Bill asked. "Wouldn't it be much simpler where things are more accessible?"

The two visitors exchanged glances, then turned bright smiles on Bill.

"The Guyanese people, represented by Deputy Prime Minister Reid, invited us to come here," Carol emphasized. "Mr. Reid espouses the same kind of philosophy our own leader does, and he welcomed the opportunity to have us in his country as an example of what can be accomplished by people of diverse races and backgrounds who choose to live, love, and work together to create a new and better world."

"I understand that," Bill said calmly. "But it still doesn't explain why the Peoples Temple felt it couldn't provide the same example while staying in California, or at least somewhere else in the United States."

"Are you familiar with scripture?" Robert asked.

"Yes, a little. To which part are you referring?"

"The verses in the New Testament where Jesus Christ alluded to persecution in His own country. Because Father Jones teaches love, equality, and living a life not bound by prejudices and strife, he has been persecuted to the point that he felt it necessary to seek another place to establish and carry on his ministry, a ministry that is also being persecuted by those who wish to destroy its effectiveness."

"As far as I know, everyone in the States has virtually absolute freedom to pursue their faith in any manner they choose," Bill countered. "Their 'beliefs' vary widely."

"Not true," Carol protested. "As long as religious, or even ethnic, groups conform to a preconceived idea of what the established 'norm' is, they are allowed to exist. Let someone or some group step away from those norms— that's when the trouble begins."

"You are aware, no doubt, of the strong racial prejudices still existing all across America," Robert added. "And the same is true for any group, really, that is different or apart from the mainstream."

"Yes," Bill agreed. "There is prejudice and there are groups in opposition to almost everything. But I still say there has to be some powerful incentive for such a large group to leave families, friends, and even their country to start a new life in a strange land."

"You would have to know our Head, our Christ, in order to understand the depth of our sincerity and conviction in this," Carol responded.

"I would have to know much more than that," Bill admitted, seeing in the young couple before him an unreal commitment to their beliefs. They reminded him of other young adults he had encountered in airports soliciting money for their religion, wearing orange robes and sporting shaved heads. Bill was tiring of the conversation.

Bill shook his head. "I'm sorry, you still haven't convinced me. I find it difficult to fathom what would motivate the leader of a group to undertake such a thing, and in Guyana of all places."

"You seem to know more about us than we thought you did at first," Robert said, his tone cooler now. "What did you say you do here in Guyana?"

"It didn't come up before," Bill answered. "I'm a vice-consul at the American embassy here in Georgetown."

"I see," Robert said, almost formally. Again he exchanged glances with Carol, and this time Bill caught the negative signal he gave. "This was enjoyable," Robert added, standing, setting his glass firmly on the table before him.

Nodding, Bill agreed. "Please, sit back down and let's continue."

"We'd like to, but we can stay only so long with each household." Robert assisted Carol to her feet. "Perhaps we can come back later and answer more of your questions."

"You're welcome to do that," Bill said pleasantly, trailing the couple as they retreated rather hastily down the staircase to his door.

"Thank you for sharing your time with us," Carol said lamely, "and for the drink," she added with more sincerity, as Robert nudged her forward.

Bill stood on the front steps, watching them, noting that they did not stop at the next several houses. They seemed to be hurrying away from him.

Huh, Bill thought, returning inside. *I wonder just what they're hiding?*

As he was clearing away the young couple's glasses, he realized that they had never even asked for their donation.

Chapter 18

August 1977

"Come on in, Priscilla," Jim Jones called through the open doorway of his Ukiah office. "I've been meaning to talk with you about Guyana."

Priscilla entered quickly, shutting the door behind her. Jim stood to greet her and she kissed him quickly on the lips, pressed her body against his, and said, "It's been a while. I missed you."

"Thank you, dear. You mean so much to me." Jim patted her hair and ended the hug, drawing her down to sit beside him on a small sofa. "Now, I'm thinking about leaving within the next few days, dear, and I want you and Katrina to follow me. I don't think it would be a good idea for us to travel together, although nothing would make me happier. Do you understand?"

"Whatever you say, Jim, it will be done," Priscilla responded. "I understand completely. This can't be easy for you either. You've done so much for the people here in California, and now the system has turned against you. The accusations, the lies—they don't understand you. I'll make the reservations as soon as we have your travel confirmed."

"Just call Sharon," he instructed. "She will take care of everything on that end." He touched Priscilla's face with one hand. "Those bastards just won't let up. This will never stop. It will be so much better in Guyana, you'll see. Have you seen the latest photos that were in the mail? Let me see where I put them . . ." He stood and began to rifle through the papers on his desk.

Priscilla watched him sift through memos and envelopes, his hands trembling slightly. She pushed the observation from her mind and cleared her throat. "What about my ex-husband, Dad? Should I let him know that I'm leaving? I know he'll be worried if I don't call."

Jim righted himself, seeming to forget what he was hunting for. "Look, Priscilla, calling him is only going to give us a headache. Do you think he's going to wish you a bon voyage? I don't think so." He walked forward and put his hands on Priscilla's shoulders, shaking her gently and smiling. "Let him be tormented. The son of a bitch deserves that, at least."

Katrina knew that something strange was going on, but she didn't know what. Her mother had photos taken of her early in the summer, but she wouldn't tell Katrina what they were for. Priscilla had also asked the school to prepare a copy of Katrina's school records.

Katrina had heard about a place called Jonestown from the other children attending Temple events that summer, but it never occurred to her that the word would affect her. So she hadn't thought to mention it to her father, whom she continued to talk to daily on the telephone. Then one night, after she'd gotten off the phone, her mother called her and asked her to sit down; she had something to tell her.

"Sweetie, we have to talk about what's going to happen over the next few days," Priscilla began. "We've been invited to visit Jonestown in Guyana and will be leaving tomorrow morning. Doesn't that sound exciting?"

"What? Tomorrow?" Katrina felt a panic rise up inside of her and heard her voice rise in response. "You've got to be kidding me, Mom! For how long? Why are you only telling me now?"

Priscilla patted her daughter's hand and answered soothingly, "Not long at all, honey, about ten days. I've already talked with the principal and there's no problem with school. You'll only miss the first three days, and then you'll be back to catch up. That won't be too bad, now will it?"

"But I don't want to go!" Katrina protested shrilly. "Why don't you go? I'll stay with Daddy while you're in Jonestown."

"Don't make this difficult, sweetie," Priscilla countered. "I see the trip as a wonderful opportunity for you to learn about a new country, new people, customs, and a new way of life. It should really be interesting. I'm told that there is a group of girls your age down there already, and I'm sure you know some of them from the Temple. I just know you'll have a good time. It'll be an adventure!"

Katrina was shaking her head. "Maybe you didn't hear me, Mom . . . I said *I don't want to go.* Maybe *you* like all the Temple rules, but I hate them! They just get me into trouble, no matter what I do. I'm not going!"

Priscilla leapt to her feet and glowered down at the flushed twelve-year-old. "Well, get used to the idea, missy, because I'm going and you're coming with me. It's all set. That's final. Now go to your room and start packing. You won't need any sweaters or heavy jackets. Get moving!" She yanked Katrina to her feet and gave her a push toward the hallway.

"Don't grab me like that. It hurts, Mom," Katrina protested, and whirled away from her, shouting over her shoulder, "I hope this makes you happy! You're the worst mother ever."

Priscilla waited until she heard the door to Katrina's room slam, then sank down onto the worn tweed couch and held her head in her hands. She looked up and gazed around the tan and yellow living room of the modest apartment she'd rented upon moving to Ukiah. When had her sweet little girl become this hateful, rebellious creature, she wondered? And how would Katrina react when she learned that they wouldn't be coming back in ten days, or even ten months? She planned on extending the trip bit by bit, letting Katrina adjust to her new home in Jonestown before telling her that the change was permanent.

The rest of the evening was spent getting packed for Jonestown. Katrina stayed in her room, dragging clothes out of her dresser and choosing outfits for the trip. Periodically, Priscilla would come into her room to check on her progress and to ensure that she wasn't taking any clothing that was too worn or too small. She rifled through her shoes and selected those that would serve her best in a tropical climate—sturdy but comfortable.

Later in the evening, Priscilla walked into the kitchen and switched on the lights to discover Katrina kneeling down next to the counter, the telephone in her hands.

"What are you doing, young lady?" Priscilla snapped, grabbing the receiver from her daughter and lifting it to her ear. She could hear her ex-husband's voice, distant and anxious: "Hello? Hello? Katrina—" She hung up quickly. "I've just about had it with you," she yelled. "Get to your room and stay there for the rest of the night!"

As a precaution to prevent Katrina from calling John again, Priscilla unhooked the two extension telephones in the apartment and brought them into her bedroom. When all of the packing was finished, she waited until Katrina had bathed and was sleeping soundly before dozing off herself. The taxi would arrive at 6:30 in the morning.

CHAPTER 19

September 1977

By September, the number of newly arrived residents at the Peoples Temple at Jonestown had grown and was approaching one thousand in total. The Reverend Jones had relocated to Jonestown in August amid a storm of controversy surrounding him and the Temple back in the States. Plans were that another three hundred members of the Temple would arrive within weeks.

It was the influx of Americans that kept the embassy attuned to Jonestown; the controversy that followed Jones hardly mattered. In August, a heated custody battle erupted involving Jim Jones himself, when a woman who had recently defected from the Temple claimed that Jones had taken her son to Guyana against her will. Papers surfaced identifying Jim Jones as the father, and Jones's wife, Marceline, had even signed them as a witness. Evidence of Jones' affair and illegitimate child only underscored the accusations being made about him in the States—that he was a fraud and a fanatic who bullied his flock into submission. Two or three other custody cases were soon filed in the Guyana courts involving other children who had been whisked off to Jonestown by one parent without the consent of the other.

"Do you think it's just one big harem?" Bill mused one day, in reference to the illicit affair that had led to Jones' custody battle. "I heard he's got a slew of kids, and only some of them were born by his wife."

"You have to remember that most of them were adopted," Alex pointed out. "Still, I wonder. Especially when you see him trotting out those little tarts to curry favor with the Guyanese."

Bill nodded. He'd also heard accounts of women from Jonestown showing up at parties that the Georgetown politicians attended, wearing revealing clothing and making themselves available to the officials. Nonetheless, the rumors surrounding Jonestown and the goings-on of the settlement became a sideshow of minor interest to the consular officers, who were concentrated on their primary tasks of issuing immigrant and non-immigrant visas to Guyanese.

One morning over coffee, Alex asked Bill, "This Jonestown thing has me intrigued. I wonder why the Guyanese would welcome them in the first place."

"Well," Bill commented, "it's not hard for me to figure out. Prime Minister Burnham was motivated by politics. You see, it was the perfect opportunity for him to generate negative publicity about the United States at the same time that he's promoting his own brand of socialism."

"Maybe you're right. He could also be thinking that this is an opportunity for Guyana to raise its stock in the Non-Aligned Movement," Alex said. "Burnham is well known for finding ways to make his point, no matter what."

"It seems to me that Jones suits Burnham's purposes to a tee. After all, he still fully believes the United States sponsored the Cubana Airlines bombing," Bill reminded him. "This may be his way of striking back at us, the superpower, and getting away with it."

"But why?" Alex asked. "Why would a religious man want to get himself and his followers tangled up with a man like Burnham, in Guyana of all places?"

Over the following months, the circumstances of Jones' departure from the U.S. became known in the embassy through the visits of Californians to the consulate—Californians whose loved ones were members of the Peoples Temple in Jonestown. From what the embassy learned, the Los Angeles District Attorney's Office had begun an investigation into several mysterious deaths in California—deaths alleged to have been linked to the Peoples Temple and Jim Jones. The relatives judged that this investigation apparently compelled Jones to flee and to seek out a sanctuary where the U.S. legal arm couldn't touch him. Guyana was that sanctuary.

Topographically in Guyana, civilization was mostly limited to the coastal plain, where buses and taxis served the population's transportation needs. Getting around at one's own initiative anywhere else in the country, especially in the interior, was practically impossible. Roads were nonexistent. Transport was limited to irregular flights from one jungle landing strip to another or to Georgetown. As such, there was virtually no outside contact with the settlers of Jonestown. The members of the Peoples Temple were trapped by the surrounding jungle and totally dependent on Jones and the infrastructure he had established for their survival. The Guyanese didn't even have a policeman assigned there, no mailman or any other kind of official—no outsider whatsoever.

Early on, the embassy wanted to centralize any contact with the members of the Peoples Temple so that it could maintain one voice concerning U.S. citizen services that were available. The consul, Alex Manus, was designated to be that voice: a central point of contact appointed to handle all matters related to Jonestown and to prevent passport fraud at the least. It would also help ensure that the social security checks the embassy received monthly were going to people who were actually alive and living at Jonestown.

On another front, the Peoples Temple and Jim Jones were being hounded by several parents wanting to regain custody of their children, who were in Jonestown.

One case was that of Thomas and Greta Marks and their son, Jason. Six years prior to arriving in Jonestown, they had given custody of Jason to Jim Jones. In an effort to get their son out of Jonestown and returned to them, Thomas and Greta Marks hired the best lawyers in Guyana to sue Jim Jones to win back custody of their son.

Just prior to the case making headlines in Guyana, the Congress of the United States passed the Freedom of Information Act into law. Under the FOIA, any U.S. citizen could file a petition with the federal government to obtain copies of all records pertaining to him or her.

As soon as FOIA had become law, Jones' lawyers filed a petition on behalf of their client and updated the request at regular intervals to ensure that they received any existing U.S. government records on Jones, past and present. In effect, any telegrams sent to the Department of State from the embassy that mentioned Jones' name had to be turned over.

Initially, the consulate had reported to Washington the substance of Guyanese newspaper articles concerning the Jason Marks case due to the political significance of the case in Guyana. Then the embassy received guidance from State asking it not to report on the activities of U.S. citizens in Guyana, unless the embassy was acting within its authority to discharge consular services to them.

The legal consensus was that while not focusing on the trial in any way, or deliberately acting maliciously, the embassy had come dangerously close to violating the rights of U.S. citizens living in Guyana. These rights were derived under the Privacy Act, a law passed by Congress about the same time as the

Freedom of Information Act, that guaranteed the privacy of U.S. citizens living abroad and protected all U.S. citizens from any governmental monitoring of their activities while overseas. Essentially, if an American citizen wanted to "disappear" in Guyana, it was his right to do so.

Concerning the Jason Marks case, Jones' lawyers had successfully obtained the court's decision to dismiss the suit as frivolous. The newspapers let the case die, and the Marks returned to California broken and dejected.

Bill followed closely the details of the Marks case. He had personal motives. Walter Solomon, an attorney whom Bill had befriended from the Georgetown Rotary Club, was at the same time handling another child custody case involving Jonestown. Walter represented a businessman from California who had divorced his wife in 1975 for incompatibility. The wife got custody over their only daughter; the father had weekly visitation rights.

After their divorce, the wife and child became ensconced members of the Peoples Temple. She was among the first to place her name on the list of members to go to Guyana, along with her daughter's. In violation of the divorce settlement, the wife took her daughter to Guyana, denying the father his right to weekly visits. The father just wanted his daughter back in the United States.

CHAPTER 20

October 1977

It took two weeks and dogged persistence to get Sharon Amos in Georgetown to agree to John's visit to Jonestown, but at last he had her word. After arriving in Guyana, his first stop was the Peoples Temple offices.

When he knocked on the fence around the house, a guard came. "I'm supposed to see Sharon Amos," John said. "I'm John Olsen from the United States." He waited while the guard retreated under the stilts of the house to talk on an intercom.

"She will be right with you, sir," the guard responded.

John didn't have to wait long before a woman exited the house and descended the stairs. She was attractive, in her mid-forties, he guessed, and didn't wear a trace of makeup.

"Let him in, please," she said. The guard nodded and returned to unlock the gate.

John approached Sharon Amos with a tight smile. "Hot weather you've got down here," he ventured. She ignored his attempt at small talk and waved him toward the house.

"Please come in," she said. "My office is to the right."

Amos took a seat at her desk, and John situated himself opposite her, under a slow-moving ceiling fan. She got right to business. "I guess you've come to make arrangements to visit with your daughter, Katrina, right? You're lucky that Priscilla didn't object to your visit."

"I guess I am. Just how does this work? Are there scheduled flights?" John asked.

"Here's the deal, Mr. Olsen," Amos began. "There're two flights a week—on Tuesdays and Thursdays—to Port Kaituma, a small airstrip close to Jonestown.

We don't like visitors to stay more than a day or two, because that interrupts the settlement's routine. You can schedule a flight with Guyana Airways on this coming Tuesday to go down, and return on Thursday. How does that sound?"

"That's fine," John responded, relieved he'd been granted two nights in the settlement. "Tell me, would it be okay for me to spend some time with Katrina here in Georgetown on my next trip down? I'd like to plan a weekend together, maybe go do some touristy things."

Looking at him without any real interest or concern, Amos slashed the idea to ribbons. "It's against the Temple's policy to allow any travel unless it's related to Temple business or a personal emergency. I'm afraid that is not going to happen. Try to understand that we're building a community down in Jonestown and we need everyone totally committed to it."

John felt his face burn at the abrupt refusal. "I know," he started, "I was just hoping—"

"Listen, it's a rough life down there. No one is sugarcoating that. If we allow some of our members to start visiting Georgetown, it will cause resentment among the others," she explained. "That's what we're trying to avoid. Look, I'll set everything up so that someone is there to meet you at the airport in Port Kaituma next Tuesday. Is there anything else?"

"No, I guess not. Thank you, Ms. Amos. I really appreciate it." John grappled to appease her, sensing that he'd somehow offended the gatekeeper to Jonestown. At the same time, his mind reeled with the phrase "a rough life down there." He was more anxious than ever to see the conditions in which Katrina was living.

The Guyana Airways flight to Port Kaituma was only half full—eight passengers, including John. He was the only visitor headed to Jonestown, though two other men on the flight were Jonestown residents. One of them had been involved in an accident while working on a tractor. He had severely lacerated his leg and broken it in two places and had to use crutches. John and the other men assisted him in descending the airplane steps in Port Kaituma.

As they deplaned, one of the men from Jonestown pointed to a flatbed trailer being pulled by an Allis Chalmers tractor. "Hey, this is your ride to the settlement," he shouted to John.

"This is incredible," John commented as the tractor made its way over the wet and muddy trail to Jonestown. "Are you doing all right?" he asked the man with the cast. He received a thumbs-up in response.

After about forty minutes and a lot of bouncing, the tractor entered into a clearing in the jungle and John spotted Priscilla and Katrina in a group of onlookers.

"Daddy! Daddy!"

John stepped down off the trailer just in time to catch the gangly girl, marveling at how different she looked from when he'd last seen her two months prior. Had she grown? Was she thinner? Or was it the deep suntan that made his little girl look so much older?

"Hello, angel. How are you doin'?" John asked with a quiver in his voice. Turning to Priscilla, he said, "What a trip!"

"Welcome to Jonestown," Priscilla offered. "We're just getting started, so don't expect too much." Priscilla put an arm around Katrina's shoulders and turned away, leaving John to trail behind with his bag. She leaned close to their daughter and he heard her caution, "That's enough hugging and kissing. Remember, we have to keep our distance."

It was late in the afternoon and clouds were gathering. One of the young men at Jonestown took John's overnight bag and told him that he would be staying with them in the men's sleeping quarters.

"I'll show you where that is after dinner, okay?" Priscilla affirmed. "Grab your umbrella—it's going to rain. Why don't you and Katrina go over to the pavilion, where you can sit and talk? I'll join you for dinner." She then reminded Katrina, "No hugging and kissing."

John was amazed at how much Katrina had matured in the space of three months. He noticed that when there were others around, she was subdued and not very animated in talking about Jonestown and her experiences. When no one was nearby, though, she aired her grievances openly.

"The food here is awful, Daddy. There are no snacks and no popcorn, even though we have movies on Saturday nights," Katrina commented. "The kids are really nice. We're sorta in the same boat, you know? I have one best friend—her name is Judi and we're in the same level at school. We try to have fun together."

"Are you okay with all of this, angel?" John asked.

Even though Katrina answered him, he knew that it was a canned response. She talked on and on about her "jobs" and the other girls in her sleeping quarters. She explained that there wasn't room enough for families to live together, so they all lived in individual groupings, men with men, women with women, and children with children.

"We have some girls as young as nine years old in our dorm room," Katrina explained. "We sleep in bunk beds, three beds tall. I'm on the top. There are twelve of us in the room, and it gets really hot at night. If it rains tonight, it will cool off some and make it nicer to sleep."

Katrina clammed up when Priscilla found them to lead them to the dining hall. Over dinner, John tried to ask Priscilla questions about the settlement and her plans for returning to the U.S., but she was unresponsive and defensive by turns. She spoke with a kind of arrogance about her decision to leave the material comforts of the U.S. behind for a more purposeful life in Jonestown. At nine o'clock, Priscilla told John it was bedtime and escorted him to the men's quarters for the night.

In the morning, the wake-up call came at 6:00 A.M. The men were already up and moving just before dawn to have breakfast and to start another workday.

John met up with Priscilla and Katrina an hour later at the pavilion. After having some fruit, breakfast rolls, and coffee, Katrina offered to show her father around the settlement.

They spent the next three hours walking around and talking. Katrina proudly showed him where her sleeping quarters were, noting that the top bunk was where the air flowed through best. In spite of appearances, John could sense that she was holding herself back from sharing her thoughts.

When they returned to the pavilion, Priscilla was there, waiting for him with a stocky, muscular young man.

"What's up?" John asked warily.

In response, Priscilla pulled Katrina to her and launched into a verbal attack: "I tried to accommodate you by letting you come down here, all because of Katrina. But you weren't honest. You want more than to just see your daughter. You're trying to take her from me. You want to convince her that this is all a big mistake. Listen, John, we're here to stay, do you understand me? There's no going back."

John stepped back and lifted his hands, trying to speak calmly. "Priscilla, slow down. I'm sorry if I said something last night that upset you, but I swear, it was all part of my natural curiosity about Jonestown and your lives here. You're not going to blame me for that, are you?"

"All I know is that you are here to collect information for a lawsuit against me to regain custody of Katrina. Your little plot is not going to work, pal! This gentleman is here to escort you out of the settlement. Here's your bag."

The young man slung John's suitcase forward, dropping it at his feet, and Priscilla turned to Katrina. "Say goodbye to your father, honey, and behave yourself."

Katrina stepped forward to shake her father's hand. "Bye, Daddy," she said in a wavering voice.

John held her hand tightly, savoring the contact with his daughter for as long as he could. But in the end, all he could say was "I love you, angel."

As the tractor-trailer bounced down the jungle road to Port Kaituma, John's thoughts were on Katrina and Priscilla's abrupt change of heart regarding his visit. He wondered what had happened between his arrival and his sudden dismissal to make Priscilla so suspicious. He'd bet his bottom dollar that Jim Jones was to blame.

Only when he could no longer see the settlement behind him did John dare reach into his pocket and withdraw the object concealed there—a small silver cross necklace, given by John's mother to Katrina on her seventh birthday. He turned it over in his hand, touched and saddened that his daughter would slip him this treasured keepsake during their goodbye handshake.

Then his eyes detected an unfamiliar texture on the back of the pendant. Lifting it closer, he stared at the crude engraving until tears blurred his vision.

Scratched into the silver cross were two words: *help me.*

CHAPTER 21

November 1977

One Sunday afternoon, attorney Walter Solomon was seated at the pool bar at the Pegasus Hotel when Bill stopped by to say hello.

"Bill, I'd like you to meet John Olsen," Walter began. "Bill's with the American embassy here in Georgetown."

"Pleased to meet you," Bill said, extending his hand to greet a heavyset, balding man about his age. John Olsen set his drink down and clasped Bill's hand lightly, smiling and agreeing, "Nice to meet you, too."

"Staying out of trouble, Walter?" Bill asked his friend, adding, to John, "You know Walter's the most dishonest attorney you can find in Guyana, don't you?"

Laughing with hurried denials, Walter asked, "Have time for a drink?"

"Sure, why not?"

After Bill placed his drink order, he turned to his new acquaintance. "Tell me, John, what brings you to Guyana?"

"John is here trying to get his daughter back; the custody case I told you about," Walter explained.

"Ah. Stop right there!" Bill held up one hand. "I don't want to hear anything about it, not with all the hassle about the Privacy Act and the Freedom of Information Act. I don't want even to feign being interested." Then, suddenly realizing the predicament he was joking about, he added to John, "Although I can imagine the stress you must be going through."

"Thanks," John responded. "It hasn't exactly been easy."

Both John and Walter expressed an interest in the two new U.S. laws and their implications, and before long, Bill was invited to have dinner with the men.

"Sorry, I'd love to, but there's a reception tonight at the Japanese consul's residence. If I don't get goin', I'll be late," Bill said. Looking at John, Bill joked with a wink, "Look, if you need any off-the-record advice, look me up rather than relying on Walter. At least my advice is free!"

The laughter of the two men lingered as Bill left. He wondered how a sincere, likable guy like Olsen was mixed up with the Peoples Temple.

Before John left Georgetown, he stopped by to see Bill at the consulate to ask him if there was anything he could bring back from the States on his next trip to Guyana.

"Yes, there is," Bill replied half-jokingly. "Four pounds sirloin steak, five pounds potatoes, five pounds onions, and a half-pound of garlic!"

Laughing, John said, "The only thing you're going to get out of that order is indigestion, pal!" Then he continued in a more serious tone, "By the way, I saw my daughter and ex-wife down at Jonestown early during this trip. No breakthroughs, unfortunately. The courts are the only solution to this and I'm sure Jim Jones and all his cronies will stand behind Priscilla all the way to make this as difficult as it can be."

"That's too bad," Bill said.

"You should see Katrina," John continued, attempting a smile. "Boy, has she grown since the last time I saw her. She's getting to be a big girl." Then after a long silence, John added, "She wants to come home." His eyes began to mist over as he fished in his pocket for what Bill assumed would be a handkerchief. But instead he withdrew a silver chain, which he passed to Bill.

Bill took it and fingered the delicate cross pendant as John explained, "Katrina wouldn't give me a hug or a kiss me when I had to go. Rules, I guess. She only held out her hand to shake mine. When our hands met, I felt this. Turn it over."

Bill read the plaintive message and was speechless for a long moment. Then he handed the cross back to John, saying, "Well, I just know you'll be successful getting your daughter back." But the words sounded hollow even to him. Both men knew from the Marks' case that the odds weren't stacked in his favor.

Bill bid John goodbye, wishing him the best of luck. "Let's keep in touch," he said, more out of empathy than sincerity. In his job he was used to fleeting acquaintances. He felt for the man, but he doubted he'd ever cross paths with John Olsen again.

CHAPTER 22

November 1977

"Okay," Bill said, as they exited the plane, "out with it! What did I do wrong?"

Roland shook his head and answered glumly, "Where do I start?"

"What? That's bullshit! That flight was one of my best from beginning to end," Bill protested.

"Yep, it was," Roland admitted, his dark eyes twinkling as a grin spread across his face.

Bill laughed. "Whew. For a minute there you had me."

"You're ready," Roland announced. "Go ahead and contact Chip Roberts to set up your check ride. No sense waiting any longer."

"That's great! Thanks, Roland! I'll call him as soon as I get home. Come on, I'll buy you a drink," Bill added.

"Let's wait and have a real party when you get beyond the check ride," Roland suggested. "Jenny and I already have plans. Got to get going." As he talked, he walked toward his car.

"Okay, sounds good," Bill answered. "I'll call."

Feeling great, Bill jogged lightly to his car. As he drove toward home, he mused to himself, thinking that, on balance, Guyana had been quite an experience so far.

He parked his car in its customary place beneath his house built on stilts and bounded up the stairs to make the phone call to the Director of Civil Aviation. When he had completed the call, he was even more exuberant. He had an appointment to meet with director Chip Roberts at Ogle Airport for his check ride next Saturday morning.

Bill passed his test with flying colors, and once he had his Guyanese license in hand, he looked around for a way to barter his license in exchange for access to an aircraft. He eventually made a deal with the owner of a small air charter company in Georgetown to work as a backup pilot when no one else was available. Instead of a fee for his piloting services, Bill would be allowed to fly the company's aircraft anytime he wished, free of charge, pending availability. Alex Manus cooperated as well, letting Bill take annual leave on those occasions when the charter company needed him. Not only did Bill have an outlet for enjoyment, he was also able to visit parts of Guyana that few Americans ever had the opportunity to see, with Celeste at his side.

With the beginning of 1978, the time came for Bill to submit his choices for an assignment following Guyana. When he requested a one-year extension, nearly everyone at the embassy thought he was losing touch with reality. They just didn't appreciate the seriousness of Bill's relationship with Celeste.

Alex Manus welcomed Bill's extension and recommended its approval out of hand. Within a few weeks, Bill's position had been extended until September 1979.

He and Celeste celebrated the decision over drinks with Roland and Jenny. It was also a going-away party: Roland and Jenny had been married at a small civil ceremony in December, with Bill and Celeste as witnesses. Now the newlyweds were relocating to Florida to start a family in a more promising economy. Roland was qualified to immigrate because his mother was a U.S. citizen. Bill saw to it that their visas were processed correctly and issued expeditiously.

Once in Florida, Roland found a job with an air charter service flying Twin Otters out of Fort Lauderdale to the Bahamas, and from what Jenny wrote in her updates to Celeste, they were happy as clams in a shell built for two.

CHAPTER 23

April 1978

It was a surprise when John called Bill at the consulate, announcing that he had arrived "with some goodies" and giving Bill his room number at the Pegasus. After work, Bill picked up Celeste and went straight to the hotel.

When they arrived, John greeted them with a big grin, his arms full of groceries.

"How did you ever manage to get all this through customs?" Bill asked as they set the bags down. "Good God, man! Steak, potatoes, onions, garlic, and toilet paper! Look at all this stuff!"

Then Bill remembered, "John, I'd like to introduce Celeste Campalena. Celeste, meet John Olsen from California."

"It's a pleasure, a real pleasure to meet you, John," Celeste remarked. "Look at all these groceries!"

"Well, at least I'm good for something," John responded. "Nice to meet you."

"Okay, how much did you have to pay to get this stuff into the country?" Bill insisted.

Chuckling, John answered, "I packed everything, all of this, into a white plastic cooler, sealed it with white cloth medical tape, and labeled the cooler in big red letters, *FRAGILE, HYDRO-KINETIC ANALYZER*. When the customs officer asked what was in the container, I began to explain the function of the Hydro-Kinetic Analyzer and the importance of getting it to the engineers in the Ministry of Communications and Public Works to help them plan the Mazaruni Hydroelectric Project. Apparently the details weren't very interesting, because they waved me through without further questions."

"What a great idea! But how did you know about the Mazaruni Project?" Bill asked.

"All you have to do is read the *Guyana Chronicle*," John admitted.

After an hour or so of getting reacquainted at the hotel bar, Bill said, "Those steaks sure would taste good for dinner. What do you say, John? Let's go over to my place and I'll have Serita cook them for us."

Celeste helped Serita in the kitchen so that John could catch Bill up on the latest U.S. gossip about the Peoples Temple, as well as the new developments in John's custody case.

"Things are moving at a snail's pace, Bill. It's not Walter's fault, but he was only recently able to get a court date set for the preliminary hearing, on Wednesday, April 25th at 10:00 A.M."

"So, that's why you're here. At least you're making progress and getting this thing to court. Have papers been served to Priscilla?"

"Yes, I think so. They have to have been," John said.

"Well, I have the utmost confidence in Walter's skill as a lawyer. Let's hope that this will all be over very soon," Bill said.

John seemed to wilt a little under Bill's obvious bravado. He gripped his hands in front of him and said, "There's a group of relatives forming in California—people like me, who have family down here. They're claiming all sorts of bizarre things are happening down in Jonestown . . . " He cleared his throat before continuing: " . . . things like beatings, and torture. Especially the kids . . . " his voice trailed off and he sat staring at his hands.

Bill wanted to laugh the accusations off as sensationalist press, but it wasn't the first time he'd heard such claims. After an uncomfortable silence, he pressed gently, "What else did you hear in California?"

"Well, they say that all of the mail to and from Jonestown is being censored by Jones' inner circle. Any criticism of Jones or the settlement just doesn't get through, and any sign of dissent is punished harshly. But I don't know, it would be awfully hard to hide this kind of thing, don't you think?" He looked up at Bill hopefully, as though asking him to corroborate the absurdity of such rumors.

"Yeah, but you have to remember that Jonestown is a closed society, John," Bill cautioned. "It's living under Jones' thumb, his rules."

"Some of these concerned relatives are talking about traveling to Guyana as a group to visit Jonestown and to talk with their family members, as if that will do some good. I couldn't have a real conversation with Priscilla when I was there. What bothers me so much is that all these things could well be true! The setup down there is perfect to control people. I guess seeing the place lends some credence to it all. I don't know."

Bill, too, was troubled. While John had been talking, Bill couldn't help but think about the social security checks the consulate sent every month to over seventy retired Americans living at Jonestown. How easy it would be for anyone to send those checks off to some unauthorized bank account for deposit, whether or not the recipients ever saw them.

Another thought crossed Bill's mind. Would the consulate even know if an elderly American receiving those checks at Jonestown should die? He made a mental note to discuss these concerns with Alex Manus, pronto.

"Our steaks are ready," Celeste called, putting an end to the discussion about Jonestown. Dinner conversation turned to more pleasant topics.

After the preliminary hearing the following Wednesday, John called Bill at the office. He began, "No sooner had the judge heard the opening arguments in the case than he adjourned the session. It was incredible! That pompous blowhard. He said that he needed time to study the facts to determine if the circumstances of the case warranted the suit."

"When are you due back in court?" Bill asked.

"Not until next week," John answered. Anticipating Bill's next question, he continued, "Don't worry, I'm staying. I just can't leave until I have Katrina with me."

"This is really a shock, John. How are you holding up?"

"I guess I'm fine, just disappointed. Walter has been super—it's not his fault, the delay, I mean. I'm going to push for another visit to Jonestown, if I can get permission," John said. "Isn't it ridiculous that I have to get permission to see my own daughter?"

"You gotta do what you gotta do," Bill lamented lamely.

"Yeah. Walter advised me to follow their rules and to be on my best behavior," John said bitterly. "I'll get back in touch, okay?"

"Sure, John. Hang in there, and good luck!"

Now concerned over what had transpired in court, Bill called Walter at his law offices. "Walter, what happened?"

"John told me he was going to call you," Walter said. "This is the damndest thing I've ever seen. No judge in my time has ever cut me off like that. Confidentially, I think there's something going on behind the scenes in this case, but I have no idea what! The way the judge handled the hearing today was just not proper, regardless of how he made it look. I just don't want to worry John right now. I could be wrong, too."

"This just doesn't sound good to me, Walter. Is there anything you can do at this point?"

"No. I've thought of everything. We just have to wait for the judge's decision next week. In any case, I'll check around to see what I can find out. You know, Bill, I've got as much law on my side as I can muster, but that might not help in a situation like this. We're dealing with the laws of two very different countries here, and one country may not be willing to accept the legal precepts of the other—international agreements in force or not."

"Do you think it's a good idea to have John go down to Jonestown unescorted?" Bill asked.

"Oh, yes, there shouldn't be any problem. Why, it may even be good for him, and there's an outside chance that his ex has had enough of Jonestown. We'll never know if he doesn't talk to them."

"Guess you're right," Bill replied. "Hang in there, Walter. I know these things can get messy."

"Thanks, Bill. See you soon."

Four days later, Bill got a telephone call from John asking him to come to the hotel. Bill could tell from the sound of his voice that he was upset, and went over immediately. He knew that John had been to Jonestown for another visit with his daughter and ex-wife, because he had made the flight arrangements with the air charter company Bill worked for. Sharon Amos had arranged ground transport from the airstrip to Jonestown.

With a heavy sigh, John began telling Bill about his visit. "Katrina is not eating well at all," he reported, "and she's becoming despondent over her living conditions. I can tell she's unhappy with her life there, even though she said she was enjoying herself and the challenges she's experiencing. Bill, I can tell when my daughter's lying! She's going through hell down there!"

"Did you talk to Priscilla about all this?" Bill asked.

"I tried, but it was no use. At first, she said she didn't want to see me, but I stayed there as long as I could, and she finally came to talk with me. I told her I didn't like the changes I saw in Katrina, and she basically blew them off as part of being a teen. I tried to reason with her, assuring her that I wouldn't interfere with her religious beliefs, and that she could spend as much time with Katrina as she wanted each time she returned home, but that I wanted to take Katrina with me.

"She told me that I was wasting my time coming to Guyana, and she was so angry, I thought she actually was going to lash out at me. She didn't, of course, because we were in public. I pleaded with her, but she only spit in my face. I mean actually spit at me and shouted uncontrollably. I don't believe she's rational anymore."

"My God, John . . . that's awful."

"It was like she was rabid or something," John went on, "calling me the devil, accusing me of trying to destroy everything she believes in. It was no use, Bill. Finally one of the Jonestown thugs came and took her away from me and asked me to leave. It was incredible . . . Whatever happened to her? Whatever happened to my wife?"

"Are you going to be okay, John?"

Ignoring his question, John continued, "I told this guy that I'd be ready to leave as soon as I could tell Katrina goodbye, but he refused, escorted me to the truck, and hurried me back to Port Kaituma. Just like my first trip down there, I had to sleep on the floor of the general store that night and flew back to Georgetown the next morning." He sank down onto the edge of his bed and began to weep.

"John, listen to me," Bill responded. "You're doing everything in your power. You have to think positive about this. The courts here have to support you. It'll only be a matter of time. Let's wait and see what the judge says. Okay?"

John wiped the back of his hand over his eyes. "You're right. Hopefully it will all be settled at the hearing. It just got to me, having to leave Katrina there. I didn't even get to tell her I love her."

Officially, Bill knew there was nothing he could do. But his heart went out to John.

Wednesday morning, Bill and Celeste went to the courthouse to hear the judge's decision but were told that the proceedings were closed. They waited in the vestibule for John and Walter to appear.

CHAPTER 24

May 1978

Inside the courtroom, John and Walter sat at the litigant's table, reviewing the facts of the case one last time.

"Isn't it strange that no one from the Peoples Temple is here? At least their lawyer should show up, don't you think?" John said.

"It's hard to say what they're doing. I'm focused on the fact that they haven't filed a respondent's brief yet. Maybe they're waiting—" Walter was cut off in mid-sentence.

"Hear ye, hear ye. Given, this day of our Lord, the second day of May, nineteen hundred and seventy-eight the presence of the Honorable Mohandas Ramdahal, all shall rise and be silent," the court crier announced. He turned and lowered his head as the judge entered the courtroom, then continued, "All may now be seated."

Looking down from the bench, Judge Ramdahal addressed Walter; "Mr. Solomon, please approach the bench with your client."

Walter and John responded immediately, rising from behind their table and walking up to the judge's bench. "Your Honor, may I present Mr. John Olsen," Walter offered.

The judge's eyes met John's for a passing glance, and then he looked down and began to read a prepared text.

"The matter of custody of the minor child of John Olsen and Priscilla Olsen, known as Katrina Olsen, has its roots in the divorce settlement as set forth in the divorce agreement between the parties dated and signed in Los Angeles, California, and given in evidence to this court. As such, a procedural question arose that needed to be decided prior to any court action in Guyana relevant to instant matter. After careful review, the court judges that without the filing of a compliance suit in the County of Los Angeles in California to compel Priscilla Olsen to discharge her responsibilities as custodian of said minor child in accordance with the divorce agreement, there is no basis in law for contention in Guyana. Therefore, it would be presumptuous for the Guyana courts to consider any custodial suit on behalf of John Olsen under prevailing circumstances. No conveyances concluded in Guyana are in dispute, nor has there been any violation of Guyana law to warrant a separate suit. Until such time as the court of record in Los Angeles rules in this matter, there is no issue to litigate." The judge slowly placed the prepared statement down and closed the leather-bound file before him. Looking down at Walter, Judge Ramdahal said in a firm voice, "Mr. Solomon, please join me for a moment in my chambers." He rose from the bench and left the courtroom.

Walter and John were frozen for a long moment. Then Walter said, "I'll be right back," and walked toward the anteroom to the courtroom to join the judge in chambers.

The moment that John and Walter walked out of the courtroom, Bill could tell things had not gone well. They agreed to meet at Walter's office to go over the details.

In his office, Walter began, "When Judge Ramdahal came into the courtroom, there was no one there for the defense, no one. He read from a prepared statement. In sum, it was his view that no Guyanese laws had been violated to warrant a separate suit. Then, he asked me to join him in his chambers."

John turned to Walter. "Did the judge give you any idea why he was in such a hurry to dismiss the case?"

"Not really," Walter answered. "The judge told me that politics were influencing how the courts were going to handle Jonestown-related suits. Then he told me, 'Walter, take my advice and stay out of these matters. You have too much to lose.' I was livid and confronted him. I asked if this was why we fought so hard for our independence, so the politicians could make our courts into a rubber stamp. Then I walked out of his chambers, not giving him the chance to respond. Boy, does this disgust me!"

"Walter, what does this mean for us—for our case?" John asked.

Walter confessed, "There's really only one thing to do, John: you're going to have to return to California and start the legal process there. We need to get a compliance order issued in California. Only then could a summons be sought to bring Priscilla and Katrina to court here, provided the Guyanese court accepts its obligations under international law. Please understand that there are no guarantees here. It's a crapshoot of the worst kind."

John shook his head. "I'll do my part. Just let me know what I need to do."

Both Celeste and Bill pledged their continuing support. Bill simply could not shake the look of pain on John Olsen's face that morning. He had seen it before on other men's faces—a sure sign of hopelessness and despair.

Chapter 25

May 1978

The delivery of fifty fertilized eggs to the settlement was a big event. The incubator was ready and these eggs would start Jonestown's own egg and poultry production—at least, that was the hope.

Having been assigned to help out with the farming chores, Katrina and Judi were more interested in having fun than doing chores. They slipped an egg out from the incubator and decided to play a trick on their dorm monitor, Rose. Knowing that she came into the dorm around 9:00 P.M. every evening to count heads, turn off the lights, and say good night, the girls rigged the egg on top of the door to fall on her head.

All of the girls in the dorm were giddy with anticipation. When Rose approached—*splat!* The egg hit Rose on the head, broke open, and soiled her blouse.

After some commotion to ferret out who was responsible, Katrina and Judi stepped forward to take the blame. They immediately apologized; it was a matter of wanting to have some fun. But Rose was not amused.

The next morning the girls were brought before the disciplinary council, made up of two women and a young man. The small group sat down at the pavilion to discuss what had happened, to pass judgment, and to decide any punishment if the girls were found culpable.

After Rose spoke, the man who managed the incubator had his say: "We lost five years' productivity of one future hen because of this prank, and that impacts our future. That hen would have laid about 280 eggs for each of its first two years and about 190 eggs a year for the next three years. At five years old, the hen's egg productivity falls off, and it is used for food. These girls need to think about the long-term effects of their actions on the community."

When asked if they had anything they wanted to say, the girls quietly said that they were just playing a joke and didn't mean anything by it. Both expressed their sincere apologies for what happened. The girls were taken away from the pavilion while the council considered the matter. After only ten minutes, they were called back in.

"The council has reached its decision," the older woman said. "Katrina and Judi, you have been found guilty of stealing an egg from an incubator for devious purposes; it doesn't matter that your intent was playful. Given the severity of this offense as measured by the loss of productivity in support of the settlement, the punishment you each will receive is as follows: twenty strikes with a man's belt over your bare bottoms and three days in isolation in our confinement box with your food rations cut in half. Because this is your first offense, I will suspend the belt strikes. Do you have any questions?" she asked.

The girls broke down in tears before the councilwoman finished speaking. Katrina looked around for her mother, but she wasn't there. How could all this be happening, she wondered?

For the first time in her life, Katrina felt alone and totally abandoned. By the time the girls were led away, Katrina's small body was shaking with fear and sobs. The woman who held her by the arm patted her shoulder and shushed her gently: "There, now. It won't be that bad."

They wrapped a twin sheet around each girl to keep her from resisting. The confinement box was dark and moist, and it smelled like fresh vomit. Together with a plastic bucket for their waste, the girls were lowered carefully into separate boxes isolated from one another.

The wood of the box was rough-cut timber and felt hard against Katrina's tailbone and back. With the lid lowered and latched, the cramped interior of the box was plunged into darkness interrupted only by faint rays of light that sifted through the thin slits between the boards.

The first night was the hardest. It had taken Katrina nearly an hour to wriggle free from the tightly wrapped sheet, and after trying numerous positions, she found that she could lie somewhat comfortably in a fetal position, using the sheet as a blanket. Only after everything became pitch black did she realize that this was not a joke. She cried out and yelled for help, but no one seemed to hear her. She called out for Judi, but again, there was no response.

Then it started to rain. Huddling with the sheet around her, Katrina was wet and cold. She began to sob, and eventually dozed off.

At first light, the caretaker opened the door and handed down a plastic bowl of oatmeal and a plastic glass filled with water. "Here's your breakfast," he said, and closed the door.

Katrina ate the oatmeal quickly, a habit she'd developed after months of shoveling down bland, unappetizing food. She didn't realize it would be ten hours before she was fed again.

The second meal was a bowl of rice with beef-flavored gravy and another portion of water. Famished, Katrina finished every drop.

By the second day, Katrina was calling out her apologies for having stolen the egg and promising to be good, but no one came.

The third day dragged by ever so slowly. Exhausted, she kept falling into and out of sleep all night, sometimes waking with a start because she imagined some bug was crawling on her. Then, at mid-morning, the caretaker came one final time and set her free.

Her eyes were not used to the light. As she crawled out of the confinement box, Katrina expected to see her mother, but she wasn't there. Her muscles stiff from being cramped up for three days, she leaned on the caretaker for balance until she could manage on her own. Then he told her to walk over to the pavilion.

Seeing her mother waiting at the pavilion, Katrina picked up her pace.

"How could you, Mom?" she cried out. "Where were you?"

Priscilla crossed her arms in front of her as Katrina approached. "Hush. I'm right here," she said. "You know I couldn't interfere. You girls never should have stolen that egg. Stealing is a major offense down here—you know that. You know we all have to work together. If your punishment served to remind you of that, then it's a good thing. But I'm glad you're all right. How are you feeling?"

She reached out to touch her daughter's face, which was streaked with dirt from the night it had rained, but Katrina whirled away from her.

"You don't really care about me, do you?" she cried, tears forming again. "All you care about is Jim Jones and the Temple. Look what they did to me!"

Priscilla closed her eyes. "You're just angry about your punishment. You're not angry at me. Let's go get you a shower. You'll feel better afterwards."

Priscilla opened her eyes in time to see Katrina stalking off toward her dormitory on her own. Then she turned back and shouted, "If you don't care about me, why don't you at least let me go live with Daddy? Why do you make me lie to him? Why do you want to keep me here if you hate me so much . . ."

Priscilla didn't answer. She had already turned and was walking in the opposite direction, away from her daughter. She didn't want Katrina or the other onlookers to see that she had begun to cry.

CHAPTER 26

July 1978

Following the departure of Chargé Blacken back to Washington, D.C., Ambassador John Burke arrived in Guyana fully aware of the dilemma he faced concerning Jonestown. On the one hand, the testimonies of Temple defectors and the concerns of families back in the States created a cloud of suspicion regarding the treatment of people at the settlement. On the other hand, U.S. laws prevented the embassy from directly monitoring or investigating the activity in Jonestown.

Burke argued forcefully for Washington to take some action, but the bureaucracy would not be pushed for fear of repercussions. Consul Alex Manus suggested that the embassy could share the information from the Jonestown defectors with the Guyanese government and let them chart their own course—a tactic that would be better than nothing. But Ambassador Burke had faith that Washington would buckle to common sense over time. The consulate was told to do nothing for the moment.

Bill watched on helplessly, with a bitter taste in his mouth. He had witnessed this kind of inertia before, during the fall of Saigon. He was certain nothing official would be done given the circumstances, and he pitied the poor folks like John Olsen, who were suffering for it daily.

One afternoon in late July, Bill and Celeste had been invited for dinner by Bill's neighbors, Anil and Chitra Nayak. Chitra had promised to prepare Guyanese-style hassa fish, and pepperpot for the main course.

The evening passed quickly, with Bill and Celeste enjoying themselves and the company immensely. As they strolled back to Bill's house, the night was clear, with stars twinkling above and the light of the moon illuminating their way.

To their surprise, when they arrived home, they discovered John Olsen asleep on the reclining front seat of Bill's car, and Bill's embassy-provided guard, Mr. Kissoon, not far away.

While John slept on, Mr. Kissoon explained, "The American arrived by taxi at about 10:30 P.M., sir. He asked for you and I told him you were out. Since I recognized him from the other time he was here as your guest, I allowed him to enter the yard to wait for you and Ms. Celeste. He sat down in your car and dropped off to sleep around midnight. Would you want me to wake him?"

"No, that's okay, Mr. Kissoon," Bill responded. "You did the right thing. I'll take it from here. Thank you."

When Bill tapped the car door, John sat up with a start. Then he recognized Bill and a smile came to his face. "Man, am I glad to see you," he said.

"Good morning, John. Would you like to come in?" Bill invited.

"When did you return to Guyana?" he questioned as they took seats in the den.

"Just tonight. I didn't take the time to make any advance reservations, and when I arrived, I couldn't get a room at either the Pegasus or the Tower," John admitted. "I finally decided to come over here as my last resort. I got a taxi to bring me over. Hope you don't mind."

"Of course not. You know you're always welcome," Bill assured him.

"I'll open the guest room," Celeste offered.

"Oh no," John protested. "Just let me sleep right here on the couch. I don't want to be any trouble."

"You're not, John. Come on. We can talk in the morning, after we've all had some sleep," Bill said. "My God, it's almost 1:00 A.M."

Bill led the way to the guest room, and John was soon settled in, content to have a clean bed to sleep in.

The following day was Wednesday, and when Bill got up, John was still asleep. After a jog along the sea wall, Bill showered and dressed for the day. He just had time to bid John a good morning before heading to work. They agreed to catch up over dinner that evening.

When Bill arrived home, John was in the living room, his attention focused on Henrietta, Bill's pet orange-winged Amazon parrot. He couldn't get over her clear speech. About that same time, Celeste arrived carrying a grocery sack full of fixings for dinner. Her interest in John's legal case had piqued her curiosity to learn the latest from California.

When Bill joined John, Henrietta paced back and forth on her perch, looked at him and said, "You should plan a trip to California."

"Did you hear that?" Bill called. Celeste popped back into the room in time to hear Henrietta repeat her new sentence, and they all laughed.

"That parrot is amazing," John commented. "She picks up words so fast!"

"Yeah, sometimes even the really bad ones, too," Bill agreed.

"Well, I hope you guys are ready for my special chicken curry," Celeste announced.

"Sounds great," John replied.

"Okay then, I'll call when it's ready. But first, Bill, you're in charge of the piña coladas."

"Thank you, love," Bill said as he grabbed three glasses.

After blending the drinks, Bill handed one to John and led the way to the verandah. When they had settled into chairs, he said, "It's always good to see you, John, but I wasn't expecting you back so soon. How long has it been, almost three months?"

"Time . . . time is flying by. It is going to take at least another six months for the Los Angeles Court to even put my case on their docket . . . just incredible," John lamented. "I came to Guyana for one reason," he admitted, pausing to carefully choose his words. "Did you know that there have been several defections from Jonestown?"

"No, I don't think so. Why?"

"Let me start in a different place, okay?" John said. "One of my lawyers is close friends with an investigator from the Los Angeles District Attorney's Office. This investigator was assigned the job of looking into several suspicious deaths of persons connected to the Peoples Temple and Jim Jones." As John talked, he became more and more intense.

"The cases being investigated are: Maxine Harp, who allegedly committed suicide after an altercation with members of the Peoples Temple; Emily Leonard, an elderly woman and former member of the Peoples Temple, who was suing Jones to regain personal property that she had given to the church, and who died mysteriously on the day she was to go to court; and Robert Houston, a former member of the Peoples Temple, who died under unusual circumstances while working for the Southern Pacific Railroad."

"What does the investigator make of all this?" Bill asked.

"Well, that's the problem. The investigator confided to my lawyer that while there is plenty of circumstantial evidence implicating Jones and several members of his church in conspiring to commit murder, there is no hard evidence that will stand up in court. Due to political pressures, the FBI is also involved."

As they responded to Celeste's call to dinner, John continued, "During the first week of June, this year, one of Jones' close associates defected from Jonestown and returned to California. This defector gave a sworn statement to the L.A. District Attorney's Office, in which she described details of sect practices there."

"Finally someone is willing to go on the record to nail down all of these damn rumors!" Bill added.

"My lawyer obtained a copy of the statement for possible use during our custody hearing. It's really incredible what's going on down there," John said excitedly.

"Wait a minute, John," Celeste implored. "That's an ideal place to put the Jonestown discussion on hold. Your food is going to get cold if you don't stop talking and eat, okay?"

Everyone thoroughly enjoyed dinner, not only due to Celeste's great-tasting curry—more importantly, John had a chance to unwind.

While Celeste and Bill cleared the table, John excused himself to go to the guest bedroom. He returned to join them on the verandah with a copy of the defector's statement in his hand.

"Here, take a look at this," John said as he handed it to Bill.

Bill took the papers and eyed them warily, not really reading. Then he handed them back to John. "I want to know what's in there," he said, "but I have to ask you to keep our conversation informal, one friend to another, okay? Then I can consider it hearsay and won't have to 'handle it' officially. Understand?"

John narrowed his eyes, but then shrugged. "If that's the way you want it, that's the way you'll have it, no problem."

"Let me start. Let's see." John then began reading from the statement: "'Jonestown is a concentration camp. We worked in the fields under the hot sun from 7:00 A.M. until 6:00 P.M. You had an hour off for a lunch of rice water soup. After work, we went to a religious meeting and listened to Jim Jones preach for hours upon hours . . . one time until four in the morning. With just a few hours' sleep, we returned to the fields to work. This was the routine, day after day. We were isolated from our loved ones. You didn't dare speak to anyone, because it looked treasonous. There was no one to trust. Jones wanted it that way so he could maintain absolute control over us. Most of us were sick from diarrhea, very weak and tired.'" Here John paused, steeling himself for the next sentence. When he continued, his voice was shaky. "'When Jones started holding white night rehearsals to practice revolutionary suicide, people never knew if he was fooling, and they really didn't care. As I'd drink the prepared mix, I'd say to myself, *God, at last. I'd rather be dead than go on living here.*'"

Bill was taken aback as John read, and Celeste gasped. John pressed on.

"'Jones has a great capacity for being brutal. Even children were beaten with as many as 150 cracks with a paddle during one beating for offenses against the community. Jones teaches that community self-destruction, what he calls revolutionary death, is the only means to a better life. He uses sexual favors to blackmail government officials both in California and in Guyana . . .'" John interjected: "I take it that means he's loaning out women from the Peoples Temple to politicians and other men in power, then turning around and blackmailing them, saying he'll tell their wives or go public . . . 'Jones ordered his followers to commit homosexual or adulterous acts, believing that through their guilt feelings, they would be easier to control and to manipulate.'"

Bill interrupted, "Frankly, John, this sounds a little farfetched, don't you think?"

"There's more: 'Jones smuggled large quantities of drugs and arms into Jonestown with no interference from Guyanese officials. Jones is a drug addict. He salts tranquilizers into the food in Jonestown. Grilled cheese sandwiches were often used as the host to drug sect members to keep them docile and under control. Jones does not allow sex between married couples. Spouses live separate from one another. Jones created an armed security force at Jonestown to prevent defections. There is no way to escape. He has amassed a fortune in real estate assets and in cash—all given to him by his followers. The total is estimated at over eighteen million dollars. Jones holds the fear of death over the heads of the sect members. Dress rehearsals for mass revolutionary suicide are held regularly to psychologically defeat any resistance to his will. His paranoia runs deep and has become the primary factor that influences his actions.'"

As John continued to read the long list of accusations, Bill felt stunned by the things he was hearing. Not since the killing fields of Cambodia in 1975 had he felt so cold inside.

"What I've quoted is just the beginning. There's much more to the statement. I chose only the items I thought were most important." Standing, John walked over to look out toward the sea wall. His voice sober, he said, "My daughter is in Jonestown right now, suffering through the schemes of this demon."

Celeste's eyes began to fill with tears. She stood and went back inside.

Turning to Bill, John pleaded, "Even if only one fourth of those things in the statement are true, I have to do everything possible to get Katrina out of there, now!"

"But, John," Bill protested, "it's going to—"

"We don't have time to wait for the legal process to produce results," John interrupted, anticipating his response. "I can't stand by and do nothing as my daughter is beaten, drugged, maybe even raped, God forbid. Every moment she spends in Jonestown, I'm one moment closer to losing her forever."

"I know you want to do something, John. But what?" Bill said.

John walked closer, his eyes lighting up as though he'd been waiting for that question. His voice was desperate. "That's why I came here, Bill. The law isn't working in my favor. I need to go in and get her, without any court orders. Will you help me? You're the only pilot I know, and I feel like I know you pretty well now. I need someone I can trust to fly me into Port Kaituma to get Katrina out of there!"

Bill felt a tightening in his throat as he started to speak. "Maybe you should take your suspicions officially to the United States government, if you feel Katrina is being abused at Jonestown."

"Don't cop out on me, God damn it," John said coldly. "The group I told you about, these concerned relatives, they've already gone to the FBI and to their congressmen to express their fears. Several Jonestown defectors have spent days in Washington telling everyone who would listen about what's happening down there, but what has been done? Absolutely nothing!"

"But, John, there's just no authority to investigate these kinds of allegations. The Privacy Act—" Bill began.

"I'm sick of hearing about that! They tell us that the very people this law protects are the ones abusing our children at Jonestown. I've had it with this so-called Privacy Act and the federal government! There's only one way to get my daughter out safely, and that's to go to Jonestown myself and get her," John declared in a tone that left Bill with no doubt that he meant every word.

"Even if you could get into Jonestown, how would you bring Katrina back with you? You know that no one is going to allow you to just walk in and leave with your daughter."

"All right," John conceded. "So, do you know any other way of getting Katrina out? Just sneak into Jonestown and get her? Don't you see? I'm at the end of my rope!"

"John, I'm afraid that it's just not possible," Bill said. "There's no way into Jonestown except by way of Port Kaituma, and the Peoples Temple has control of that entire area."

"There's no other way in?" John pushed. "None?"

"A well-trained military unit could possibly do it overland from Matthews Ridge. The whole operation would be risky, though. Getting there is one thing, getting out is another—this time with a thirteen year-old girl in a weakened condition. I don't see any way to do this. It's just next to impossible, no matter which way you turn."

John again pushed the issue: "There's got to be a way to get to Jonestown and get Katrina out. I'd rather die trying than know I didn't try everything to save her from this hell."

Bill was growing uncomfortable under John's anguished gaze and went inside to pour himself another drink—whiskey this time. He empathized with John's fear and desperation, but what could he do? He found that he was almost angry at John for hanging his hopes on him, asking him to play the hero in a situation that had so little chance of success. He wanted to explain to John that he wasn't a hero, but that would only invite questions.

John had followed him inside and was watching him closely. Then, as if reading Bill's mind, he said, "Come on, Bill. You're the big war veteran; I know you've seen worse spots than this before."

That was the spark that set Bill ablaze. He turned on John. "You're right, I have. And I know how quickly things can go wrong in situations like this. You want to get your daughter home safely? Then go through the proper channels like everyone else. Don't go pretending to be a Goddamn G.I. Joe when you're anything but. You're a businessman. So you just focus on filing your papers instead of asking your friends to risk their lives on some dangerous, harebrained scheme that could very well get your daughter killed."

John's shock had turned to anger as Bill ranted. Now he glared as Bill turned and stalked down the hallway. "So that's it? You just refuse to help me?" he called out.

His answer was the slamming of Bill's bedroom door.

When Celeste asked what all the commotion was about, Bill begged off talking on account of a headache, and she went home to let him rest. After she'd gone, Bill lay in bed trying to sleep, but his mind was active. One significant factor was that the mission had to be conducted in Guyana, a country relatively hostile to the United States and apparently sympathetic to Jim Jones. Not only would any stranger coming into Guyana draw a lot of attention, it would be a significant problem getting any operational equipment—weapons and other specialized gear—into the country.

Then there was the matter of getting out of Guyana. Given the influence that Jones had with the Burnham government, there was no doubt that there would be a nation-wide search for Katrina as soon as she turned up missing. She could never just fly out of there with John.

The more Bill thought, the more convinced he became that this was all a pipe dream. He remembered the failed attempts private citizens made to locate and rescue American prisoners of war held in Laos, and the hard lessons they learned. Good men had died. He knew he had to try again to discourage John from pursuing any rescue attempt.

CHAPTER 27

July 1978

Over lunch the next day at the Tower Hotel Restaurant, Celeste was eager to hear the results of Bill's discussion with John the previous night. As Bill talked about significant obstacles that were in the way of any viable rescue plan, he could sense that she was becoming more and more distraught.

"And so you decided that it just couldn't be done. Is that it?" Celeste concluded. "I can't believe you're not going to even try to help him. What is going on with you? I never thought for one moment that you were totally heartless, but now I'm beginning to wonder."

Bill closed his eyes and took a deep breath. He couldn't believe he was going to have to defend himself to her, too. "Look, sweetie," he said, "I know that's how it might look to you, but I've considered every angle. There are too many obstacles. It's just not feasible."

"I'm not that willing to write off the life of a little girl because it may be a little difficult to pull off," she retorted, her voice strained.

Bill realized Celeste needed the facts, so he attempted to lay them out for her: the lack of manpower, the difficulty of finding a country from which to launch the rescue, the risks involved in landing to refuel, the risk of being caught in an illegal act while crossing international borders, the sheer danger of trying to sneak past armed guards in a settlement so far removed from the outside world that it functioned by its own laws. Finally, he'd exhausted his list of reasons. But Celeste didn't look convinced. She looked angry.

"I'm beginning to understand what you're saying," she began. "You're giving up too easily, that's all. What's the matter, Bill? Have you lost your passion for doing what's right? Where's your courage, for heaven's sake?"

Bill stared at Celeste in dismay before throwing down his napkin and pushing back his chair. "I apologize for not sugarcoating this, my dear, but those are the facts," he said bitterly. "I think this conversation is over." Then he stood and walked away, leaving Celeste alone at the table.

Knowing that John was still at Bill's house, Celeste called Serita. When John got on the telephone, she didn't waste any time.

"John, we have to talk as soon as possible. Can you get a taxi to the Pegasus Hotel?" she asked.

"Actually, I was just getting ready to leave. The Pegasus had a room open up and they'll give it to me. What time do you want to get together?" John responded.

"I'll be waiting for you in the lobby of the hotel when you arrive," she said quickly. "Please hurry, though; I have to get back to work, okay?"

When they met in the lobby, Celeste gave John a quick hug and then moved to the bar to sit down.

"I just finished talking with Bill," she began. "He explained to me all of the obstacles that any rescue attempt would have to overcome to be successful. To summarize, it just can't be done . . . at least, that was Bill's conclusion."

"Yeah, Bill and I discussed things last night and again this morning and reached that same conclusion," John said.

"We need to talk with someone who knows Guyana and who could possibly help you get Katrina out of Jonestown." Pausing for a moment, she then said, "I know a man who may be able to help. No promises, understand, but at least he knows the country, and that could be a big advantage. I won't rest until we've done everything possible—and talking with this man is definitely worth a try."

"Who do you have in mind?" John asked.

"Obviously, I'm speaking way ahead of myself—" Celeste didn't want to encourage John too much "—but the man I'm thinking of is Roland DaLuz. Perhaps Bill mentioned him to you before. He's the pilot who gave Bill flying lessons to get his Guyanese pilot's license?"

"Yes, I remember."

"Trouble is that Roland and his wife have moved to the States," Celeste continued, "but we keep in touch. Please understand that this is a shot in the dark—maybe our only shot! I know this, though: you can trust Roland implicitly. He knows how to keep his mouth shut."

The more Celeste talked about Roland DaLuz, the more convinced John became that Roland could help him. He made plans to fly out to Miami on the first available flight and then rent a car to drive to Fort Lauderdale. Celeste passed along Roland's contact information and instructed John to call him after 6:00 P.M. since Roland wouldn't be home during the day. She promised to call Jenny to let her and Roland know that John was going to stop by.

One of John's concerns was whether or not to offer Roland compensation for his time and trouble. "I feel I should pay the man for the time he spends on this," he said. "Don't you agree?"

"You'll have to make your own decision on that one," Celeste answered. "Roland is sort of funny about money. You'll have to work out an arrangement when you talk with him."

"I really appreciate all you've done to help out here, Celeste."

Celeste replied, "You'll do just fine. You'll see!"

CHAPTER 28

July 1978

After his clash with Celeste over lunch, Bill felt out of sorts. He left the restaurant and, instead of going back to work, took a walk around Georgetown to clear his head and ended up at the ambassador's residence, where he lay down on one of the pool's lounge chairs. He closed his eyes and tried to let the chatter of people and the sound of traffic drown out the argument playing over and over in his head. Before long the noise of the city became a dull hum, and he drifted off.

When he woke up, the sun was beginning its descent. Bill stood to straighten his shirt-jac and decided it was time to go home.

Celeste's car wasn't in the driveway, but then, he hadn't really expected it to be. She never came over without checking with him first.

He'd scarcely walked in the door when the phone rang. It was another vice-consul, calling to invite him along for a bachelors' night out on the town.

Bill glanced at his answering machine to see if there were any messages that might be from Celeste, but there weren't. "What the hell," he said into the receiver. "I could use a night out."

First, they went to the popular Chin-A-Sue Chinese restaurant, then to the Pegasus Hotel bar, finally finishing the evening at the Belvidere Hotel. When they got to the Pegasus, Bill scanned the room and kept one eye on the door, wondering if Celeste would be drowning her sorrows the same way. There were only so many bars in Georgetown.

But whatever Celeste was doing, she wasn't doing it in any of the drinking holes Bill passed through that night. And by the time they made it to their last stop, Bill was so far gone, he barely thought about Celeste or the fight they'd had.

The Belvidere had a reputation as the place to meet women in Georgetown. It catered to sailors from the ships that made port in Georgetown, and always had a live band playing the latest dance music.

Bill wasn't usually much of a one for dancing, but tonight he made an exception. His buddies quickly paired off with young women, leaving Bill alone at their table, and when a thirty-something-year-old Guyanese woman in a tight yellow dress grabbed his hand and began pulling him toward the dance floor, he suddenly felt like Fred Astaire. He bumbled a little in his inebriation, even stepping on her sandaled foot at one point, but she just laughed and toppled against him, grabbing his chest for support. Before long, they were both in hysterics, laughing and swirling, bumping into other couples and nearly falling over. Eventually the music stopped and the lights came on; it was 2:00 A.M., and the place was closing.

Hours later, he awoke in bed with a horrible odor hanging over him. Even though the lights were on, he had a difficult time focusing. The room was spinning. Half dressed, lacking his shoes and pants, Bill struggled to make it to the bathroom. To his surprise, lying on the bathroom floor in a fetal position was a Guyanese woman wearing only her undergarments, the one with whom he had been dancing.

He stood in the doorway wondering what to do when his knees buckled, sending him to the floor in a heap. He lay there, surprisingly comfortable, until the bathroom got dark.

Time passed, and Bill woke up a second time. He struggled to his feet and grabbed hold of the sink to steady himself. *Cold water*, he thought, and turned on the faucet.

After splashing himself thoroughly, Bill bent down and tried to rouse his lady friend. She moved and mumbled but didn't come to. Bill's only concern was that she was alive.

He returned to his bed and found that it was soiled with vomit. Collecting all the bedclothes into a bundle, he walked through the kitchen, opened the back door, and dropped the bundle onto the porch, just to be rid of it. In turning back around, he lost his balance and almost careened over the stair railing. Noticing that Bill was awake, Mr. Kissoon called up to him. "Good morning, sir. Are you okay?"

"What happened?" Bill responded as his guard ascended the back outside staircase.

Mr. Kissoon told him that he had arrived home by taxi with the young lady at about 2:30 A.M. and appeared semi-conscious and drunk. He and his lady friend had helped to get Bill up the stairs and into the house.

"Kissoon, I think her name is Christine. She's sleeping on the floor in my bathroom. Would you mind waking her up and helping her to collect all of her things? We're going to need a taxi for her as well. Meanwhile, I'm going to try to make some coffee, okay?" Bill said.

"Right you are, sir," Kissoon responded as he entered the house and walked toward the bedroom.

After they got Christine dressed and served coffee, the taxi arrived and she was gone. It was 6:00 A.M., just after sunrise. Bill returned to the bedroom to take a shower, hoping it would help him wake up.

"I'm just not feeling well, Alex," Bill explained into the phone, clutching his forehead in his free hand. "Don't worry, I'll be back to work on Monday for sure." Hoping Alex hadn't noticed a slurred word or two, he retired to the guest bedroom to make up for lost sleep.

When he awoke, he had a throbbing headache. Instead of reaching for aspirin, he reasoned that gin would probably help balance his body chemistry and relieve the onslaught of pain. Besides whiskey, gin was the next best thing in his mind for relaxation.

Not needing any more of an excuse than that, Bill went on a binge, drinking steadily through Friday and well into Saturday. This time, he didn't know what was compelling it. He just knew that it was somehow justified and needed. As an added measure of security against having to explain anything that had transpired, he unplugged the phone. It felt childish and cheap, but he couldn't face talking to Celeste. He couldn't sit across from her and apologize for his behavior or attempt to justify it, knowing that he had lost her already.

Thinking of his car, Bill called a taxi and went to the Belvidere Hotel to see if it was still there. *Eureka*, he thought. It was still parked where he had left it and all in one piece. He knew he shouldn't be driving, but then, he'd done many things he shouldn't in the past forty-eight hours, so what was one more? He slid behind the wheel and pulled out onto the road, taking care to drive slowly.

By the time he was headed down the coastal highway toward home, though, he'd gained confidence and allowed his speed to pick up. As he rounded a bend a little too fast, his car drifted over to the right side of the road.

"What the—" He yanked the wheel sharply, barely missing the herd of goats that were wandering onto the road. There was no time to correct—the vehicle careened into the deep drainage ditch on the left, and Bill's head connected hard with the window frame as the car toppled onto its side into the soft embankment. He was aware only of a throbbing in his skull before he lost consciousness.

Bill realized he must be okay, because he was walking. But this wasn't the country road he'd crashed on. No, this was a hot, bustling, sunlit street in Saigon. He smelled fish and spices. He heard the clamor of cars and bicycles and people shouting to one another. Looking to his left, he saw peddlers selling vegetables and handmade souvenirs. Then he looked to his right and saw Co Hoa, walking in stride beside him, smiling and wearing the last dress she'd ever worn.

"It's Buddhist ritual," she explained, "to rid house of 'cong ma.' Family prepares meal—rice dishes, and putting flowers on table. Must put table across main entrance to house, light joss sticks, say prayers to Buddha to help. All people in family must pray for Buddha to force cong ma out." Bill nodded, realizing he knew what she was talking about. They'd had this conversation before. Lying in a hotel bed, wrapped in his arms, Co Hoa had talked about ghosts—cong ma—and described how to perform an exorcism using ceremonial red joss incense sticks.

"It's sort of a cleansing, huh?" Bill asked, the sense of déjà vu accompanying every word.

"More than that. Cong ma will not come back to house," she emphasized, believing fervently in this tradition. "Come, let's sit in park for while," she suggested, leading him off of the street and onto the well-manicured grass at the base of the Notre Dame Cathedral.

They settled onto the ground cross-legged, facing one another, surrounded by the park's statues, trees, walkways, and benches. They seemed a world apart from the noise of the city.

Taking Bill's hand in hers, Co Hoa began, "I know cong ma visit you all the time, right? These visits not good. Make life hard!"

Bill nodded in confirmation, feeling a familiar sense of relief wash over him. Co Hoa had always seemed to understand the turmoil inside him. He never had to explain himself to her.

"You must understand: cong ma come to you because you don't let go. You see, cong ma have place to go to be happy. If people hold on too tight to memory, they trap cong ma, can't leave. You understand?" she asked.

Bill wasn't sure he did, but he nodded, trying to wrap his head around it.

"Now I help you let cong ma go to happy place," she said, taking some red joss sticks out of her purse. "You must join me praying to Buddha to help you free cong ma from your spirit, okay?"

Co Hoa then lit three joss sticks for Bill and three for herself. "Hold them like this and we pray to Buddha together. Don't worry. He'll hear my words," she said.

Bill did as Co Hoa asked. She began bowing and chanting in Vietnamese. He followed her lead, bowing when she bowed, feeling the incense smoke curl around them. This continued until the joss sticks had burned out.

Co Hoa took the sticks from Bill and caressed his face with her hand. She raised her head and kissed him. Then she stood and walked away, disappearing into the remaining tendrils of smoke. Bill watched her go, heartbroken, but with the knowledge that Co Hoa wanted him to be free.

Bill came to with a sharp pain in his head and the smell of incense lingering in his nose. The glass of the driver's side window was cold and hard against his face, but miraculously unbroken. He reached up and felt the tender spot on his skull where a bump was forming. He realized that in spite of the pain, he felt strangely alert. The fog that had consumed his brain the last few days was gone. And something else was missing too—the weight he'd been carrying around inside him for years.

Pulling himself up, Bill crawled out of the car and scaled the sides of the ditch until he reached the top. Wet and dirty, he walked for some time down the highway before a taxi slowed to offer him a ride. He got in, gave the man directions, and settled back into his seat, grateful to be alive.

On Sunday afternoon, Celeste drove to Bill's house, concerned and upset that his phone had been disconnected since Friday. Mr. Kissoon informed her that Bill had returned home late Saturday night looking disheveled, as though he'd been in a fight. Entering the house, she found him asleep in his bathrobe, facedown on the covers. He woke with a start, and Celeste told him to get dressed; she'd be waiting in the living room.

When he walked into her sight, she could tell that he was unsteady. "What on earth happened to you? You've been drinking, haven't you?"

Bill sighed heavily and sank onto the couch, wondering how much to divulge. Finally he opted for full disclosure. He told her everything that had transpired since Friday—the drinking, the dancing, the Guyanese woman in the yellow dress, the subsequent drinking and accident.

When he'd finished, the appalled look on Celeste's face told him he wouldn't be getting any brownie points for honesty. She stood speechless for several moments as Bill stared into his folded hands. When she spoke, her voice was ice cold.

"So let me get this straight. We have one little fight—a disagreement—and you get stinking drunk, bring another woman home, and *crash your car*. What in the hell is wrong with you? I thought you were being cowardly, but now I don't know what to think of you. I feel like I barely *know* you." She lifted one hand to her brow, and Bill could tell she was fighting back tears. "Look, Bill, I thought we had something special, but apparently you were ready to flick it in at the first sign of conflict. Talk about cowardly. I need to get out of here. You just go on enjoying yourself."

Bill had opened his mouth to protest, to tell her that they *did* have something special, but the words wouldn't come. He didn't have the first clue how to defend his behavior. Then, as Celeste turned to leave, he decided to call upon the one thing he could think of that might work in his favor. "Before you go, can I say something?"

She paused but didn't turn around to face him. Bill took this as a yes.

"I know this doesn't change anything. I know I behaved like an ass, and you've got no reason to trust me. But I want you to know that I changed my mind. When I was lying in the ditch after the accident, I wasn't sure if I was going to live or die, and I wasn't sure if I really cared. But something happened to me out there. I can't explain it. It was like something inside me got cut loose, something that's been holding me down a long time. When I came to, I realized you were right . . . about everything. I was just scared. I've been scared since I can't even remember when. You're right, John needs my help. I shouldn't have turned him away like that. That was selfish and cowardly. I've decided to do whatever I need to do to help him get his daughter back safely."

At this Celeste let out a delicate snort, her back still to him. "Well, that's great, Bill. I just hope that it's not too late."

With that, she took the first step down the staircase to the front door.

"Celeste," Bill pleaded, "Wait a minute. Am I going to see you again?"

She looked back at him and said, "Of course you are, if you really have had a change of heart and aim to be a part of this. When you refused to help, I called Roland, and he was at least willing to listen. I plan to help John any way I can. But don't you go expecting more than that from me."

And then she was gone. Bill heard the front door slam shut. He moved to the verandah and watched her drive away.

"Hey there, old sport," Roland began when Bill called him the next day, "I guess you want to talk about this fellow, John, right?"

"Among other things, yeah," Bill answered. "How are you guys doin'?"

"Just fine, thanks." Roland was brief. "Look, this chap came to see me. Interesting case, his. He called to invite us to dinner, but Jenny didn't really want to go out, so he came over."

"How did it go?" Bill asked.

"Well, he basically laid out the circumstances he faced in Guyana," Roland said, "and how he met you, and so forth. We talked until well after midnight. He even had photos of his daughter and his ex-wife that he showed us. It was all really interesting. The real kicker was that sworn statement. Just incredible, isn't it?"

"I know. John told me all about it, too."

"Okay. I told the man that first, I'd have to study the situation and decide whether something could be done or not, you know," Roland said. "*If*, and that's a big if, there's any possibility, then I'll have to decide whether I'm interested. We left it like that."

Agreeing with what Roland had told John, Bill asked, "When are you guys coming down for a visit?"

"I'm working on that," Roland answered. "It's pretty slow this time of year, so it shouldn't be that difficult to get away for three or four days, maybe toward the end of the month, okay?"

"We'll be looking forward to seeing you," Bill said. "Just make sure you bring Jenny with you!"

"That's a given. Look, I'll get into more detail with you when we're face to face, understand? I just don't feel right talking about things on the phone."

"No problem, Roland," Bill assured. "Let us know when you're coming and I'll get the guest room ready for you guys to stay with me."

"Okay then. Cheers, man!"

Bill couldn't wait to talk with Roland about John's predicament and the ideas that he had.

As he promised, on August 25th, Roland and Jenny arrived in Guyana.

They went straight to Bill's house, where Serita greeted them and helped them unpack and settle in. The big surprise was that Jenny was about four months pregnant and had just begun to show it.

CHAPTER 29

August 1978

Early on the morning after Roland and Jenny's arrival, under a clear sky, Bill and Roland took off from Ogle Airport in a Cessna 206 to fly to Port Kaituma and Jonestown for an aerial reconnaissance of Jonestown and the surrounding terrain.

Upon arrival over the area, Bill began snapping photos with his 35mm camera from four thousand feet altitude. He shot another roll of photographs from two thousand feet as well to ensure that they had enough detail to work with.

Speaking over the intercom, Roland commented, "It looks as though Port Kaituma is the only airstrip close enough to Jonestown to use for a rescue. Matthew's Ridge is way too far."

"Boy, this is rugged terrain too, either thick jungle or mangrove swamps," Bill remarked. "I suspected as much from how John described his trek from the airstrip to Jonestown and back. Look, you can't even see the road from up here, it's so thick."

"Interesting . . . Look over there." Roland pointed to an area just southwest of Jonestown. "Looks like the Kaituma River cuts through fairly close to Jonestown on its backside. I'll bet you that it's within three or four kilometers of the river. What do you think?"

"That's certainly worth a look. Still doesn't provide much to work with, though, does it?" Bill asked.

"It all depends on how wide the river is," Roland answered. "Let me take it down for a look-see."

After bringing the plane down to thirty feet over the water, Roland followed the contour of the river itself. "Looks good," Roland said over the intercom. "Nice and wide with no rocks showing. See the bend in the river? That could be a landmark, even at night. Looks like there're plenty of big trees along the bank as well—that's good. I'll have to check to see if this is high tide or low tide right now. It really matters."

After making their low pass over the river, Roland took the plane to 1,000 feet. "You know, the trick in using the river is the approach to landing. It would have to be silent and done against the current; otherwise, you'll have control problems as soon as you hit the water." With that, he positioned the plane where he wanted it and cut the engine back to idle. "Let's see how this would work."

It was clear that Roland had an idea and wanted to ensure that there was enough room for landing and for takeoff at the potential spot in the river he had identified. As they descended, Bill watched Roland control the plane's altitude and observed his use of flaps.

After satisfying himself that the river was usable, Roland turned the plane over to Bill to survey the jungle area between the river and Jonestown. From the air, the distance did not seem far. They couldn't gauge exactly how dense the jungle was because of the double canopy growth overhead. The few open areas they spotted looked wet and were identified as the mangrove swamps on the flight charts. They flew farther south and found higher ground, which would be drier and easier to negotiate.

After loitering for about twenty minutes, flying out of hearing range of anyone at Jonestown, they finally decided on a possible ground route that ran directly east from the river on an azimuth of ninety-seven degrees for almost a kilometer, then slightly north on an azimuth of seventy degrees, following the contour of a small ridgeline that petered out almost at the southern edge of the Jonestown settlement. This route, while not direct, avoided the worst of the swampy areas and the thickest part of the jungle.

With this reconnaissance under their belt, Roland and Bill were confident that they had collected the information they needed to decide a course of action.

Celeste and Jenny were deeply absorbed in conversation when Roland and Bill returned from their flight over Jonestown. Without skipping a beat, Celeste got up and welcomed Roland with a hug and then asked if anyone wanted lemonade.

Bill smiled at Jenny, trying to shrug off Celeste's coolness toward him. He had filled their friends in on things to an extent, telling them that he and Celeste were "taking a break" and were shelving their issues until John's problem was resolved. He certainly hoped it was just a break.

Bill cleared the end of the dining room table and laid out his flight chart for the area around Port Kaituma. "Here's what we've got," Bill said softly, and proceeded to outline for the girls the results of the flight. "I took plenty of photos of Jonestown and of the surrounding area, so that's done."

Roland then stepped up. "The best approach to getting a team close to Jonestown without anyone knowing is to use an amphibian aircraft to land on the Kaituma River here." He pointed to the place on the flight chart. "I could put a Grumman Goose in there without much problem. The landing would have to be at high tide, though, to minimize the risk of hitting an underwater obstacle."

Bill agreed. "Would the plane be safe on the river after the landing?"

"Yeah, I think so," Roland answered. "We'd have to make sure that it was out of the main current along the river's bank. It'd be okay."

"Tell me about the Grumman," Bill prompted.

"The G21A Grumman Goose is a commercial aircraft that we used here for years to settle the interior of Guyana. I've flown at least a thousand hours in it . . . a really reliable and responsive airplane. It has two powerful engines and carries eight passengers with a full load of baggage easily," Roland explained. "I've heard of two places in Florida that lease the G21A. I'll have to check into what's required to get one and the costs involved. If we get serious about this, I'll lease the one that's in the best condition."

"That's it, then!" Bill said.

"Well, not quite. Fuel. Fuel is going to be a problem. I told John that any rescue attempt from inside Guyana wouldn't work—just too many complications. The staging area—the place where we start, and hopefully finish—will have to be somewhere outside of Guyana." As Roland spoke, he moved his gaze north on the chart to the Caribbean Sea to survey the best potential staging area.

"Are you thinking about Trinidad?" Bill asked.

"Well, we have to consider all the angles here," Roland responded. "Customs officials in Trinidad are generally pretty strict and thorough in their inspections. They never liked the Guyanese. I know the customs officials in Barbados reasonably well. They don't usually give me any hassles, or close inspection inside the airplane. Barbados has promise. What they're mostly interested in is cargo aircraft coming in so they can collect tariffs."

"How far are we talking about, Roland?" Bill asked.

"Well, let's see. I'd estimate about 630 kilometers, just under 400 miles one way from Barbados to our landing site. Yep, Barbados is definitely in the running. There are some small islands right here." He pointed to the chart just south of Barbados. "They're sometimes used by these Caribbean yacht clubs for overnight stops. We could use one of them for our staging area after we leave Barbados."

"Won't we be missed by the flight center in Barbados?" Bill asked.

"Good question! When we file our flight plan out of Barbados, we could always say that we will be island hopping and camping for four or five days, and identify Saint Vincent as our final destination. Because we'll be flying an amphibian, no one will question it. How 'bout that?"

"That sounds really good, guys," Jenny commented.

"At least it's a start," Bill said with a satisfied look on his face.

Celeste then spoke up. "Getting back to landing on the river, wouldn't we run the risk of being seen by the Jonestown people? After all, we'll be landing awfully close."

"Exactly," Roland responded. "For that reason, we'll have to do it very quietly at night. It's a higher risk, perhaps, but safer for us in the long run."

"How would this work, Roland?" asked Bill.

"Okay . . . once we have a plane, I'll pre-position it in Barbados and we'll be set. We'll have to carry fuel containers with us, enough fuel to get us back to the island staging point, then onward to Saint Vincent. I'll figure it all out so we don't cut ourselves short. No problem."

"That's getting in. But dealing with the jungle is another thing," Bill commented. "I figure it will take about eight hours just to get to Jonestown, if we move slowly. We're going to need a plan to take control of Katrina and to get her out. Coming out will be much quicker."

"Hey guys," Jenny spoke up, "I just realized that John Olsen is going to have to go along to get Katrina out. None of us even know her!"

"Yeah, I think you're right, Jenny," Roland responded.

"What about timing?" Bill asked. "When can everything be ready to go?"

"There's still a lot to consider before we decide whether or not this can be done," Roland replied. "At this point, we don't have much to go on. It seems to me that the most difficult part is getting Katrina out of there without everybody in Jonestown knowing about it. According to John, Jonestown has armed guards 'protecting it.' Anyone have any ideas?"

Bill nodded and said, "You're right. It's going to be dicey, but there are options open to us." He knew that his army experience would come into play in deciding the best plan to snatch Katrina from Jones' isolated jungle hellhole.

Taking a break, Roland and Bill went outside to look at Bill's papaya crop growing in the back yard. Bill asked, "Tell me, Roland, have you decided to do this or not?"

"It looks pretty good to me—at least the flying part," Roland responded. "Yeah, I'm in. I just have to cash in on any opportunity that comes my way to make some money. With the baby on its way, and all of the expenses of living in the States, we're going to need every penny we can scrape together just to get by. You know, Jenny is going to have to stop working when the baby comes. That's going to really hurt. I'll have to negotiate an appropriate fee with John. I wish I didn't have to think this way, but reality is reality."

Bill nodded and was silent for a moment. "I had no idea. So things aren't working out as you'd hoped?"

"It's not that, it's just that at work, I'm at the bottom of the seniority list. If business is slow, I'm the one whose flight time is cut. Believe me, I'm looking for any other flying job."

"I really hope that things improve for you guys, especially with the baby coming," Bill said, adding a silent prayer for his own happy ending.

"Me too, man," Roland said. "Me too."

Bill and Roland spent the remainder of the day developing a detailed plan and identifying the gear they would need.

"We're going to have to use some mild gas to get Katrina out of her dorm without worrying about another girl waking up," Bill announced.

"Isn't that dangerous to the kids?" Celeste asked.

"I've used it before. It's perfectly safe, sort of like strong laughing gas. We even used to use it in training against live targets. The only danger is with older people. There's always the chance of inducing a heart attack. But for kids, there's no risk at all. Katrina will be unconscious for about twenty minutes or so. That will allow enough time to carry her out of the immediate area—"

"If we don't run into interference from anyone," Roland interjected, finishing Bill's thought.

They made a list of items that John and Roland would have to buy either at gun shops or at army surplus stores. Besides the basic clothing and personal jungle gear, the items included the following: two Browning semiautomatic hunting rifles, caliber .270 Winchester with a twelve power scope; eight spare magazines and two hundred rounds of ammunition for the Browning rifles; two Model 870 Remington twelve-gauge pump shotguns with 30" barrels; and one hundred rounds of buckshot.

Bill and Roland continued to add other items to the list: four Silva Ranger compasses; two sixteen-power binoculars; two heavy-duty machetes; and six waterproof flashlights with red filters and extra batteries. In addition, they decided upon six high-quality crystallized GE portable transceivers with battery charger, carrying cases, headset earphone/microphones, and six extra batteries.

Roland, thinking of the plane and fuel, wrote down six ten-gallon plastic gasoline tanks with spouts. After looking over the list, they thought of one complete set of durable clothes for Katrina, to include a pair of high-quality, high-top leather sneakers.

Bill turned to Roland. "When you get back to the States, you're gonna have to brief John on what we've done. I'd split up the list so that you don't have to get everything yourself. Tell John that quality reigns, okay? I think it's best if you get the guns, so that John won't have to transport them across the U.S. from California."

"Don't worry; I know exactly what to do," Roland responded with a smile. "What else?"

"John's going to have to send you some money," Bill cautioned.

Roland nodded. "Yeah, you're right. Don't worry. We'll have it together in no time."

"Oh, almost forgot!" Bill exclaimed. "When you talk with John, tell him to apply for a new passport for Katrina. She'll need a travel document after the rescue and he shouldn't have any trouble getting one for his daughter if he says the old one has been lost. I hope he has some photographs of her—maybe some from school last year."

Bill handed Roland the rolls of film that he had taken of Jonestown and the surrounding area, and asked him to get them developed, to make the best selection of the shots, and to have 11" by 15" blown-up prints made of them. They would be important aids in preparing everyone for the rescue.

"Okay," Roland said, "One thing we haven't established—how are we going to get our hands on sleeping gas? That stuff isn't exactly available in your average corner drugstore."

Bill smiled. "Well, now, I've been thinking about that. See, I'm not convinced that you, John, and I have the muscle to pull this off on our own, especially with John being hopelessly out of shape. Would you agree to do this if I asked an army buddy to help?"

"Of course. Who do you have in mind?" Roland asked.

"My old team sergeant from Special Forces, Master Sergeant George Kladensky," Bill responded. "He's out now, but if I ask him, I know he'll say yes in a heartbeat. And he has contacts at Fort Bragg to get us anything special that we need. I'll take leave the first week in September to go talk with Ski personally. It's time I paid that man a visit anyway."

CHAPTER 30

September 1978

George "Ski" Kladensky was born in 1931 on a farm near a little town in Czechoslovakia called Písek, located south of Prague along the Vltava River. At eighteen years old, he left Czechoslovakia for Germany as a refugee, where he enlisted in the U.S. Army. After advanced training, he was assigned to the First Ranger Battalion at Fort Benning, Georgia, which deployed as a unit to Korea. Wounded twice, he was awarded the Silver Star, two Bronze Stars, two Purple Hearts, and a Presidential Unit Citation, among others.

Upon recovering from his wounds, Ski was assigned to the 77th Special Forces in Bad Tölz, Germany, where he trained specially selected indigenous commandos for top secret intelligence gathering missions into Eastern Europe, behind the ominous Iron Curtain. In 1962, he was assigned to the First Special Forces Group, Okinawa. President John F. Kennedy had given this newly constituted unit the distinction of wearing the green beret. The flash for the First SFG was a rich yellow color, almost golden, with a border trim of the same color, sewn on the beret and positioned over the left eye. In 1964 the flash was modified; a black border was added to symbolize mourning for President Kennedy.

In Okinawa, Ski married a petite, eighteen-year-old Japanese girl named Yoshiko, and together they had five children, three boys and two girls. The early years of marriage were rough for Yoshiko. Ski drank heavily when he wasn't deployed off-island and often found himself in the stockade as punishment for "conduct unbecoming an NCO," as the military called it. While in Okinawa, Bill had heard Yoshiko's pleas for help more than once; she would often call him to help her locate Ski at one of the Okinawa bars and deliver him home to her inebriated. Ski was a competent team sergeant, but he couldn't shake "the beast."

Bill and Ski had kept in touch over the years, especially at Christmas. In 1977, Ski decided it was time to retire and pursue a quiet, wholesome existence for the benefit of his wife and children. At the ripe old age of forty-six, he had already spent twenty-seven years in the army. Bill still found it hard to believe that Ski had actually retired to a farm in North Carolina.

Ski answered the phone in a bland voice: "Good afternoon."

"You old cockroach, how are you?" Bill shot back.

Recognizing Bill's voice, Ski became much more animated. "What a surprise. It's good to hear your voice, Bill. Is everything okay?"

Bill swapped cordial remarks with him and then got down to the reason for the call.

"I'm going to be passing through Fayetteville tomorrow and thought I'd stop in to say hello. Are you busy?" Bill asked.

"Not so much that I can't take time to see you!" Ski boomed. "You coming into the airport or what?"

"Yeah, I should be there at about noon. Can you meet me?"

"Sure thing. And you're welcome to stay here as long as you want," Ski offered. "We've got a lot of catching up to do."

"Thanks, Ski. I'm looking forward to seeing you, too. I'll be on the noon flight from Miami."

Inside the terminal, Bill was greeted with a bear hug and a kiss on each cheek—a Czechoslovakian tradition. Swallowing back the emotions that sprang to the surface, Bill and Ski held each other close for a moment. Bill's mind flashed back to the days in Vietnam when they had relied upon each other to stay alive.

Next, Bill turned to Yoshiko, standing next to Ski, waiting patiently to welcome him also. The two embraced.

"You look great, Yoshiko, more beautiful than I remember," Bill commented. Both Ski and Bill smiled broadly as the shy Yoshiko turned her face aside, hiding her reddening cheeks with her hands.

Ski was still in top shape. He had lost a little hair, but that was to be expected with four teenagers in the house and one pre-teen to contend with.

Before going to their house, Ski showed Bill around his farm of 460 acres. It was within an easy forty-minute drive of Fayetteville. He and Yoshiko had obviously made the right decision in retiring.

All except Ski's two youngest children remembered Bill from Okinawa. They were soon playing the piano and showing off their collections of stamps and coins. The time passed swiftly. It wasn't until after dinner that Bill and Ski had a chance to talk.

To Bill's surprise, Ski brought him a beer from the kitchen and a glass of iced tea for himself. Plopping down on the porch swing across from him, Ski said, "I kept my promise to Yoshiko that I wouldn't have any alcohol until after the kids are in bed. I frequently fall asleep early because I'm pooped from all of the farm work, and that's caused me to cut back on my drinking. And, you know, when all's said and done, I feel a hell of a lot better now than when we were on Okinawa."

"You know the best decision you ever made in your life," Bill commented, "was when you proposed to Yoshiko. I'm so happy for you both."

They clinked glasses to that. "What've you been doin' for yourself?" Ski asked. "I remember your last letter. Are you still in Guyana?"

Bill updated Ski on the highlights of his career with the Department of State. He briefed Ski in detail on the North Vietnamese invasion of South Vietnam, and belittled the federal government for standing by and letting it happen. He then briefed Ski on Guyana and its politics, including the Burnham government's version of socialism and the circumstances surrounding the Jonestown commune. Seeing that Ski was listening attentively to every word, he described his personal involvement with John Olsen and gave a detailed explanation of the problems John faced in light of overwhelming evidence that his daughter was at risk.

"How old is this girl, Katrina?"

"Thirteen," Bill answered.

"My third oldest, Toshiko, is also thirteen," Ski said quietly.

"Then you understand how much John wants to have her safely at home with him, and why I've gotten myself involved to try to help him."

"Just what do you have in mind?"

"We're going to go into Jonestown and snatch the girl, bring her out, without anyone knowing," Bill answered. "Right now, there are three of us involved: me, a pilot friend of mine, and the father. We've come up with a plan that I think will work."

Bill and Ski talked long into the night about Roland, John, and the rescue plan. Bill went into the house long enough to bring out the aerial photos he had taken.

"It's not going to be easy, even if everything goes right," Ski commented after thoroughly reviewing the photographs. "When are you planning to go in?"

"There isn't a fixed date yet, but if everything goes our way, we should be ready sometime in October. We're hoping that you'll help us. Fact is, we need a few essential items from Fort Bragg. Without 'em, our chances for success are greatly reduced."

"Okay . . . what items are you talking about?" Ski asked uneasily.

Bill withdrew the list of items from his wallet. "Here it is."

Ski looked over the list carefully: one portable gas tank filled with "knockout gas" and dispenser; two gas masks; two .22-caliber tranquilizer pistols with silencers and twelve tranquilizer cartridges; six trip flares; four white smoke grenades; and six tear gas grenades. He smiled. "Is this all?"

Bill nodded.

"I don't think there'll be any big problem here."

"Then I can count on you to help?" Bill asked hopefully.

"I said there'd be no problem!" Ski said sternly. Then, warmly, he asked, "Are you ready for another beer?"

Upon returning from the kitchen with a cold beer in hand, Ski remarked, "You're going to need more muscle. You know that, don't you? Just securing the site for the actual retrieval will take two men minimum, and you're going in with a rookie."

"Yeah, I knew you'd say that. Do you know anyone who might be interested in throwing in with us?"

"You son of a bitch! What about me?" Ski shouted.

Even though Bill had suspected all along that Ski would be willing to take part in the rescue, he laughed with relief. "I hoped you'd say that! Here's to going back to the jungle!"

The two men clinked glasses again, and as they were settling back in their seats, Ski asked, "Have you read much Shakespeare?" Before Bill could respond, Ski began quoting:

"This above all, to thine own self be true, and it must follow
as night the day, thou canst not then be false to any man . . ."

Pausing to study Bill's face, Ski added, "If that were my own child at Jonestown, I would not hesitate to go in after her, regardless of the consequences.

I just can't turn away from another man's need, especially one who can't help himself. It'll be an honor to go with you all!"

"You're absolutely certain?" Bill asked. "I almost hated to ask, knowing how well it's all going for you now."

"Yes, sir, it is," Ski said, "but that makes it that much more important to me to help someone else." Then, leaning forward in his chair, Ski asked, "Tell me sir, how are you doing? Are the nightmares still with you?"

Bill took a swig of beer and savored it for a second before answering. He smiled at the ease with which Ski posed the question, how natural it sounded coming from a fellow soldier's lips. "Let's just say that I'm getting better," he replied. "No prize yet, but I'm getting better, thank God. Things are moving in the right direction."

"I'm really glad to hear that, sir. Those things can tear a man apart," Ski offered. "You know, I'm still struggling. Do you still have your nerve? That's the part that bothers me the most. It's the reason I got out—just couldn't risk letting someone down."

Bill didn't answer. Both men were thinking the same thing: It was going to take a great deal of nerve, and no small amount of luck, to get Katrina out of Jonestown and through the wilderness to safety. And if they failed, they'd be doing worse than letting John down. No one knew just how dangerous the people guarding Jonestown could be, and the truth everyone was afraid to voice was that if the little girl's rescue took a bad turn, she might get hurt, or even killed.

After a long silence, Ski spoke up. "Listen, sir, whenever you need support, I'm here for you. Now, what's next on the agenda?"

"Well, we'll need to meet in Fort Lauderdale," Bill responded, "—you, me, John, and Roland—to discuss the rescue plans in detail. Roland has suggested Saturday, September 30th at his place. Is that all right with you?"

"Yeah, I'll be there," Ski said. "Now, let's get some shuteye. That is, unless you want to talk through what's left of the night."

"Nope. I'm about talked out!" Bill confessed. "I'll need to fly back to Miami tomorrow. I only have a four-day weekend, so it's back to work at the embassy on Tuesday."

The next day, Ski accompanied Bill to the airport. At the sound of Bill's flight announcement, the two men again shook hands, embraced, and Bill turned to hurry toward his plane. He stopped once to look back, calling out, "See ya on the thirtieth."

CHAPTER 31

Late September 1978

As John arrived in Miami on Friday, September 29th, he was hoping that the gear for the rescue had already arrived at Roland's house. It had been ten days since he sent it by airfreight, and he was concerned.

Hours later, Bill and Celeste also arrived in Miami, ostensibly to do some shopping over the weekend. Bill welcomed the chance to get out of Guyana and to spend some quality time with Celeste. He would be back to work on Monday morning.

Although the meeting to discuss Katrina's rescue from Jonestown was set for 10:00 A.M., everyone involved was anxious to get going.

Ski drove down from North Carolina and was met at the door by Jenny. As he wove his way through the house to the pool verandah, Bill came to greet him. "Welcome aboard," he said.

"Great to see you again, sir," Ski replied, shaking his outstretched hand.

Turning to Roland, Bill introduced his two friends. Just after 10:00 A.M., John Olsen was at the door. After everyone was acquainted, Jenny invited the group into the house to sit around the dining room table and talk.

John had been in sporadic contact with Roland since they had first talked in Fort Lauderdale, and the men had concluded an agreement for Roland's support of the rescue. John would pay Roland $15,000 up front in view of the risks involved and to cover all operational expenses. Upon the completion of the rescue effort, Roland would receive another $15,000 that John set up in an escrow account. It was easy for John to agree to Roland's terms.

"Before we begin, may I say a few words?" John asked. "First of all, I want to thank each of you for your good will in attempting to get my daughter out of Jonestown." His eyes filled with tears and his voice was unsteady. "It means so much to me that you care enough to be involved, not even knowing Katrina. We are forever grateful for—" Then John began to weep, taking out his handkerchief to wipe his tears.

As he composed himself, there was a moment of silence around the table. Then Bill spoke for the group. "John, we realize there's just no other choice. If there were, we wouldn't be sitting here today. God willing, we'll return your daughter to you and save her from this madness."

"What can I say besides thank you," John responded.

There were nods and murmurs of "Of course," around the table.

"Now, let's get started," Bill concluded.

Sitting forward in his chair, John reiterated the facts that he had discussed with Roland and Bill concerning Jonestown, including the reports from those who had escaped, which described it as a "hell on earth."

"There's been another defection since I talked with you last," John said. "According to this woman's testimony, the situation in Jonestown has gotten much worse since June. Apparently Jones is more paranoid than ever and the people there are really frightened for their lives. The point is, I don't think we have any more time. We have to select the earliest possible date to go in."

Bill nodded in agreement and said, "Well then, down to the details. Our purpose today is to finalize our plans, make sure we've thought of everything. I suggest that we consider Roland in charge of the airborne portion of the rescue and Ski in charge of the ground portion. That way, the most experienced among us will make the operational decisions."

"Good!" John said. "Are we all in agreement, then?"

Both Ski and Roland joined their voices in assent.

"I've completed all of my purchases and sent them here via airfreight," John said. "Roland told me on the phone that he's done with his stuff as well."

Roland nodded in confirmation. "First, I decided on a plane. There's a small airport near Fort Myers, Florida, that will rent me a 'Goose' for $250 an hour, actual flight time. I've already taken a check ride with the owner and reviewed the plane's logbooks. Everything looks good. I've already test-fired all of the weapons and had the rifles zeroed in by a local gun shop so that the sight picture through the scope is true. Basically, we're ready to go."

Looking at Ski, Bill asked, "Have you been able to get the stuff from Bragg yet, Ski?"

"Well, I brought the two gas masks with me, the trip flares, smoke and gas grenades," Ski said. "We'll have to wait to get the knockout gas and the tranquilizer pistols until just before we're ready to go. These items are closely controlled, and my contact can cover for them only a few days at a time. We'll be *borrowing* these items, so once a go date is set, I'll let him know. That way, we can work out the details for actually getting the gas and the pistols delivered on time. That's the best I can do."

"Sounds good," Bill commented. "Any questions?" After a silent pause, Bill continued, "I think it would be a good idea to lay out the plan to give everyone an overview of how this will go. Roland . . ."

"Okay," Roland began. "I'll rent the Grumman Goose from an outfit in Fort Myers, Florida, for a three-week period beginning five days prior to the date we decide to launch the rescue from Bridgetown, Barbados. That, by the way, is where we'll all need to link up.

"I'll bring the plane to Barbados loaded with all of the gear. I'll take the weapons apart and put them into a plastic container that I've already painted white and labeled *survival kit*. I've seen many of these in small commercial airplanes that fly over jungles, so it shouldn't raise any interest at all. I'll find a way to attach it to the rear of the baggage compartment. I'll pack the rest of the stuff into duffel bags and carry them as 'camping gear' for some wealthy clients who want to go camping on an isolated island in the middle of the Caribbean."

"We're the clients, right?" Ski asked.

"That's right," Roland answered. "It's important that everyone act the part. You're coming to the Caribbean to do four days of peaceful island camping and getting away from it all. Ski, John, Celeste, and Bill will arrive in Bridgetown the day before our launch date so that we can all review the plan and make any last-minute changes."

John looked to Bill. "Do I understand correctly that Celeste is going with us?"

Instead of answering, Bill raised his eyebrows at Celeste. This was news to him. Celeste ignored his gaze and nodded to John.

"That's right, John," Roland said. "We need someone to stay with the airplane to make sure nothing happens to it during the time we're on the ground."

"There must be another way," John objected, looking at Celeste. "You could be in harm's way!"

Celeste leaned forward to speak. "Look, gentlemen, I can take care of myself, and I'm not going to just sit home when there's a job to be done. Please understand, John, this wasn't forced on me. I volunteered."

Roland added, "Celeste knows how to use my 9 mm Browning. In fact, she has wanted to be in on this from the beginning, and encouraged all of us to be involved. If Jenny weren't pregnant, she'd be going as well. The bottom line here is that leaving the plane unguarded while we're in the jungle could spell disaster for all of us."

John nodded. "I guess it isn't a good idea to involve anyone else in this, right?"

"Yeah, John, that's how we feel," Bill said, fielding the question.

John Olsen swallowed hard. "I know, and I agree totally. I was just hoping that we might spare Celeste from being so deeply involved, just in case things don't turn out . . ." He quickly changed the subject. "How soon do you think we can meet in Barbados?"

"I don't know exactly, but I think we can aim for mid-October at the earliest," Roland replied.

"That's it, huh?" John asked, his face reddening. At Roland's nod, he exhaled heavily. "All right, then. That's it."

Bill agreed and added, "The biggest factor is to determine the exact dates and times of the tides."

"No problem," Roland volunteered. "Consider it done. I'll tell the air controller that the group is going to go camping for three or four days on one of the deserted islands just south of Barbados. That way, the tower won't expect me to contact them again until 'the end of the camping trip.' The island will be our staging area for the rescue. We'll fly under the radar from Barbados and arrive over the Port Kaituma River at eight thousand feet altitude, when high tide peaks. I'll cut the engines to idle and land on the river as silently as possible, given that Jonestown is close by. After the rescue, we'll fly back to the island to change clothes and reorient ourselves. When we're ready, I'll contact the tower in Bridgetown and ask for clearance to take off to fly to Saint Vincent, a tiny island nation in the West Indies chain. We can dump all of the weapons and gear used for the operation during that leg of the flight home. That is, all except the things we borrowed from Fort Bragg. The tranquilizer guns can be stored with the actual emergency gear for the aircraft, and the empty gas bottle can be explained as medical gear that I used for a medical evacuation flight days earlier."

"Whew, you've thought of everything," John said appreciatively. "How long a flight is it?"

"We're looking at somewhere around three hours," Roland answered. "I'll have exact flight times and fuel consumption figured out by the time I leave Fort Lauderdale. Concerning radar on the Guyana end, we shouldn't have any trouble at all. The Guyanese rarely turn it on. It's used primarily during inclement weather to direct aircraft landing at Timehri Airport. We'll need to paddle the plane to a mooring spot under the overhang of the trees where it won't be easily spotted and refuel the aircraft right away for the return flight."

"After we fly back to the island, then what?" John asked.

"First, we'll fly to Saint Vincent to refuel the aircraft again. We won't return to Barbados, but will fly back to Florida following the West Indies-Bahamas route. No one will be the wiser that we have an extra passenger on the return trip. You did say you have Katrina's new passport, right, John?"

"Yeah, I have it. And she will be with us at that point," John said hopefully.

"Don't worry, John; mid-October will be here before you know it and she'll soon be safely at home with you," Bill said firmly.

Holding out the prints from the overhead photographs of the Jonestown settlement, he asked John to point out exactly where Katrina normally slept.

Studying the pictures intently, John oriented himself to the way he had come into Jonestown on the jungle road from Port Kaituma. He then moved his finger to the pavilion and then to the target building, located on the northeast side of the settlement. It was in a cluster of five identical rectangular buildings standing together. Although set apart, these buildings were relatively close to the pavilion, where all of the activities in Jonestown took place.

"John, what does the inside of this building look like?" Ski asked.

"Well, the inside is divided by a partition, with twelve children sleeping on either side," John said. "They all sleep on narrow bunk beds built right into the wall. I made it a point to get inside when I was visiting so I could see Katrina's bunk."

"Is there a window near her bunk?" Ski asked.

"Yes, toward the top of the wall," John answered. "There are windows on all sides, obviously built for air circulation, not for looking out. The roof overhangs the outside walkway by three or four feet, pretty much covering the windows like an awning. There is screening on the windows, but no glass and no shutters."

"Hmmm," Ski murmured, turning to Roland. "Will the air in Jonestown be still this time of year, or windy?"

"Hot and humid, with heavy air—the breeze dead still at night," Roland surmised. "It usually begins to rain about 5:00 P.M. and continues for four or five hours. It comes down hard at first, and then gradually slackens off to a stop. Before the rain, the air is turbulent, but afterwards, it's perfectly still."

"That's what I wanted to hear," Ski said. "It's important that the knockout gas doesn't disperse too much. Even with a lot of open windows, it sounds like it'll work just like we want it to." Ski continued, "Bill, you'll also be in charge of the knockout gas and the dispenser. Each of us will have a radio, smoke grenade, and a tear gas grenade. We'll take turns chopping our way through the jungle."

"Just to be clear, Ski," Bill interrupted. "John and I will be the ones going in after Katrina, right?"

"That's right." Ski then warned, "Movement through the jungle is going to be difficult. It'll test our physical stamina. I expect all of you to get out and get your bodies conditioned for this." His words seemed to be for all of them, but were directed mostly to John, who colored a bit, promising he would be as ready as the others by mid-October. "We'll also need mental toughness. Resign yourselves now that you may have to do things to get Katrina out of there that you would never do otherwise."

"How long do you estimate it will take us to travel from the river to the settlement?" John asked the question on everyone's mind.

"I anticipate we'll be moving about eight hours to reach Jonestown. We'll move slowly and quietly to avoid running into anyone unexpectedly. Under cover of darkness, we'll head to the northeast side of the settlement and move into a safe holding area. Then Bill and I will try to determine movement patterns in the settlement, both by day and night. In the meantime, everyone but the man on recon will stay together, resting on their stomachs, weapons ready to use. Each of us will form the spoke of a wheel, with our feet being the hub of the wheel. There will be no moving around or talking. We're calling upon self-discipline here. If everything goes as expected, we'll move from the holding area to the building where Katrina will be sleeping around 2:00 A.M. on the second night. John, remember that once you have your daughter, you'll need your arms and hands free to carry her because she will be unconscious and nothing but dead weight."

He again paused, waiting for this statement to make an impact. "Questions?" Ski asked.

"How long will it take to dispense the gas?" John asked.

"You should hold the key open for a full two minutes, but not a second more, to ensure that everyone is out," Ski answered.

"How long will it take for Katrina to wake up?" John asked apprehensively.

"She should come around within twenty to thirty minutes after the gas is released," Ski said. "The sooner she is able to walk on her own, the better it'll be for everyone. Remember though, we can only move as fast as the slowest member of our team. Hopefully, we'll get in, get Katrina, and get back out without anyone being the wiser."

Meeting their eyes, Ski's face became stern. "Weapons are to be used only as a last resort. Our objective is not to inflict casualties on anyone, but rather to rescue Katrina. That brings up another point everyone has to understand. If we're discovered on our way into the settlement, all bets are off and we'll abort the rescue plan and retreat, using the tear gas if necessary, and return to the river with all possible speed. Any other questions?"

"Just one, Ski," Jenny said. "Are we certain that this 'knock-out gas' is safe for children? I'd hate to think that we might harm those girls."

Ski hesitated for a moment before answering. "Okay, let's talk about this so that everyone is confident in what we're doing. The knockout gas that we will be using is called hexane gas, a petroleum-based gas that is a neurotoxin that deepens an unconsciousness state. In large doses, it can cause serious brain damage. I've used it operationally only once. It comes in a small, pressurized bottle about the size of a quart thermos. Hexane gas will put a person into a deep stupor, the deepest stage of sleep, called REM sleep. Used properly, it's perfectly safe."

Listening intently, Celeste finally spoke up. "I don't know, Ski. It sounds potentially risky. I don't think we should use it."

"How does everyone else feel about this?" Ski asked.

John was the first to speak. "This is a hard one. What we may be sacrificing here is certainty for hope. I'd rather be certain that what we do is going to work. Let's use the gas . . . that's my vote."

Bill and Ski accepted John's opinion as definitive. They all finally agreed.

When no other issues were raised, Ski's features softened. "I'm proud to be a part of this effort. With God's grace, I know we'll be successful."

John's eyes filled, but his voice was steady as he asked, "Can we select an exact date now to do this?"

Stepping over the ottoman in the den, Ski reached for the calendar that Jenny was holding out for him. Looking at it pensively, he said, "I think we should aim for mid-week to stage the actual rescue. The routine they follow will probably stay the same on week days, but may vary somewhat on weekends."

"We could probably be ready for the 14th, as long as the tide is right," Roland said.

Ski concluded, "That would make our launch date October 16th, Monday, the day we leave Bridgetown. If that's the case, the actual rescue would take place the night of the 19th, almost three weeks from now."

Everyone sat in silence as Ski looked around the den. Finally, Bill concluded, "It's about the best we can do. We have to remember that it'll take several days for Roland to fly the plane to Barbados. Let's hope the morning high tide doesn't come in too late."

"Everything has to be right before we begin, or there's no use in starting. One miscalculation and we all may wind up in serious trouble or dead," Roland warned.

On that ominous note, the group retreated to the garage to look over all of the gear that John and Roland had acquired for the rescue.

After the day's activities, John drove back to Miami and settled into his hotel. He was exhausted mentally from the strain of the day. Considering everything, he was satisfied that this effort had a good chance of success.

Packing his things for his flight back to California, John picked up the photograph of Katrina and Priscilla that he always carried in his suitcase. Then, all at once it hit him: *What about Priscilla?* He couldn't escape the thought that he was abandoning her at the moment when she needed him the most.

"Oh, God," John murmured into his hand. "What will Katrina think of me if I leave her behind?"

The question lingered on his mind until the small hours of the morning, when he at last fell asleep.

CHAPTER 32

Mid-October 1978

To obtain leave, Bill requested time off to attend his sister's wedding. His sister had actually been married years earlier, but nobody at the embassy knew that, and his request was approved. Celeste obtained the same time off and made reservations for them to fly to Port of Spain after work on the night of October 12th. They would then take an early flight to Barbados on the 13th to link up with Ski, John, and Roland at the Barbados Hilton Hotel. Jenny had already made reservations for all of them at the Hilton.

Time seemed to stand still for Bill during the next several days. Then, because of last-minute preparations, the last two days passed quickly. A phone call from Ski made him even more eager to begin. Ski reported that he had just delivered to Roland the knockout gas and the tranquilizer guns. Roland now had all of the needed gear.

After talking with Ski, Bill went to Celeste's apartment to update her. She sat on the sofa and Bill joined her.

"Well, Ski says everything's ready to go. He spoke with Roland and is eager to get started," Bill said, adding, "I just want you to know how impressed I am by the way you've handled all of this—how you brought everyone together to help John."

She interrupted him and put her finger on his lips. "And you thought you had me all figured out," Celeste responded.

"No, I never claimed that," Bill laughed nervously. "Look, I've been wanting to talk about this for some time and didn't know how to start. But we're about to go into a very dangerous situation, so I feel like it can't wait. I just need you to know how sorry I am for everything. These last few weeks have been awful—like being in limbo. I love you, Celeste, and if there's any way forward for us, I want you to know that I'm ready to reengage and take our relationship to the next level."

Celeste held up a hand. "Please stop, Bill. I understand what you're saying." She took a deep breath. "But I'm just not sure how I feel about you anymore, and that bothers me. I'm still wrapping my head around all this. Don't push things, okay?"

Bill nodded. "Of course. You mean so much to me."

Then Celeste stood up, and Bill knew it was time for him to go.

———

To their surprise, Roland and Jenny were waiting for them at the Hilton Hotel when they arrived in Bridgetown. That evening, they all had dinner together, drank a little wine, and caught up on events.

On October 14th, John and Ski arrived on the same early morning flight from Miami. Everyone was on schedule. Once they had settled in, it became apparent to the others that John was all nerves. When he pulled out Katrina's new passport to show the group, his hand shook.

Instinctively, Bill reached out his hand to steady John's arm, and as he did so, his eyes met Roland's a few feet away. They were both wondering the same thing—in this state of anxiety, and in his physical condition, would John end up compromising the mission? Bill just hoped that they could succeed in reassuring him over the next few days.

Listening to Ski rehearse their plans that afternoon brought back memories of Okinawa to Bill. He remembered the practice sessions Ski used to conduct prior to their missions to Vietnam. Ski would coach the detachment like an elementary school teacher to make sure everyone knew exactly what the plans were, and precisely what duties and responsibilities were assigned to each team member. This time, he was even more patient and precise, since he was coaching people who were not accustomed to the discipline required.

Slowly, each member of the team was absorbing the details. After two hours of work, Ski called a break, declaring they were all on the right track, concentrating and cooperating, and that they would begin again fresh at 8:00 A.M.

The following morning, they went over the entire plan step by step, but this time each person recited the overall plan as well as confirmed their individual responsibilities. When John, the last to stand, had completed his part with few errors, Ski got to his feet, smiling broadly.

"I'm impressed! Thank you for your cooperation," he said. "We're ready. We'll have the final review tomorrow morning."

A chorus of groans met his words, but all nodded at the same time, knowing there could not be too much rehearsal for something so important. As they stood and stretched, Roland moved toward the door. His hand on the knob, he called out, "The last one in the pool buys the drinks!"

The next morning, after the final briefback, they all packed and met in the lobby of the hotel to go to the airport. Roland was organizing everyone with Jenny looking over his shoulder.

As everyone was loading into the van, Jenny spoke up: "Hey, sport, aren't you going to say goodbye?"

Roland turned toward her and smiled. He gently took her in his arms and gave her a lingering kiss, saying, "Have a safe trip home, my love. I'll be thinking of you."

"I love you, Ro . . ." Jenny responded as Roland got into the van.

John sat down next to Celeste, closed his eyes, and rested his head against the van window to calm himself. Each member of the group carried one bag and looked as if they were out for fun and relaxation. John wore his loud Hawaiian shirt, the tail flapping out over white Bermuda shorts. Large sunglasses hid his eyes. Ski had on a yellow-and-orange rugby shirt with the sleeves cut off, and a red plaid pair of Bermuda shorts. Adding a straw farmer's hat and sunglasses, he was a sight for sore eyes and typified the American tourist.

Celeste was dressed for the beach, her tanned skin and hair setting off a chic swimsuit underneath a brightly colored beach cover. Roland and Bill were the most conservative, with their cut-off jeans and tennis shoes. Immigration took one look at this motley crew and gave them clearance after only routine questions.

CHAPTER 33

October 16, 1978

Within a few minutes, Roland was cranking the engines of the Grumman Goose. Bill checked the time. It was 3:25 P.M., October 16th.

Airborne, they flew for thirty-five minutes to a small, uninhabited island directly southeast of Barbados, pre-selected by Roland. He closed out his flight plan with the control tower in Bridgetown and looked for the best cove to put the plane down. There were many little coves around the island, and Roland chose the largest one. The water was calm as he landed and taxied the aircraft toward a white-sand deserted beach.

When he had stopped, they took the time to look about, admiring the beauty of their tropical surroundings. At Roland's signal, all turned to the plane and began unloading their equipment. The gear had to be thoroughly checked, readied, and stored properly. They also had to change into their camouflage clothing, check the radios, and test-fire weapons.

At 7:00 P.M. Ski inspected everyone. He bent back the pins on the smoke and gas grenades to prevent them from being activated by a hanging vine in the jungle. One by one, he checked out each weapon, which he then handed back to be reloaded. Satisfied with the inspection, he pulled from his grip two tubes of grease paint, one green and one black.

"This will come off only with alcohol, so we won't worry about it until we're back in the plane. I have a big bottle in my suitcase. Now, who's first?"

Roland stepped forward, and Ski began applying the grease paint, face first, then neck and throat. When he had finished, Bill could hardly recognize him. After his turn, Bill helped Ski put on his camouflaged face. Celeste gladly passed up the makeover.

When all seemed ready, Ski said, "There's one more thing." Turning to his gear, he handed out two self-contained ampoules of morphine to each man. "Each of you can give an injection, even to yourself," he began, demonstrating the technique as he talked. "We'll carry these in our right breast pocket so that we can find them quickly in case of an accident or injury. They are to eliminate pain in order to move the wounded man to safety. We gotta use these sparingly. Don't give more than three ampoules to anyone over the short term. This is something I realized we needed and secured from Fort Bragg. Of course, we all hope it isn't necessary to use them," he added as everyone nodded soberly.

Once Ski was finished, he began piling up the driftwood Celeste had been gathering, and soon they had a picture-perfect fire burning on the beach.

Celeste settled into the sand a few feet from the fire and began working a hotdog onto a skewer for dinner. Bill hesitated, considered taking a seat next to John on the opposite side of the fire, then approached Celeste and lowered himself down next to her. She didn't look at him, just kept her eyes fixed on the blaze, rotating the skewer meditatively while the hot dog turned deep brown and blistered. Neither of them said anything.

Tentatively, Bill reached an arm out and wrapped it around Celeste's shoulders. There was no response at first, but after a moment, she softened and leaned into him, resting her head on his shoulder, careful to avoid the greasepaint.

They ate their simple dinner in silence, gazing into the fire, until Roland announced that it was time to board the plane again. They had to leave at exactly 10:45 P.M. to arrive over the Kaituma River at 1:37 A.M., when the tide was at its highest.

Ski stood first, holding his hand up for the others to wait. "Before we go, let's all join in a prayer," he suggested. Bowing his head with the others, he simply said, "We humbly ask you, Lord, to bless our undertaking and to keep everyone safe." All echoed his fervent "Amen."

The plane's takeoff was timed to the minute. Bill sat in the copilot's seat, gazing into the clear night sky as they flew low over the dark water below. A quarter-moon helped to light their way. Once out of Bridgetown's radar coverage zone, Roland increased their altitude to eight thousand feet to cruise to their destination.

When they were within a hundred miles of Guyana, Roland swore and pointed out the window. "Looks like a line of thunder cells rolling in from the southeast over Venezuela," he shouted over the intercom. "Everyone hold onto your dinner. It's going to get choppy."

The next hour and a half of the flight was excruciating. The Grumman Goose bounced roughly in the storm. As soon as John vomited from being airsick, Celeste and Ski followed in turn.

Roland tried to escape the rough air by changing altitudes, but to no avail. Now flying on instruments, Roland had to rely upon dead reckoning and only one ADF channel to judge when it was time to descend. When the altimeter hit just under five hundred feet above the ground—the abort altitude for an instrument approach—Roland gave power and climbed to two thousand feet.

"This isn't going to work, even if the ceiling improves," Roland said to Bill over the aircraft's intercom. "Without at least some moonlight, we're never going to find our landing site. We've got to go back to the coast."

Once the ADF signal indicated that they were over the Caribbean Sea near the Guyana coast, Roland again made a descent. This time the plane broke out of the cloud ceiling at three hundred feet.

"That's better," Roland cried out.

Now flying west along the coast, Roland alerted Bill when he had found the mouth of the Kaituma River. "That's it—all we have to do is follow this thing to our landing site. It will be only another twenty to twenty-five minutes and we'll be there."

The rain, lightning, and thunder continued unabated, rocking the aircraft mercilessly. Finally, Roland spotted the unique bend in the river that he sought.

"There you are, my sweetie," he said. "Now, let's put this thing down." He banked the aircraft to the right and flew a downwind leg to better gauge his approach to landing.

Bill turned and yelled to the others, "We're landing—get ready with the paddles!"

Unable to see his surroundings in the pounding rain, Roland turned on the landing lights. "I hate to do this," he said, "but it's better than crashing into some tree." Looking out the aircraft windows himself, Bill understood completely.

The touchdown was hard but certain. The aircraft came to a quick stop due to the river current. Roland had to use the aircraft engines to steer the plane to the east side of the river before cutting off the landing lights.

When they were almost stopped, Ski and John opened the doors on the aircraft and began paddling as well. As soon as Ski saw the riverbank, he used a rope and grappling hook to act as an anchor.

"I've got it," Ski yelled out to Bill as he stepped out of the aircraft into the water and walked onto the riverbank. Knowing that the aircraft was secured, Roland then shut down both engines. Even though it wasn't pretty, they had landed in one piece.

Despite the hard rain, Bill noted with relief the lack of current when he stepped out of the plane and into the river near the bank. Nonetheless, it took nearly an hour for Ski, Roland, and Bill to locate an appropriate anchoring point for the plane underneath overhanging tree branches and to tie off the front of the plane as well as anchor its tail.

"If we tie off both ends, it won't turn in the water," Roland advised. "We'll avoid running the risk of damaging a wing tip." The red-filtered flashlights helped the men get their bearings and select the best mooring site.

After the plane was unloaded, Roland and Bill concentrated on refueling the aircraft, using the extra gas containers they had on board. Out of habit, they filtered the fuel through a chamois to collect any moisture left in the gas as they emptied the ten-gallon containers one by one.

"Do you think the people at Jonestown heard the plane coming in?" Bill asked.

Roland responded, "That was a pretty heavy thunderstorm we came through. Imagine sitting inside one of those shacks at Jonestown with the rain beating down on those sheet metal roofs. I'll bet you it was deafening."

Finally, the rain began to subside. Bill and Roland sat down with the others to await the dawn. It was 4:30 A.M., October 17th.

Despite the miserable conditions, they all managed to doze until about 6:00 A.M., when Ski alerted them that the time had come. During the night, the river's water level had gone down appreciably as the tide ebbed, but the aircraft was still treading water.

Roland looked over everything carefully now that there was light and confirmed that the plane would be safe as they had secured it. He then took Celeste around the plane, pointing out critical areas that she should monitor and discussing solutions to problems that might arise. In the end, he was satisfied that the plane was in good hands.

As Ski stood and conducted a last-minute review of each man's responsibilities for the first leg through the jungle, Bill turned toward Celeste and whispered, "Be safe, sweetie."

"Take care," she said. When they embraced, Celeste noted the tension in his body.

At Ski's signal, Bill moved out, following a compass heading of ninety-seven degrees. He turned for one last look at Celeste, who seemed impossibly small where she stood by the riverbank, her arms wrapped around herself. Then the jungle overtook him and the other men and she disappeared from view.

As soon as they were within the line of the trees, Bill was overcome by a familiar sensation. This was how he had felt when he stepped off of the helicopter on his first long-range patrol in Vietnam, and here it was again, all the stronger for the dense, dark foliage that isolated them from the open air and sky. It was the sense of having been transported in time and place to another jungle, one in which every tree and shadow was a potential source of enemy fire.

Bill shivered to think that in a few hours, that might well be the case here, too. He glanced over at Ski, wondering if he was experiencing the same sensation; but Ski's expression was blank beneath the thick black greasepaint. Bill swallowed his anxieties and pressed on.

Tangled vines and wet, swampy undergrowth limited Bill's visibility to only a few meters, but he led his party away from the river, into the jungle, hacking a path as they advanced. After about 1600 meters, Bill turned north onto a heading of seventy degrees to try to find higher ground.

They continued in the swamp for another thousand meters. The going was challenging and physically exhausting. Just as Bill was questioning himself, visibility opened up to twenty or thirty meters, and the swamp's quagmire turned to solid, albeit soaked, ground. Feeling more in control, Bill was confident that they were at last on the right path.

The team continued to move slowly and cautiously along. They paused at regular intervals to rest, conserving their water as much as possible. Finally, they stopped long enough to eat and to readjust their gear.

As they were sitting in a close grouping, Roland began scratching his lower leg muscle.

At first Bill thought nothing of it, but after a few minutes, the look of discomfort on Roland's face set off an alarm in Bill's head. "You okay there, Roland?"

Roland grimaced. "My leg's burning up for some reason."

"Let's take a look."

When Roland lifted his left pant leg, there was a silver-dollar-sized welt on the side of his calf, bright red, with a small white mark in the center. His calf had already started to swell.

"Looks like you've been bitten by a spider of some sort, Roland," Bill speculated. "Looks like the work of a banana spider. What do you think, Ski?"

Ski took a close look as well and confirmed Bill's suspicions. "They have those things all over Okinawa and people get bit all the time," Ski offered. "Here's the deal. You're going to start to feel dizzy, have swollen limbs and throbbing muscles; then it gets nasty. As your body absorbs the poison, a high fever sets in, accompanied by a splitting headache that will make you wish you were dead. This thing will totally incapacitate you within twelve hours. You will be over the worst in about seventy-two hours and back to normal within a week or so. And no, there's no antidote or treatment. If you were in a hospital, they'd ice down your leg and keep you comfortable. The only thing that you can do is to drink plenty of water, stay off your feet, and keep your leg raised higher than your heart." Ski shook his head in frustration. "You're going to have to go back to the plane, and quickly, while you can still walk. You're going to be on your own. Use your compass as a double-check and follow our trail back and you'll be okay. Follow 250 degrees initially, until you reach the wetlands, then 277 degrees. Just take it slowly, that's all."

"I agree," Bill added. "The sooner you get going, the better. Give me your tranquilizer pistol, the smoke grenade and your tear gas. You won't need them back at the plane. Here, take one of my morphine ampoules—you may need it for the headache. I'll keep my radio on. Report in when you make it back, okay?"

Cursing himself but realizing that he had limited time to moan about it, Roland left the group and began his trek back to the river, already feeling a shooting pain in his leg with every step.

Time seemed to pass even more slowly once the remaining three men were again on their way. The heat and humidity became ever more oppressive as the afternoon sun bore down on the entangled vines and trees all about them.

By late afternoon, Bill had begun to wonder if they had miscalculated the distance to Jonestown. Just after 5:00 P.M. he spotted an open field ahead of them with rows of papaya trees growing in a clearing.

Motioning Ski forward to join him, they consulted their aerial photos and scouted a bit of the surrounding area before deciding they had somehow moved too far east. Given the situation, Bill agreed that he and John should wait where they were while Ski moved northwest to see if he could locate the settlement. They sank down in a thicket, hidden from view, and tried to make themselves comfortable yet stay alert.

Around 6:30 P.M. a soft rain began to fall, relieving their discomfort from the heat. Steam rose from the matted floor of the jungle as the rain soaked in. After nearly an hour had passed since Ski had gone, they heard someone moving slowly about twenty meters away. Bill moved out from cover and pursued the sounds of movement, finding Ski.

Ski related what he had discovered in a whisper. "We're not far from Jonestown. It's only about four hundred meters that way." He signaled with his arm. "I've found a spot right over there that'll make a perfect rallying point after the rescue. There's a big old hardwood tree that we should be able to find without any problem at all. Let's move over there now, and then we'll wait till late tonight before moving to the other side of the settlement." At that, Bill moved out slowly in the direction that Ski had indicated. The rain seemed to renew their energy.

Reaching the newly identified rallying point, Ski motioned for them to find places where they could rest until late that night. He judged that they would need total darkness to safely circumvent the settlement without being heard or spotted.

Just then, the radio crackled to life. Roland had made it back to the river safely. As time ticked by, the men kept still and remained alert.

Near 9:00 p.m., Ski was ready to go. With Bill once more in the lead, they moved out, cautiously and quietly making their way around the perimeter of the settlement.

Once they had moved well north of the settlement, Bill turned east to find the road between Port Kaituma and Jonestown. They crossed the road carefully, trying to avoid leaving any obvious footprints. While the jungle undergrowth helped them, the earth was nonetheless soaked, and it was difficult not to leave traces.

They breathed more easily as they moved along, finally arriving on the northeast side of Jonestown. While Ski and John patiently waited, Bill located a thicket some 150 meters from the edge of the jungle that the team would use as their staging area for the next day or two.

CHAPTER 34

October 18, 1978

The rain continued unabated as John and Bill hid beneath giant foliage, attempting to get some sleep. Ski, on the first watch, climbed a tree and used binoculars to scrutinize activity around the cluster of five buildings. They had to become familiar with the movement patterns in that area to finalize their plans for the actual rescue.

He was able to get a clear view of the target building, the one in which Katrina Olsen slept. As he watched the movement to and from the area, he determined there must be a gathering in progress in the pavilion. Although it was well past midnight, he could hear music and the sound of voices singing.

At about 1:30 A.M. on October 18th, just as the rain was finally letting up, the gathering ended. Ski could see a large group of adults and children walking into the target area. As they drew closer, some of the young girls turned toward the target building and entered it. The others continued on to other buildings. Only one guard remained within the area.

By 2:30 A.M. all was quiet. The lone guard, a young black man armed with a rifle, moved from one end of the courtyard to the other at irregular intervals. Twice he walked in the direction of the pavilion, and was gone for nearly an hour each time. Later, another guard approached from the south to stop and talk with him. After a few minutes, the second guard returned in the direction he had come, and the guard on duty near the dormitories resumed his pattern of walking about.

His routine did not change during the remainder of the night; nor, to Ski's disappointment, did the young guard fall asleep while on duty. He rarely stayed in one place even long enough to sit down. These men were apparently carefully selected and well trained for their duties.

Just as dawn was breaking, Ski was startled to alertness by a voice booming over loudspeakers, ordering everyone to get up and go to work. It was exactly 6:00 A.M. and things rapidly began coming to life in the settlement.

When the guard left his post at exactly 7:00 A.M., Ski realized it was time for him to return to the staging area. As John and Bill finished their morning rations, Ski briefed them on all he had seen and heard during the night. After answering some questions, he ate his own food and sank down to get some sleep. Bill departed to take his turn at watch.

Bill observed Katrina's sleeping quarters from his perch in the tree for some time. When he realized there was no activity there during the day, he decided to scout out Jonestown itself. He first moved toward the Jonestown–Port Kaituma Road and observed that their tracks had already been wiped out by the rain. A large flatbed truck rumbled by, but he crouched low and stayed out of sight. Moving slowly and deliberately, he paralleled the road and finally arrived at Jonestown's vehicle park. There was space for six to eight vehicles, but only two were parked there—the flatbed truck and a pick-up truck. A line of buildings formed the western perimeter of the settlement, with a sidewalk of wood planks that connected the buildings to one another.

Moving to another tree, Bill could see a steady stream of adults moving between the pavilion and the main road. Even though he could not see where they were going, he figured the mess hall must be in that direction.

Returning to his first tree perch, Bill heard what sounded like group recitations, apparently coming from an open-air building being utilized as a school. In late afternoon, the loudspeakers were again put into service, broadcasting what appeared to be a sermon.

Just before it started to rain, at about 5:45 P.M., Bill returned to the staging area. They huddled over the enlarged photograph of Jonestown, and Bill pointed out what he had observed. They figured that there were about 140 adults and children housed in the cluster of five buildings, all female.

The broadcasts continued until 8:00 P.M. The moment the loudspeakers were silenced, Ski noted from his perch that everyone began moving in the direction of the pavilion. About the same time, he spotted the young guard he had observed the previous night. The guard was wearing a poncho and advanced to the target area to begin patrolling as before.

Within a few hours, Ski reached a decision and hurried back to the staging area. Based upon his observations, he judged that the guard would either have to be tranquilized, or they would have to go in and get Katrina during one of the guard's trips to the pavilion. He preferred the latter way, since it would mean not directly confronting the man and minimized the possibility that he might sound an alarm.

Ski whispered, "As soon as the guard moves in the direction of the pavilion, I will position myself behind the building nearest the inner entrance to the area to provide cover while you get Katrina out." Indicating another path, he said, "This is where the visiting guard entered last night. Just be aware—that's all. If he should come along, Bill will stop him with the tranquilizer pistol."

At Bill's nod, Ski added, "If the guard doesn't leave the dormitory area by 2:30 A.M., I'll move in and put him down. Regardless of how we get rid of him, Bill, at two-thirty, you and John will be positioned within fifty meters of the target building, ready to go. Once all is clear, I'll radio you to move in. If there's a radio malfunction, I'll move to where you can see me and give you a hand signal. Make sure your watches are synchronized so that we're all on track at two-thirty."

Ski returned to his surveillance post. The time was 12:10 A.M., October 19th.

The evening's prayer meeting did not end until almost 1:00 A.M. By 2:00 A.M., the settlement lay in apparent stillness; only the young guard remained on duty.

Ski carefully lowered himself from his perch in the tree to move back to the staging area. Their heads close together, Ski said, "I think the guard will leave the area soon, so be ready from the moment we approach to move in and get Katrina. Good luck!" he added, then motioned for them to follow him back to the edge of the settlement.

When they arrived, Ski moved forward alone, cautiously. The guard was nowhere in sight. Ski continued creeping over the open field surrounding the dormitory complex, pausing at the side of the building nearest the pavilion to watch for movement.

As if on cue for the rescue, the rain stopped, and only the occasional dripping from the leaves could be heard. When three long minutes had passed without any guard appearing, Ski judged that the man had indeed gone off to the pavilion.

Ski's radio signal, "All clear, it's a go!" came through loud and clear. Bill acknowledged the order, and he and John moved forward.

Bill stepped out first, his eyes scanning for any signs of movement. John followed closely behind him. Moments later, they were in position alongside the target dormitory.

They put their gas masks on and Bill removed the bottle of knockout gas from his backpack. He slipped the plastic dispersal tube under the door and opened the key on the bottle.

John began timing the release. After only forty seconds, the gas stopped flowing—the bottle was empty.

Bill stepped forward to open the door, but the knob wouldn't turn. It was latched from the inside. Cursing silently, he took out his KA-BAR knife, cutting the wire mesh diagonally on the bottom of the door and pulling it back to permit entrance. The rip hardly made a sound.

John dropped to his hands and knees and crawled through the opening. Finally standing up, he looked about and hurried to where Katrina's bunk was located, praying her sleeping arrangements hadn't changed since his last visit. Shining his red-filtered flashlight on the young girl lying there, he held his breath. It was Katrina!

Relief flooded him as he scooped his daughter into his arms and lowered her carefully from the top bunk into a carrying position. Without hesitation, he returned to the door, fumbling with the latch for what seemed like an eternity before he was able to unlock it. Stumbling a bit as he exited, he nodded his head to signal that he had her.

Unbeknownst to John and Bill, while they were inside the small dormitory, the young guard had re-entered the far side of the area, coming back from the pavilion. Ski kept him in constant view. When he began walking toward the target building, Ski waited until he couldn't miss, then shot the guard in the back with the tranquilizer pistol. The guard grabbed his back, reacting as if a bee had stung him. Then, with a low moan, he crumpled to the ground.

Reloading the gun, Ski moved carefully toward the man. Certain the guard was unconscious, he caught him under the arms and dragged him to the side of the building, placing him out of sight from the path. He had just finished when he heard a voice calling softly: "Thomas? Thomas?"

When the second guard appeared, he turned and looked right at Ski. Ready for him, Ski fired the tranquilizer gun again, hitting him in the chest. He, too, cried out and collapsed to the ground while trying to gain control of his rifle from underneath his plastic poncho. Then his limbs stopped moving and he slumped motionless on the grass.

Ski moved forward, grabbing the downed man under the arms to drag him over behind the first guard. At that moment, he heard the radio crackling. John and Bill were already out with the girl. Ski sighed with relief and gratefully retreated back to the staging area.

When Ski caught up with Bill and John at the staging area, he growled, "I had to tranquilize two guards."

"What? Where did they come from?" Bill asked.

"The first one was the regular guard we were expecting. I have no idea where the second one came from. He took a hit in the chest. I think he'll be okay. There's no doubt that he got a good look at me. Hope no one comes looking for them any time soon. John, how is Katrina?" Ski asked, walking over to where John Olsen sat on the ground holding his sleeping daughter.

"She hasn't awakened yet," John said. "I'm going to let her sleep as long as she can."

Ski leaned over and examined the girl, felt her skin. "She's fine. Give her fifteen to twenty minutes or so and then we'll wake her up. One of us will help you with Katrina," Ski offered, reaching out to take the girl so John could stand.

"Thank you, but I'm fine now," John said, holding his daughter closer to his chest. "If you're ready, I am. Guess we shouldn't hang around here any longer than we have to."

Bill had gathered his gear and stood up, ready to go. In a matter of minutes, they were on their way.

Bill led the way with John and Katrina behind him, and Ski bringing up the rear. Moving back to the southern side of Jonestown was relatively easy, except for the wet, slippery mud. Ski made every attempt to cover their tracks, but the ground was just too soft, their footprints too deep in the muddy earth. He only hoped any pursuers would conclude that they'd come from Port Kaituma and head in that direction.

Katrina continued to sleep as they went. John reluctantly accepted Bill and Ski's offer to help carry her, as the wet terrain made for uncertain footing and he was tiring quickly under the load. By the time they reached their rallying point some four hundred meters southwest of Jonestown, Katrina had begun to stir. When her eyes finally opened, a horrified look crossed her face as she took in the strange men around her, their faces black and green with grease paint.

The moment she heard her father's voice, though, she hugged him tightly and began to cry. John held her and spoke softly, assuring her she was safe. "These friends of mine have helped me get you out. You won't ever have to go back. I promise!"

After a minute or two, Katrina sat up and dried her eyes with her father's handkerchief. John helped her to her feet and into the change of clothes they'd brought for her.

It was getting close to dawn, and the men were anxious to be going. A tranquilizer cartridge lasted only about twenty minutes, so the guards were likely awake again. No doubt a search party was being organized. They decided to eat quickly. Once they got going, there would be no stopping until they reached the river.

The young guard named Thomas sat up groggily. He shook his head, attempting to clear it. At the same time, his hand automatically moved toward his back. Something had bit him there and it still hurt. His heart began to pound. He would need to report this to his supervisor, and he dreaded having to admit that he'd been unable to do his duty, even for a moment. There would be hell to pay if any small thing had gone wrong while he was incapacitated. He hoped nothing had.

A groan from a few feet away startled Thomas. He froze, trying to peer through the darkness, until a faint voice called out, "Help me, I've been shot!"

Thomas moved forward slowly and almost fell over someone lying on the ground.

"Thomas, is that you?"

"Yeah, who's that? What happened?"

"Man, it's Avery. I think someone shot me in the chest."

"Are you hurt bad? Are you bleeding?" Thomas asked.

"No, I don't think so," Avery responded. "It hurts really bad."

"We got to report all this to the chief," Thomas said. "Lie right here real still. I'll go get help." Then he was off toward the main compound, trying to run.

When Thomas returned with two other guards, Avery briefed them on what had happened. As best he could remember, there was an intruder dressed in black who had shot him. Avery remembered trying to get a shot off at the intruder, but couldn't recall whether he'd been successful.

Next, the young men awoke the head of the guard force, Mr. Manny Robinson, and relayed the story.

"Do we know what this intruder was after?" Mr. Robinson questioned the group.

They all stood in silence.

"Okay. Let's alert the rest of the guards," he ordered. "Tell them to search the entire compound. If someone was here, he came for a reason. Now go!"

Meanwhile, Mr. Robinson sent one of his guards to alert the Jonestown executive team to report to the pavilion for a meeting. Priscilla Olsen was the last to arrive.

"Sorry for getting you all up," he began. "It appears that we were visited by at least one intruder. It's unlikely that the intent was robbery. My guess is some kind of an escape attempt. Anyone have any other ideas?"

When no one said anything, Mr. Robinson continued. "I've asked the guards to conduct a thorough search of the compound. I'd like you all to check with your group leaders to verify that no one is missing. Get back to me as soon as you can. I want to have a full story in the morning when I brief Father Jones. Are there any questions?"

Before the meeting ended, Rose, Katrina's dorm monitor, appeared out of breath at the door and reported that Katrina Olsen was missing. A startled cry issued from Priscilla, and the others turned to look at her. "Do you know anything about this?" Mr. Robinson asked.

She shook her head. Then her face blanched and she nodded. "It has to be my ex-husband. He's been going through the courts to take Katrina from me. But I never thought he of all people . . . There's no way he did this alone. There must be others with him."

Bringing all of his guard force together, Robinson barked, "We have to catch the intruder as quickly as possible. Just remember that he has a thirteen-year-old girl with him. We've got to find her and bring her back. I want ten of you to go immediately toward Port Kaituma. Do whatever you think is necessary. Just bring them back—now, go!"

As the group dispersed, Priscilla left the pavilion, walking past the picnic tables and into the darkness. Strange, she thought, that no one had consoled her about Katrina's disappearance. For the committee, this was just one more incident to manage. Suddenly, her body felt wracked by a wave of loneliness and despair. Her lips began to tremble. Before she could brace herself, her legs went limp and she sank down onto her knees.

"Oh, God," she murmured. "Oh, God." Crumpling over, she laid her head on her arms and began to weep. She wasn't sure if she was crying because Katrina was gone from Jonestown, or because she was still there, left behind. Somehow, in her heart, she knew she would never see her daughter again.

CHAPTER 35

October 19, 1978

Meanwhile, the members of the rescue team had finished their meal and were putting as much distance as possible between themselves and the settlement.

Before moving out, Bill radioed Roland and Celeste their location. Roland reported that he was in bad shape—his head throbbing and his leg swollen to twice its normal size—but assured them he'd be ready to go when they arrived.

Katrina seemed much stronger after eating some solid food, and she followed her father almost cheerfully as the team set off for the river. Bill realized that the girl was probably so happy to be away from Jonestown that a walk in the jungle with her dad seemed like fun.

Ski was the last to leave the rallying point. He would set his three trip flares at certain distances along the trail to warn them when someone else reached those points. When Ski set the last one, he would call Bill by radio to change places with him so that Bill could also put down his trip flares.

As they moved with urgency along the trail, Bill kept his attention focused on listening for any strange noises. All he heard for some time were the usual sounds of an early morning cacophony of jungle creatures as the sun came up and the day began to warm rapidly. Then the sounds abated, and it seemed eerily quiet.

Katrina tired rapidly due to the oppressive humidity and rough terrain. When she sank to her knees, John picked her up and carried her, and their pace slowed to a crawl.

They had been on the move for about two hours when the first trip flare ignited.

Urging them on, Ski confirmed what Bill was thinking. The Jonestown guards had been able to pick up their trail without any trouble, and the men chasing them were probably younger and more accustomed to the heat. Before long, another flare went up; soon after, a third. The Jonestown guards were literally running after them. By the time the team reached the halfway mark, their hunters were only thirty minutes behind them.

Even with their adrenaline flowing, all of the men were reaching the point of exhaustion. They had been on the move for over three hours without a break. Worse, they were becoming bogged down in the heavy, wet jungle undergrowth. In many places, it appeared to have sprung back since they'd cleared their way in.

Something had to be done to slow the advance of the Jonestown pursuers. Collecting a tear gas grenade each from Bill and John, Ski explained his plan. He would set the grenades in succession along the path, about 150 meters apart, using trip wires. His hope was that by the time the third grenade exploded, the men behind them would be too overcome and discouraged by the fumes to continue the pursuit. The least it could do was slow them down.

Ski had completed this task and returned to the group when Bill heard a thud close behind him. John Olsen had collapsed and was lying face down in the muddy swamp water.

Katrina dropped to her knees beside him, trying to turn him over. "Daddy! Daddy!"

"Damn it!" Bill cursed. Then, in a softer voice, he said, "It's all right, sweetie. Let me see if I can help your dad."

While Bill got out his canteen and salt tablets, Ski took off John's fatigue jacket and undershirt. Melting a salt tablet in some water, Bill held John's head and poured the concoction into his mouth.

As soon as the water hit his throat, John vomited. His entire body was burning with fever, and his pulse was racing. Something more had to be done.

Stripping him of his pants and boots, Ski and Bill immersed him in swamp water. It was by no means the cold water they needed, but it might be cool enough to help bring down his fever. They began to massage John's limbs. Seeing this, Katrina began to cry.

Bill tried to soothe her. "Your father has collapsed due to the heat and is just too hot inside. We have to do this to cool him off. Don't worry, he's going to—"

"Please don't let him die," Katrina begged.

"We won't," Bill promised, "we won't."

Once John began to cool off in the water, Bill was able to get some more of the canteen's contents into John's mouth. This time, it stayed down.

John's eyelids flickered and he moaned. Soon he had regained consciousness and struggled to sit up. Eager hands reached to help steady him. As soon as he could stand, he was led from the water, clad only in his shorts. There was no time to redress him. All had the feeling that their would-be captors were about to pounce on them.

Katrina was quickly at her father's side, and he bent to kiss her forehead, telling her he was fine. The words were barely out of his mouth when his knees buckled. Ski and Bill steadied him. A few moments later, he stood again and pulled on his boots, saying he was ready to go. But it soon became clear he was too weak to walk any distance.

Although John was heavier than either man, Ski and Bill agreed they would trade off carrying him in a fireman's carry. Katrina would have to walk.

They stashed his pack in the underbrush and plunged ahead. After 150 meters, Bill collapsed under the extra weight and Ski relieved him. Though exhausted, they were able to make steady progress.

Before long, they reached a marker they had placed and knew they were only two hundred meters from the river. When it was again Ski's turn to carry John, Bill paused long enough to set his last trip flare. He hoped it would signal if their pursuers were close on their heels. The guards might have been smart enough not to follow the exact trail, especially after the first gas grenade went off. They could have bypassed the others and gained on the team.

As Bill caught up with the group, Ski leaned against a tree and Bill helped him lower John to the ground. Both men were taxed. They had to come up with another way to get John to safety. Positioning themselves one on either side, they caught him under the arms, walking him over the last stretch of the jungle.

Up ahead, Celeste and Roland had already readied the Grumman Goose for takeoff. Celeste had untied the anchor from the tail and nose of the airplane and helped move Roland aboard and into the pilot's seat, fearful that he might lose consciousness.

They waited for some sign of the returning rescuers. Then, Celeste detected movement in the trees. As soon as she recognized the men, she ran forward to help them.

"Take Katrina to the plane and get in quickly!" Bill shouted, not stopping to explain. "Tell Roland to get the engines started." They had run out of time.

Celeste ushered Katrina down the hill toward the plane. By the time Bill and Ski had reached the crest that led down to the river, they could hear the plane's left engine running. At that moment, the last of the trip flares went off. The Jonestown pursuers were a mere two hundred meters behind them.

Grabbing John's arms in a tighter grip, Bill and Ski stumbled forward with him. When it seemed neither could take another step, they finally got to the small clearing near the plane.

From the crashing in the thicket behind them, Bill could tell the Jonestown guards were right on their heels. As he and Ski waded into the river toward the plane, shots rang out. With the last bit of energy they could muster, the two men hoisted John up and onto the floor of the Goose as Celeste and Katrina pulled him the rest of the way.

Next it was Bill's turn. He pulled himself up, struggling to be free of the four feet of water. Once on board, he turned to help Ski, but as Ski's head came even with the floor of the plane, another shot sounded, and Ski yelled to him, "Throw me your gas grenade!"

He didn't need to say more than this for Bill to know his intent. He was going back. He was going to try to fend off their attackers before they reached the clearing.

At that instant, time seemed to stand still. Bill saw Val's face as Val signaled him to run for the helicopter. *No*, he thought, *this is not going to happen.*

Without a word, he jumped into the water with rifle in hand and struggled toward the bank. He could hear Ski curse behind him, but when he glanced back, Ski was boarding the plane.

Up ahead, several Jonestown men had sight of the plane and were shooting at it. Fortunately they were armed primarily with shotguns, and the blasts fell short of the riverbank.

"Start the right engine," Ski yelled to Roland above the noise. "Bill went back to slow them down with the last grenade. We'll need to be ready to take off any moment. I'm going to cover him."

Ski had barely gotten back to the door of the plane and aimed his rifle when he heard the pop of the gas grenade.

More shots rang out, causing Celeste to yell out, "Can you see him anywhere?" Ski waved a negative reply. His attention was riveted to the underbrush where he had just spotted movement.

Firing continued; six, eight, ten shots, then a burst of automatic fire. When someone crashed through the tangled undergrowth into the clearing, Ski took aim. Then, with a surge of relief, he recognized Bill, bleeding heavily from the side of his face and running toward the plane.

As he reached the water, two armed Jonestown men broke through the brush and knelt to get a shot at Bill and the plane. Ski steadied himself and squeezed off a round, hitting the guard squarely in the chest. He jerked terribly and fell. The second man fired a burst of five shots at the Goose, hitting it twice. The last shot caught Ski in the leg, and with a cry, he fell backwards into the plane. Seeing this, Bill turned, steadied himself, and took three well-aimed shots at the Jonestown man, putting him down.

Not seeing any other movement, Bill discarded his rifle and swam for his life. He reached the door after what seemed like an eternity, and with Celeste's help, got his chest, then legs, inside the belly of the plane. Once inside, he bounded up and pulled the door closed, just as he felt Roland push the engines to takeoff power. As the door slammed, Bill caught a glimpse of three more security guards swarming the clearing, guns in hand.

The Grumman Goose shuddered as Roland pushed it to the limit. Bill held his breath. They had to make it. They had come too far now to lose.

Seconds ticked by as the aircraft rose inch by inch. At last, it was safely beyond reach of the still-cracking weapons, and well into the air.

Inside the plane, however, things were chaos. Ski was bleeding profusely from his leg, and Bill from his face, where a thorny vine had grabbed him and left a gash as clean as a razor slice.

Bill knelt to examine Ski, though the pitch of the plane and the blood in his eyes made it difficult. Ski's leg showed a clear entrance wound and an ugly exit wound, but the bones appeared untouched. Bill wrapped a bandage to both sides of his leg and instructed Celeste to apply pressure to stanch the blood flow.

As Bill prepared an injection of morphine, Ski reached up and placed a hand on his arm. "Thanks, sir," he said.

"Don't thank me," Bill reasoned. "You're the one who got shot."

Ski grimaced and shrugged. "Could have been worse. You probably saved us all. I couldn't be more proud of you."

After Ski was taken care of, Celeste turned her attention to Bill. She wiped his face to determine how severely he had been hurt and then applied bandages. When Ski moaned again and reached down to his leg, Bill feared a nerve or bone had been hit. Taking out another ampoule of morphine, he prepared a needle and gave Ski a second injection in his upper thigh.

Meanwhile, John was rallying and trying to calm Katrina, who was scared to death. He hugged his daughter to him and said a silent prayer of thanks that she had remained uninjured during the hail of gunfire. Ski was right. It could have been much worse.

Then Bill refocused and thought of Roland. He stood and climbed up to the cockpit.

"Boy, am I glad to see you!" Roland said, his clenched face betraying his pain. "You need to fly this thing. I can barely see straight. I have to lay down before my head explodes."

"Go ahead, Ro. I got it."

"Keep it at three thousand feet and stay on the heading that I've set," Roland said weakly as he slipped out of the pilot's seat and moved toward the back of the plane. It wasn't until Bill was seated behind the controls that he allowed himself to breathe a sigh of relief.

CHAPTER 36

October 19, 1978

From the time they had begun their escape through jungle and swamp early that morning until the plane was airborne, they had been on the move for more than nine hours, enduring extreme heat and humidity. Though they were exhausted and battered, their success made their spirits soar.

Bill noted the time was 2:20 P.M., October 19th. They were on their way back to the small island where the rescue mission began.

When they approached Bridgetown's radar control area, Bill called for Roland to again move into the pilot's seat.

"I'm not much good now, Bill," Roland shouted over the whine of the engines. "You have to put it down without me."

"Bullshit, Roland!" Bill shouted back. "Get your ass up here and tell me what I have to do. I need the approach speeds, the flap settings."

Meanwhile, Bill reduced air speed and began a descent, flying in a lazy circle to stay out of the radar's coverage area. With Celeste's help, Roland struggled to the cockpit and sat on the floor next to Bill facing the rear, his legs stretched out into the cabin of the plane. He reached for the copilot's intercom headset.

"Bill, can you hear me?" Roland called out over the intercom.

"I'm with you Roland. We're descending from 2200 feet at 180 knots, okay?"

"Reduce your speed to 170 knots and level off at 500 feet. Stop circling and get back on course. It's important that you don't exceed 170 knots, understand?"

Roland continued to guide Bill in the procedures required to land the Grumman Aircraft. Bill flew the plane down on the deck, no more than fifty feet above the water to avoid radar detection. Spotting the island, together with

Roland's guidance, Bill pulled back on the throttle, extended the flaps, and within minutes brought the plane down in a near-perfect landing.

The first priority was to care for the injured: Ski, John, and Roland. Celeste and Bill cleaned and disinfected Ski's wounds and bandaged them using the larger emergency aid kit that Roland had prepared for the plane. They got John and Katrina situated comfortably and kept John hydrated. Roland was tending to himself, drinking lots of water and lying on his back, keeping his foot raised. Celeste disinfected Bill's facial cuts and applied new bandages.

By nightfall, John was able to sit up and take part in relating the details of the rescue to Celeste. Katrina sat close by his side. John hugged his daughter frequently, reassuring her of his love.

After a few hours of restful sleep, Bill and Roland changed into more comfortable clothing and found the alcohol bottle Ski brought in his grip. The cleanup process was quick and easy. In no time, they all looked human again.

When each had become somewhat rested, they began to discuss plans for the next step. All of them, except for Celeste, needed medical attention as quickly as they could be taken to a safe place.

"What about Saint Vincent?" Bill suggested. "We're going to land there anyway."

"Good idea. Our profile will be lower there than if we tried to get help in Bridgetown or in the States. We should be able to get what we need without any problem," Roland responded.

It was decided they would leave for Saint Vincent early the next morning. Celeste finally talked Bill into lying down to rest, but sleep wouldn't come. He kept thinking about the Jonestown men they had shot during their escape— civilians who had taken Jim Jones to heart and pledged their lives to his cause. Bill only hoped that he would never again find himself holding another man's life in his hands.

When Celeste was confident that all of her patients were getting rest, she settled in next to Bill. "Are you okay?" she asked, placing her hand on the side of his face, careful not to disturb his bandage.

"I think so," Bill responded.

Looking into his eyes, Celeste said, "I know that was hard for you. But what's important is that we're all going to be just fine." Then she kissed him, for the first time in a long time, allowing her lips to linger on his.

As the kiss ended, she pulled back a few inches and whispered, "When you ran back to stop those men from shooting at us, I was terrified . . . I didn't think you'd come back. And right then I realized, I can't imagine my life without you."

As her words sank in, Bill felt the trauma of the day slip away, and his heart leapt. "Oh, sweetie," he said, "you don't know how much I've wanted to hear that."

Sitting there in Celeste's arms, Bill finally relaxed and fell asleep.

The poor doctor in the clinic on Saint Vincent didn't know what to think. He had seen injured and sick tourists before, but this group took the cake. One was suffering from heat exhaustion, one looked as if he had been involved in jungle warfare, and the other was clearly suffering from a banana spider bite.

The story they told of how Ski had come by his wounds was a stretch. Even though the doctor was quite sure it didn't really happen that way, he wasn't about to dig into something that was none of his business. Foreigners always had what they thought were good reasons for what they did, and he was happy to have their business, always paid for in cash and in U.S. dollars.

Ski sheepishly admitted that he had been shooting a pistol while camping on a deserted island, and that the bullet had ricocheted off a rock and struck him in the leg. Silently, without question, the doctor closed the penetration points, dressed the wound, and gave him a tetanus shot. The good news was that the X-rays showed that Ski would heal without a problem.

The doctor examined Roland and assured him that he was over the worst of the spider venom symptoms, though the bite itself would take time to heal. Then he turned to Bill and John. Bill only needed five stitches to close the largest of the thorn gashes on the side of his face. John was instructed to rest, drink plenty of fluids, and take vitamins. The visit cost forty dollars total for the doctor's services.

As planned, Roland followed the West Indies–Bahamas route on their homeward flight. At last, on October 22nd, early in the afternoon, he landed the Grumman Goose at the International Airport in Fort Lauderdale. The operation was a success.

Ski would spend the next five days with Roland and Jenny, recovering.

John insisted on going to a hotel where he and Katrina could talk, rest, and be together. That evening, Bill and Celeste decided to drive to Miami for a special night for two.

There was no report made to the consulate of Katrina's disappearance, nor was there any report of an engagement between Jonestown guards and "unknown intruders" near the Kaituma River. Jim Jones, like so many other tyrants before him, accepted his losses in stride without letting his annoyance be known to the outside world. Bill felt relieved that Jones was sticking to his own rules, his own laws, rather than those of civilized society.

John expected to find waiting for him some kind of legal notice from Priscilla concerning Katrina. There was nothing, not even a letter. He concluded that Priscilla had finally realized that Katrina was better off with him, and was filled with relief and gratitude for this. Priscilla would now have to come to California to fight for the custody of their daughter, and due to the circumstances of the case, John was confident he would win a custody suit easily. Still, he spent the next month worrying and waiting with dread for the call that never came.

Then, almost exactly a month from the day of Katrina's return, John's fears were laid to rest. He awoke the morning of November 24, 1978, made himself coffee, put two slices of bread in the toaster for himself and Katrina, and turned on the news.

His coffee grew cold in his hand as he stared at the screen. How long he watched those horrifying images play in a loop, he couldn't be sure. Every time an aerial photograph of the carnage was shown, he couldn't help but search for a familiar head of dark hair.

Then Katrina came out of her bedroom, and John clicked the television off.

"What's for breakfast?" Katrina asked.

John Olsen didn't answer. He just stood up, pulled his daughter into his arms, and wept.

Chapter 37

Late November 1992

On the Saturday after Thanksgiving, Katrina sat down with her husband to begin the chore of writing Christmas cards.

Her father had joined them at their Plano, Texas, home for the weekend and was currently in the living room, holding his sleeping three-month-old granddaughter. John always joined his daughter for holidays and always came alone, having never remarried.

Katrina met her husband at the University of California, Los Angeles, where they had both been in the doctoral program in psychology. After graduation, she and her husband resettled to Dallas, Texas, as staff psychologists at a university hospital. Katrina, keeping her maiden name, specialized in child psychology and worked with children with developmental disabilities.

Whenever people asked her why she had chosen psychology as her field, Katrina would always laugh and say it was inevitable, and leave it at that. It was too difficult to explain that studying psychology had been the only way for her to explain the loss of her mother, the insidious power of Jim Jones, and the memories and dreams that continued to haunt her well into adulthood.

Priscilla Olsen lost her life at Jonestown, a victim of the machinations of Jim Jones during the merciless murder and coerced suicide of 913 men, women, and children—all members of the Peoples Temple. Following her death, John, in concert with Priscilla's parents, claimed her body and brought her back to Santa Monica for burial. They were some of the lucky relatives—under the hot jungle sun, many of the bodies decomposed so quickly that they were unrecognizable by the time they were removed. Katrina and her father were grateful to have a gravesite to visit, and they did so every year on Priscilla's birthday.

Moving through her Christmas list, Katrina came to Mr. and Mrs. Roland DaLuz. Her father had maintained contact with Roland and his wife, Jenny, throughout the years. They had stayed in Florida and had two children, Tina and Roland, Jr., both teens now. Katrina knew from their last Christmas card that Roland was still flying to the Bahamas for an air charter service.

Next was Mr. George Kladensky of Fayetteville, North Carolina. Katrina knew from her father that Ski Kladensky had recovered fully from the wound he sustained during the rescue. In 1983, he lost his devoted wife, Yoshiko, to liver cancer. In his last Christmas card, Ski had written that his eldest son had taken over the farming business and that he enjoyed looking after his four grandchildren.

Mr. and Mrs. William Hausman. Katrina remembered Celeste best from the rescue, as she hadn't had her face painted. Her father received a wedding invitation from them in 1979, when Bill had finished his tour in Guyana. They had gotten married in Lisbon, Portugal, Katrina remembered, by a priest from Guyana who celebrated a nuptial mass for them. Celeste had sent a beautiful photo of their three children with their 1991 Christmas card. She had mentioned that they were enjoying their tour in Mexico City and that she had gone back to work as a contract language instructor in Portuguese, Spanish, and French. She and Bill remained happily married.

Putting pen to each card, Katrina wrote from her heart:

> *Never will I forget you and what you did for me.*
> *You are very special, my dear friend, and I am eternally*
> *grateful. Have a Merry Christmas with your family and a*
> *New Year filled with all the happiness in our world.*
>
> *With admiration and respect, always yours,*
>
> *Katrina*

EPILOGUE

Massacre at Jonestown

November 1978

B efore beginning the account of the Jonestown massacre as it occurred on
November 18, 1978, in Guyana, it's appropriate for me as the author to
provide some insight into the story you have just read.

First of all, the characters portrayed in this book are based upon actual
people for the most part; that includes the Olsen family, though names
have been changed and artistic liberties have been taken in portraying their
personalities and experiences. Jim Jones, his wife Marceline, and his aide
Sharon Amos are real historical figures who died during the Jonestown
massacre. I have attempted to depict these individuals as accurately as possible,
drawing from public records and real-life testimonies of those who knew them;
however, scenes and conversations involving them have been fictionalized for
the sake of the narrative.

During the summer and fall of 1978, the concerned relatives of some
members of the Peoples Temple in Jonestown persisted in their lobbying
efforts with law enforcement authorities in California as well as with the U.S.
federal government. In one of these initiatives, the father of Robert Houston
made contact with Democratic Congressman Leo Joseph Ryan of California.

Robert Houston, a former member of the Peoples Temple, died under
unusual circumstances while working for the Southern Pacific Railroad.
Robert's father was convinced that his son was a victim of the Peoples
Temple and enlisted Congressman Ryan's help to investigate Jim Jones and
the settlement in Jonestown to prevent anyone else from being victimized.
Congressman Ryan and the elder Houston had been close friends for years,

ever since Leo Ryan had been a high school English teacher, and had Robert Houston as one of his students.

Given his nature to fight for unheralded causes, among them Watts, Folsom Prison, and the treatment and preservation of baby harp seals and whales, Congressman Ryan could not resist this personal request from an old friend. The congressman and his staff began to focus in earnest on Jim Jones and the Peoples Temple, especially in Jonestown.

By early November 1978, Ryan had made plans to accompany a small group of the concerned relatives to Guyana. They would visit the Jonestown settlement and talk directly with Jim Jones about the controversy surrounding his church. In preparation for the visit to Guyana, Congressman Ryan and his staff met with two former members of the Peoples Temple settlement in Jonestown. This meeting took place in Washington, D.C., on November 13th.

Both of the Jonestown defectors gave descriptions of Jim Jones' fanatical nature and the torturous practices common in Jonestown. They talked about Jones' philosophy and described the ritual of being forced to practice for an eventual revolutionary suicide, an event Jones referred to as "White Night." Congressman Ryan was also told of the members' fear and depression, as well as the distrust common among them, perpetrated by lies and deceit set up by Jones and his loyal top lieutenants. Both of the defectors agreed that if Congressman Ryan and his group were allowed into Jonestown, Jones would have staged everything, even the very words spoken to them.

After listening intently to the views and experiences related by the defectors, Leo Ryan made the decision to go ahead with the trip. He had to see for himself in order to make a judgment as to whether these allegations were true or not.

The news media quickly picked up on the opportunity for a story, due to Congressman Ryan's reputation for sticking his nose into places that were not officially his concern. They assigned cameramen and reporters to accompany the congressman to Guyana. His aides, in their efforts to cover all possible outcomes, judged that the presence of reporters and TV cameras would provide extra insurance against any potential violence.

Even before the trip, Congressman Ryan himself appeared to have sensed danger in visiting Jonestown. According to one report, on the evening before leaving for Jonestown, Leo Ryan told an associate that "one must put aside fear and do what he thinks is right." Without further consternation, Congressman

Ryan, his staff aides, seven newsmen, and ten of the concerned relatives arrived in Georgetown, Guyana, on November 15, 1978.

The party, totaling more than twenty, was allowed to visit Jonestown on two consecutive days. They flew first to Port Kaituma in a chartered Guyana Airways Twin Otter airplane, landing on the grass airstrip there, and then were transported on a flatbed truck through the jungle to the Jonestown settlement. After a gracious welcome and what appeared to be productive talks with Jones, there was trouble late in the day. While at the Jonestown compound, Congressman Ryan was assaulted by a man who held a knife to his throat, threatening his life and inflicting a minor cut. Two Jonestown men overpowered the assailant. Following this attack, Congressman Ryan became nervous and anxious to leave. Jones appeared concerned for the congressman's safety but reassured him that everything was all right.

By the second day of the visit, some of the congressman's party had begun to question whether Jones would allow them to leave. To their surprise, not only were they allowed to depart, but in addition, Jones granted permission for about ten members of the settlement to leave Jonestown with them.

At that juncture, a newsman received a note, passed to him discreetly by one of the Jonestown residents, asking for help. The newsman confronted Jones with the note during an interview to expose deep discontent in the settlement and to record Jones' reaction on camera. While somewhat embarrassed, Jones refused to budge or to engage the issue. He nonetheless appeared troubled by the allegations and responded simply by saying, "people lie."

Shortly before their transport vehicle, a large truck, pulled out of Jonestown at about 4:00 P.M. on that Saturday afternoon, November 18th, one other man, Larry Layton, joined the group, claiming he also wanted out, and boarded the truck. Several of the settlement members now in Ryan's group began murmuring, saying that Layton was there to cause trouble. They cautioned the congressman that he had always been close to Jim Jones. Despite the accusations, Larry Layton stayed on the truck with Congressman Ryan and his entourage.

When they arrived at the Port Kaituma airstrip, the two chartered planes that were to pick them up and return them to Georgetown had not yet arrived. The group waited, standing on the grass airstrip as dusk approached. They felt the tension grow but nonetheless were still hoping to fly out before the dark of night grounded them. With much relief, they heard the planes and watched as the De Havilland DHC-6 Twin Otter and a Cessna 206, chartered in Georgetown, landed and taxied over to them.

The group began gathering together their grip and preparing to board as soon as the Twin Otter's doors opened. Congressman Ryan, having been convinced by departing Jonestown residents to be wary of Larry Layton, asked that everyone boarding the Twin Otter be searched beforehand.

Learning he was going to be searched, Layton left the group briefly and returned to board the Cessna 206 without being searched. He settled into the far left rear seat of the six-seat plane. Once the plane began to taxi for takeoff, Layton allegedly pulled out a revolver and shot the woman in front of him twice in the back. Her name was Monica Bagby. He then turned his attention to the man sitting next to her, put the revolver squarely in the man's face, and pulled the trigger. The revolver's cartridge misfired. The two men seated closest to Larry Layton immediately disarmed and subdued him.

All at once, the sounds of a tractor could be heard approaching the airstrip from the jungle road. It came into view pulling a flatbed trailer loaded with armed men. When they were close enough, the tractor slowed and several men jumped down from the flatbed trailer. They then raised their weapons and took aim at the group of people lined up to board the Twin Otter. In the initial volley of gunfire, one man was grazed and the Twin Otter's left tire was shot out. Their principal targets seemed to be Congressman Ryan himself and the newsmen. People scattered in terror and ran for cover. Congressman Ryan dove behind the Twin Otter's right side landing gear, away from the hail of bullets.

As the gunfire continued, the congressman was mortally wounded. When the assassins found Congressman Ryan lying on the ground, they continued their assault on him to ensure that he was dead. Four others—three American newsmen traveling with Congressman Ryan and one of the young women from Jonestown—were also killed. In addition, there were eleven members of the group wounded in the attack. Some members of the group escaped unscathed into the jungle brush that surrounded the airstrip.

Following the flurry of gunshots and the attack that was concentrated around the congressman and his entourage, the pilots of the Twin Otter sought refuge with the Cessna 206. They booted Layton out of the plane and immediately took off for Georgetown. Reaching altitude, Mr. Tommy Fernandes, the pilot of the Cessna 206, established radio contact with Timehri International Airport and passed along sketchy details of the attack. In turn, the air controller at Timehri made certain that the prime minister was informed.

While not certain, it appears clear that Jim Jones directed one of his most trusted followers, Larry Layton, the gunman aboard the Cessna 206, to join the group of Peoples Temple members leaving Jonestown with the congressman's party. Jones' plan had been for him to board the Twin Otter with the congressman, wait until the plane was well on its way to Georgetown, kill the pilots, and then cause the aircraft to crash over the Guyana jungle. That plan was foiled because so many of the people leaving Jonestown doubted Layton's sincerity.

The improvised backup plan was simple. Those Jonestown loyalists who had weapons would wait until they heard shots fired from the Cessna 206, and then they would attack the group and seek out and kill Congressman Ryan and the newsmen.

Many theorized that had the original plan been carried out, with the congressman and his party eliminated in a plane crash and the truth about Jonestown further suppressed, Jim Jones would not have leapt to his next course of action. He might have delayed his order for the mass execution of his followers, perhaps indefinitely. But in his fear over retribution for the airstrip shootings, he decided to follow through with the threat he had so often talked about and rehearsed. His followers would be compelled to leave the world with him in an act he referred to as "revolutionary suicide." He had been stockpiling cyanide for months, and now he ordered that this poison be mixed in vats with a powdered beverage concentrate called Flavor-Aid.

What we know of the next few hours has been culled from the Jonestown "death tapes"—recordings Jim Jones made of his final sermon and the subsequent poisonings. He ordered the children to be brought first. The Jonestown guards with weapons in hand took many of the children forcefully from the arms of their frightened and resisting parents and brought them to the pavilion. There, syringes were used to inject the cyanide into their mouths. Forced to watch their children being murdered, most of the Jonestown residents fell into deep despair and hopelessness. Their will to resist the inevitable any further had been snuffed out.

Over the preceding months, Jones had taken measures to keep his followers weakened psychologically. He and selected key lieutenants were responsible for giving depressant drugs to the entire community, salted into their daily meals, for at least two months prior to this massacre. As a result, the settlement members' senses were dulled, and they became much easier to manipulate and control. The adults were collected by the guards, corralled, and led one by one to the pavilion. If they refused to drink, they were given injections of the deadly poison. Several adults were shot and killed when they resisted.

As the murderous ritual progressed, Jim Jones stood on his four-foot high podium, urging his people not to resist, not to despair. Jones' wife and at least one of his adopted children were among those who died. This was the *white night* that Jones had talked about. Even a pet monkey that rode on one of the settlement's vehicles was found dead.

There are conflicting views about the death of Jones himself. He was found lying on his back on the wooden walkway in front of the podium where he was giving his final sermon, dead of a gunshot wound to the head. The bullet entered the back of his head just behind his right ear. The impact was so severe that he flipped off the four-foot high podium, over a railing, and landed where he was found.

Some conclude that he committed suicide; however, the head wound and other evidence indicate that someone else killed him. The pistol that killed Jones was later found inside a building some twenty-five meters from the scene of his death.

It is suspected that Jones was murdered by one of the security guards who, with other survivors, stole a portion of the cash Jones had on hand at Jonestown (an amount estimated at close to two million dollars) and fled. One of the Jonestown boats that had been moored at Port Kaituma on the Kaituma River, with access to the Caribbean Sea, was unaccounted for in the aftermath of the Jonestown massacre. It was later found scuttled off the coast of Trinidad and Tobago.

The bizarre ending to the Jonestown settlement, the attack on Congressman Ryan, and the murder of 918 people total, present quite a different scene from the one painted by Jones of the paradise people could expect when they gave up everything and followed him to Guyana to become members of his special and select family. They were led to believe they could live in an agrarian paradise where they could eat fruit directly from the trees, have their own homes, and enjoy excellent medical treatment, among other wonderful advancements.

It did not take long for those who went to Jonestown to realize that reality was far from what they had been promised. By then, they had little choice but to endure the day-to-day routines of life at Jonestown, a life that many compare to the conditions of the eighteenth-century sugar plantations that ran on blood, sweat, and tears. Most residents lost weight and experienced a general deterioration of health. In such a weakened state, they were easily manipulated, drugged, and brainwashed into becoming puppet-like followers of Jim Jones, intimidated to the point that they were afraid to speak out against the injustices they suffered and the loss of freedom that had befallen them.

Afterword

The Author's Own Experience of the Jonestown Massacre

During the summer of 1976, I arrived in Georgetown, Guyana, on my second tour as a Foreign Service officer. I was to be one of the vice-consuls at the American embassy. My first tour, in Vietnam, had ended unexpectedly just fifteen months prior on April 30, 1975, when the North Vietnamese Army invaded South Vietnam and captured Saigon. During my third year in Guyana, I witnessed firsthand events surrounding the November 18, 1978, massacre at Jonestown. This book is intended to put a human face on those events and to expose the stark realities of the circumstances that drove Jim Jones and Jonestown into infamy.

On November 18, 1978, at about 6:15 P.M., Ambassador Burke asked Mr. James Adkins, the senior political officer in the embassy, who lived in a house adjacent to the ambassador's, to take him to Prime Minister Burnham's residence. The ambassador explained that his car was at the airport awaiting the return of Congressman Ryan from Jonestown. At the time, the ambassador had a premonition, or perhaps some sketchy information, that something had gone wrong with the congressman's visit and the prime minister was waiting to brief him.

After about an hour, the ambassador emerged grim-faced. He said there had been a shooting at the airstrip at Port Kaituma and that the congressman and Mr. Richard "Dick" Dwyer, the Deputy Chief of Mission who had escorted Congressman Ryan on the visit, were possibly dead. He added that at this juncture, nothing was for certain. What little information the prime minister had came from pilots who were en route from Port Kaituma back to Georgetown.

Concurrently, I had been working in the small garden planted behind my house. I was cooling off on the verandah when the phone rang at about 6:20 P.M.

The call was from the air traffic controller at Timehri International Airport. The controller knew me as a pilot who was an official at the American embassy and felt I should know about the radio conversation he had just had with Tommy Fernandes, a charter pilot who worked for the same company that I flew for part-time. He explained that Fernandes was the pilot of the Cessna 206 chartered by the embassy on behalf of Congressman Ryan for a November 18th flight from Port Kaituma to Georgetown. He said that Fernandes had taken off for Port Kaituma earlier in the afternoon to pick up some Jonestown residents and was planning to make it back to Georgetown before nightfall. I learned subsequently that these Jonestown residents were in fact members of Congressman Ryan's enlarged entourage, who couldn't all fit onto the Twin Otter chartered from Guyana Airways Corporation.

The controller related the following details to me about his conversation with Fernandes. He said that Fernandes had contacted the tower to report that he had witnessed a murderous attack at the Port Kaituma airstrip, that some Jonestown people had killed Congressman Ryan, and that many other people were killed or wounded. Fernandes judged that there were as many as twenty casualties, including a badly shot woman he was bringing with him in his Cessna, who had lost a lot of blood and required emergency care upon arrival at Timehri Airport to save her life. Fernandes further reported that the chartered Twin Otter had been disabled on the airstrip by gunfire, that the pilots from that aircraft linked up with him in the aftermath of the brutal attack, and that they were safe and aboard his plane, returning to Georgetown.

Concerned by the controller's information, I asked him to call immediately if he learned anything further. I gave the controller the telephone number at the consul's home and told him I would be there. The consul, Mr. Douglas Ellis, lived within a short walk of my residence. Knowing I would need my car, I immediately drove over to Mr. Ellis' house to brief him on this startling information.

Mr. Ellis had been appointed the "control officer" for Congressman Ryan's visit. His duties included being in touch with the Peoples Temple office in Georgetown to coordinate travel plans, and to make other arrangements as appropriate on behalf of the congressman and his group. When I informed Mr. Ellis of the details of the telephone call from the controller, he immediately placed a call to Ambassador Burke at his residence, but was unable to reach him.

"We can't sit on this waiting for official confirmation!" Mr. Ellis exclaimed, shifting his tobacco pipe nervously in his hand. "Don't you agree we should act now, just in case there's something to this?"

"Absolutely!" I responded, agreeing that we should alert the senior staff and the ambassador's secretary, asking them all to come immediately to the embassy.

Mr. Ellis began dialing, and soon plans had been made for a meeting at the embassy. Meanwhile, he and I were trying to learn more about what exactly had taken place at Port Kaituma. Upon arrival at the embassy, we briefed the senior staff on what little we knew. Everyone then anxiously awaited the arrival of Ambassador Burke. By then, we had determined that the ambassador had been called to Prime Minister Burnham's residence on urgent business and that Mr. Adkins was accompanying him.

When Ambassador Burke emerged from his second meeting with Prime Minister Burnham in less than an hour, he was ashen-faced and subdued. He and the prime minister had spoken personally with the pilots who had escaped Port Kaituma in the Cessna aircraft. According to Ambassador Burke, the pilots said that they had witnessed an attack at the Port Kaituma airstrip that may have claimed the lives of Congressman Ryan, Dick Dwyer, and others. The pilots said that a Jonestown defector, later identified as Larry Layton, had opened fire inside the Cessna as it was taxiing for takeoff and seriously wounded one woman also on the plane.

While helpful, the pilots' account was inexact and incomplete. Principally, they were not certain of the status of the congressman's entourage.

Upon returning to the embassy, Ambassador Burke sent Mr. Adkins to represent him on the U.S./Guyana Working Group that he and Prime Minister Burnham had just established to attempt to determine the magnitude of the tragedy. He was pleased that all of his staff was already there and immediately directed the response to this crisis. With an expressionless face, he called everyone into the conference room. The ambassador then began his brief. As we listened, the ambassador dictated a FLASH-precedence telegram to Washington. During the briefing, he said that Prime Minister Burnham had provided all of the details that were available up to that moment on the status of Congressman Ryan and his visit to Jonestown. The ambassador said that the prime minister trusted the information provided by the pilots who had witnessed the attack. It appeared that, indeed, Congressman Ryan had been killed. The prime minister was less sure of other details, referring to them as sketchy. His initial assessment of the situation was that the Jonestown group in fact had begun an armed revolution with the assassination of Congressman Ryan. To put down this revolt, and to re-establish law and order, Prime Minister Burnham called upon his military to seize control of Port Kaituma and then to move into Jonestown.

The ambassador said that a company of Guyana's elite Pirai Battalion, commanded by Major Randolph Johnson, was alerted to deploy by air into Matthews Ridge on the night of November 18th, under orders from Brigadier General Norman McLean, commander of the Guyana Defense Force (GDF). Brigadier McLean authorized an American embassy official to accompany Major Johnson in this military action due to heightened U.S. government interests, especially in view of Congressman Ryan's presence in Guyana. The ambassador briefed the staff that he had already dispatched Mr. Leonard Barrett, one of the embassy's seasoned political officers, on his way to link up with Major Johnson.

By 10:00 P.M., Mr. Adkins had reported to the office of the Chief of the Guyana National Police to work side by side with GDF Commander McLean, Special Branch Chief James Mentore, and Assistant Crime Commissioner Skip Roberts, among others, on the joint working group. At midnight, a call came in from Matthews Ridge, the site of an old manganese mine with an improved airstrip, located about six kilometers from Jonestown in the opposite direction from Port Kaituma. The police chief took the call but could not understand what the caller was trying to say. The caller was using a radiotelephone at the old mine, and atmospheric conditions were interfering with the signal. Frustrated, he asked Mr. Adkins to listen to the caller.

The caller continued to cut out for some five minutes or so before the line cleared up and his voice came through clear as a bell. The caller identified himself as "Rhodes from Detroit." He was clearheaded and precise in his message. Rhodes said that a suicide ceremony was taking place at Jonestown and that everyone was going to die. He said that he and six others had been waiting their turn with everyone else, when a guard from the security element pulled them out of line and gave them a task to perform, with instructions to get back in line once the task was completed. Rhodes said that as soon as he and the other six were out of the guard's sight, they ran for their lives and headed for Matthews Ridge. Rhodes estimated that as many as 450 people had died thus far and the remaining members would soon follow, if they had not already.

After briefing the members of the joint task force, Mr. Adkins called the ambassador and passed on Rhodes' information as well.

Earlier, at about 7:45 P.M., Major Gregory Gaskins, commander of the military garrison at Matthews Ridge, also received orders from Brigadier McLean to move to Port Kaituma to secure the airstrip. His troops were mobilized and moved by a seconded train to within three kilometers of Port Kaituma. When they arrived just after midnight, they entered unopposed to find five dead and eleven wounded members of Congressman Ryan's group.

Major Gaskins confirmed that Congressman Leo Ryan had been shot to death, several of his wounds being from a shotgun fired at point-blank range into his head and face as he lay on the ground close to the crippled Twin Otter aircraft. The congressman's senior aide, Ms. Jackie Speier, had been seriously wounded in the arm, and the embassy's escort officer, Mr. Richard Dwyer, the deputy chief of mission, had also been wounded.

Upon reaching the Port Kaituma airstrip, Major Gaskins also found present two Guyanese policemen from Port Kaituma as well as three Guyanese Defense Force personnel who had been guarding a crippled twin engine Islander aircraft at the airstrip at the time of the attack. The wounded had been able to take shelter under the wing of the Islander, inside a makeshift tent being used by the soldiers.

Notably, neither the soldiers nor the Guyanese policemen did anything during the attack on Congressman Ryan and his entourage. The soldiers, about 250 meters from the scene of the attack, maintained regular radio contact with Camp Ayangana. Incredibly, when the action began, they did not initiate any communication with their headquarters about what was happening before their eyes. The Guyanese had apparently been intimidated by the Peoples Temple attack, and fearing for their own lives, did nothing to intervene or to report what had happened.

Major Johnson and his troops flew into Matthews Ridge late on November 18th. Upon arrival, Major Johnson and Mr. Barrett encountered the unexpected. About ten deserters from the Jonestown settlement had made it to Matthews Ridge earlier in the day. They told the major that they had left Jonestown on Friday night after a knife-wielding member of the sect had cut Congressman Ryan on the neck. These people had bolted because they believed there would be a confrontation between Jones and the congressman, and that a *white night* would be called. They explained this meant Jones' much-rehearsed revolutionary suicide.

At first light on the morning of November 19th, Major Johnson moved his command element and light support weapons to Port Kaituma in two helicopters. The remaining troops were ferried in on defense force Islander aircraft. One of the major's first duties at the airstrip was to take charge of the evacuation of the wounded.

As the day wore on, about eight members of Congressman Ryan's group who had escaped into the jungle during the attack began coming in, seeking refuge with the Guyana authorities. They were questioned to obtain as much additional detail as possible concerning the attack and Jonestown, in order to bolster plans to move in and occupy the settlement.

Mr. Dwyer, Mr. Barrett, and Ms. Speier accompanied the body of Congressman Ryan on the flight back to Georgetown. Mr. Dwyer was the last member of the congressman's group to be evacuated from Port Kaituma. He had worked tirelessly to evacuate the wounded, in spite of being wounded himself.

By sunset on November 19th, Major Johnson had established an assault line close to Jonestown, ready to go into the settlement and do whatever was required to take control. When they moved on their target, to their surprise, they did not encounter any resistance. Instead, they discovered the grisly scene of the massacre of the people who lived there. They also found two of Jones' lawyers, alive and locked up in a holding cell. After one full day exposed to the tropical sun, rain, and humidity, the bodies of the Jonestown residents were already beginning to swell, the first stage of decomposition.

The Guyanese soldiers established a cordon around the settlement to keep out curiosity seekers from Port Kaituma. They found that some looting had already taken place. Major Johnson estimated that there were at least four hundred dead at the scene.

At the same time that these events were unfolding at Port Kaituma and in Jonestown, the American embassy staff was hard at work responding to the events that had occurred. I was one of the few officers at post who had a military background. As such, Ambassador Burke assigned me the responsibility of coordinating and controlling the U.S. military response to the crisis. Utmost on his mind was the evacuation of the wounded from Port Kaituma to the United States.

Early in the evening on November 18th, after the ambassador's briefing, I wrote a telegram to the secretary of defense requesting a military C-141 Starlifter hospital aircraft with a full complement of nurses and doctors to be in Georgetown no later than 10:00 A.M. on November 19th. I suggested in the telegram that if there was a military clash at Jonestown, there would be more casualties and a hospital aircraft would be required every four to six hours on a continuing basis to evacuate the wounded, until a field hospital could be established.

The night of November 18th was a constant flurry of activity. Early the next morning, having not slept, I went to Timehri International to await the arrival of the C-141 hospital aircraft, which came in exactly on time. At 4:45 P.M., the first defense force Islander aircraft landed, carrying the most seriously wounded Americans from the attack at Port Kaituma. It had been a long ordeal for the wounded.

By nightfall on November 19th, all of the wounded had been loaded onto the C-141, and it immediately took off for Roosevelt Roads, Puerto Rico. Soon after the C-141 had departed, the embassy received official word from the Guyanese reporting that Major Johnson had discovered the massacre at Jonestown, with an estimated four hundred dead.

With this information, Ambassador Burke sought out Prime Minister Burnham to begin negotiating a decision as to how the aftermath of these events would be handled. Initially, Prime Minister Burnham was in favor of burying the dead at Jonestown in a mass grave. After more thought, however, he ruled against this, not wanting to establish an "American memorial" on Guyanese soil.

Concurrently, the ambassador sent Mr. Adkins to Jonestown to determine if a mass burial was possible. Approaching the Jonestown site, the helicopter pilot circled the scene of the massacre several times before landing. The incredible stench of decaying bodies reached the helicopter flying 1,000 feet overhead. On the ground, the odor of death was overwhelming. By the time Mr. Adkins arrived at Jonestown, the bodies were swollen with gas and their faces bloated beyond recognition. Curiously, there was not a single child in sight. The embassy knew that there were as many as 250 children at Jonestown, and this gave rise to the hope that responsible adults had taken the children off into the jungle to save their lives.

This was a vain hope, however. When the adult corpses were moved, it was discovered that there were layers of bodies, one on top of another, with the children on the bottom, totally obscured. Mr. Adkins concluded that, given the large number and poor condition of the corpses, mass burial at Jonestown was preferable to any other option.

It was clear to Ambassador Burke that Prime Minister Burnham was against the idea of a burial *en masse* of Americans at Jonestown. While tactfully reminding the prime minister of the clear responsibility of the Guyanese government to dispose of the dead at Jonestown, Ambassador Burke suggested that the U.S. government would likely help the Guyanese government in the discharge of its duties, if it was necessary. Once Burnham recognized that his government could not handle the situation due to its limited resources, Ambassador Burke reconfirmed his offer of U.S. government assistance, and Burnham accepted.

Within hours of that decision, a unit of morticians from Dover, Delaware, was dispatched directly to Guyana to evacuate the dead at Jonestown. Other military units were ordered to action under an operations order drafted by the Southern Command in Panama. When military aircraft, CH-53 helicopters, and personnel began arriving, Ambassador Burke again turned to me to continue the role as the embassy's coordinator for this U.S. military involvement.

Initially, my major task was to mesh the Guyanese support structure with the needs of the various U.S. military units that were arriving. These included everything from housing and water requirements to fuel for aircraft involved in the evacuation of the bodies, to arranging joint military police patrols around the airport, and so forth.

The State Department sent the deputy chief of mission from Panama City to Georgetown to stand in for Dick Dwyer. He was one of the first U.S. officials to visit the scene at Jonestown. Additionally, Colonel William Gordon, chief of operations at the Southern Command in Panama, arrived with the first wave of military personnel to take charge of the body retrieval and evacuation operations. Colonel Gordon was the senior U.S. military officer on the scene.

Identification of the corpses proved problematic, even though concrete efforts were made early to tag them. Guyanese Crime Commissioner Skip Roberts was one of the first police officials on the scene at Jonestown. Roberts asked those Jonestown defectors who were still around after the shootings to identify as many of the bodies as they could. They tied name tags on the toes of the majority of the victims. In spite of their best efforts, however, a torrential rain smudged the ink to the point that the names were no longer legible.

At the first news conference held in Georgetown concerning Congressman Ryan's murder and the loss of American lives at Jonestown, the embassy spokesman announced that a total of 405 persons had been found dead. The odd number seemed to imply to the press that a count had been made. In actuality, the figure was the sum of five killed at Port Kaituma, including Congressman Ryan, and the estimated four hundred dead as reported by the Guyanese military. As the number of dead rose to a final tally of 918 dead, the embassy was haunted by its original announcement. The press believed that the embassy had deliberately misled them, even charging the embassy with an attempt to cover up the real facts.

While controversy and confusion swirled about this shocking chain of events, the embassy staff and the U.S. military units deployed to Guyana went about their duties as competent professionals. With the authorization of the Guyanese, on November 20th, I personally flew an army pathologist to Port Kaituma and escorted him into Jonestown. The pathologist performed autopsies on seven randomly selected corpses. The results indicated that the members of the Peoples Temple had been given tranquilizing drugs, some over a long period of time. Judging from the information gleaned from the autopsies, the pathologist declared that the majority of the adults at Jonestown were not fully aware of what was happening to them at the time of this so-called mass suicide.

There was only one Guyanese citizen murdered at Jonestown, one of the 918 killed. His name was Jimmy Gill, a twenty-five-year-old man who had joined the Peoples Temple months earlier and lived at Jonestown.

I wasn't able to get away from the center of activity at Timehri Airport until the night of November 21st. Gratefully returning home for a shower and five hours' sleep, I disrobed in the laundry room beneath my house and put all of my clothes into the washing machine—the stench had permeated everything. It had been a long four days, but the job I had been assigned at the airport was done. I continued in my role as the embassy's coordinator of the body retrieval operation until the evacuation of the Jonestown dead was completed, ten days after it began.

The identification of the corpses removed from Jonestown was a tedious process. Due to the rapid decomposition of the bodies, there were only two ways to establish positive identification: through fingerprints and dental records. Luckily, and unbeknownst to Prime Minister Burnham, the Guyana Special Branch of the National Police had fingerprinted between six hundred and seven hundred of the Jonestown adults as they passed through Timehri Airport upon arrival in Guyana on their way to Jonestown.

Upon learning of the existence of the fingerprint records, Mr. Adkins asked for and received photocopies of the fingerprint cards in order to identify the victims. With the full cooperation of the Police Special Branch, an FBI team led by Special Agent Robert Oglesby came to Georgetown to do the photographic work and to investigate Congressman Ryan's assassination, as well as the circumstances surrounding the Jonestown massacre.

Using these fingerprint cards and dental records provided by the victims' families, the army morticians eventually identified over six hundred bodies for next of kin to claim. The U.S. government made a concerted effort to contact the next of kin of all identified victims by publishing the names of the victims in the California newspapers and establishing a hot line for inquiries. After waiting six months for the families to come forward to claim their deceased relatives, all of the still-unidentified bodies from Jonestown—mostly children—as well as all of the identified but unclaimed bodies, were respectfully buried at sea.

In some U.S. factions, the sheer horror of the massacre inspired a need to assign blame to living parties. How could this plot have been carried out? Why had the warning signs, so clear in retrospect, gone unheeded? Why had no one intervened to stop Jim Jones from controlling and executing his followers? Certain U.S. congressmen attempted to link the Central Intelligence Agency to this tragedy, though not a single piece of paper was ever uncovered that hinted of a CIA interest in Jonestown or Jim Jones.

Failing in this attempt, said congressmen shifted the blame to several State Department officers, whose only crime was being caught in the middle of a disaster that was looking for a time and place to happen. In the process, these officers' careers were ruined. From my experience there, I can attest with certainty that there was nothing those officers could have done to avert the tragedy. If anything, the State Department was bound by Congress's passage of the Hughes-Ryan Act, coauthored by Congressman Ryan himself. Under the Hughes-Ryan Act, the U.S. government may not monitor or investigate any entity that involves an American citizen unless it is a suspected terrorist or drug trafficking activity. Furthermore, the decision to make Congressman Ryan's visit a media event could not have been more ill-advised considering Jones' reclusive paranoia and the rumors of his instability that led to the investigation. Interestingly, no blame was ever attached to Congress or the media.

In April 1979, the American embassy in Georgetown received a Superior Honor Award from the Bureau of Inter-American Affairs, Department of State. The citation read:

"In recognition of the truly outstanding performance of the Embassy of the United States of America at Georgetown, Guyana, during the period November

18 through December 15, 1978, in dealing with the tragic assassination of Congressman Leo J. Ryan, as well as four other American citizen members of his party, and the related mass murders/suicides of over 900 American citizens in the remote Northwest District of Guyana. These two horrendous events, along with the important consequences related to them, produced a crisis that could have easily overwhelmed a mission many times the size of the Embassy in Georgetown, but with quiet competence and professionalism, the ambassador and his staff discharged their many responsibilities in a manner which reflected great credit not only on themselves and their embassy but the United States as well."

SNAPSHOTS OF GUYANA

Georgetown sea wall

Hindu temple

Ambassador John Burke, Georgetown, Guyana

Rural Catholic church

Starbroek Market

The author's house in Bel Air Springs

Typical road traffic

American embassy, Georgetown, 1976

Guard Mr. Kisoon and Bob Oglesby, FBI

Joe Hartmann with his dog, Hutch